Pandora h[...]
happiness. [...]

Pandora smiled. Her gray eyes met his. "And I love you."

"Oh, God," said Sarsbrook, and kissed her passionately. The ardor with which she returned his kisses inflamed him to go even further—until the faint voice of reason forced her to weakly say, "My lord, you must stop."

"Forgive me," the viscount said. "I lost my head. You cannot know how much I want you. Say you will be mine."

"Of course, I will be yours," Pandora said.

"I will take such good care of you. You will have everything you could possibly desire. And I will look after your family," Sarsbrook pledged as he embraced her again.

Pandora snuggled in his arms. "You are very good, my lord."

He tightened his embrace. "You will be the wife of my heart. I only wish it were possible we might actually be wed."

Pandora froze as her joy shattered like crystal. She had made a dreadful mistake—and was on the brink of another. . . .

Fortune's Folly

Fortune's Folly

by

Margaret Summerville

A SIGNET BOOK

SIGNET
Published by the Penguin Group
Penguin Books USA Inc., 375 Hudson Street,
New York, New York 10014, U.S.A.
Penguin Books Ltd, 27 Wrights Lane,
London W8 5TZ, England
Penguin Books Australia Ltd, Ringwood,
Victoria, Australia
Penguin Books Canada Ltd, 10 Alcorn Avenue,
Toronto, Ontario, Canada M4V 3B2
Penguin Books (N.Z.) Ltd, 182–190 Wairau Road,
Auckland 10, New Zealand

Penguin Books Ltd, Registered Offices:
Harmondsworth, Middlesex, England

First published by Signet, an imprint of Dutton Signet,
a division of Penguin Books USA Inc.

First Printing, May, 1994
10 9 8 7 6 5 4 3 2 1

1

"Do cease fidgeting, Lizzy," cried Pandora Marsh, inserting another pin into the hem of her sister's gown. "It will take far longer if you do not keep still."

"But, Pan, it seems to be taking forever!" returned Elizabeth Marsh. "You must know how tiresome it is to stand perched up here like a trained bear."

Pandora smiled up at her impatient younger sister. "I am nearly finished," she said, pinning another section of material. "Yes, I think that will do. Now turn around, Lizzy. Slowly!" Pandora eyed her handiwork with a critical eye as her sister obliged her by rotating slowly around. "Yes, yes, that is fine. You may get down, Lizzy."

Lizzy jumped down from the ottoman on which she had been standing. Hurrying to the mirror, she examined herself with approval. "It is lovely, Pan. Indeed, I do not think that even Mrs. Rutherford could do better."

"That is praise indeed," said Pandora, acknowledging the compliment with a slight smile. Mrs. Rutherford was a well-known dressmaker frequented by Lizzy's best friend Phoebe Reynolds as well as, according to Phoebe, all manner of great ladies of fashion. Pandora Marsh, on the other hand, was an accomplished seamstress whose considerable talents put Mrs. Rutherford to shame.

Pandora had been sewing since childhood. Having early demonstrated a knack for using a needle, she had pursued sewing diligently. As her skills improved, Pandora had amazed and delighted her family with her cleverness.

She had taken up tailoring as well, a logical step for a young woman with four brothers. Winfield, the eldest of the Marsh boys, had pretensions of being a man of fashion. Skeptical about his sister's early efforts at men's apparel, he had submitted to her relentless measuring and fitting with some cynicism. When the resulting coat of olive superfine was undoubtedly the equal of any he had obtained in town, Winfield had been understandably delighted, and had pronounced his sister a veritable genius.

As the Marsh family's fortunes had declined over the years, Pandora's sewing ability had become increasingly important. Despite the fact that money for dressmakers and tailors had grown scarce, Pandora's talents allowed the Marsh family to appear fashionable and well dressed.

"You are a dear, Pan," said Lizzy, turning away from the mirror. "Phoebe will be green with envy when she sees me at Aunt Lettice's."

"It did work out nicely," said Pandora modestly. She was very pleased with her creation, an evening dress of pale-blue satin. The low-cut bodice of the short-sleeved, high-waisted gown was trimmed with French lace that had been taken from an old dress of their mother's. Lizzy looked splendid in the gown, but then Lizzy Marsh looked beautiful in just about anything.

Studying her sister, Pandora could not help but feel a slight pang of envy. Seventeen-year-old Lizzy was the beauty of the family. She had been blessed with a classically lovely face. Observers were always startled by Lizzy's exceptional prettiness—her large china-blue eyes, flawless complexion, and lustrous black hair that curled naturally. Tall and elegant, Lizzy moved with gazelle-like grace and her slender figure was much praised by even the most severe judges of feminine appearance.

Pandora did not consider herself pretty in the least. A harsh critic of her own appearance, Pandora adjudged herself too short for fashion. She thought her nose too long and her mouth too wide. Unimpressed with her own gray eyes, Pandora thought her sister's blue ones far superior. And every night when Pandora affixed curling papers to her unfashionably straight hair, she thought wistfully of Lizzy's wavy tresses.

In short, Pandora Marsh considered herself to be a rather plain, unexceptional person. She was, of course, far too hard on herself. Others less exacting found little fault with her appearance. Indeed, her acquaintances thought Pandora quite pretty, although admittedly not a great beauty like her sister. Pandora had red-gold hair, a lovely complexion, and an excellent figure. Her dazzling smile and fine gray eyes were much admired.

"Come, Lizzy, I must have the dress if I am to finish it," said Pandora.

Lizzy nodded, turning her back to her sister so that Pandora could unbutton the numerous tiny buttons that fastened the back of the dress. "But what will you wear to Aunt Lettice's, Pan? I daresay you did not have time to make yourself anything new."

"I shall wear my pink sarsnet."

"But, Pan, did you not wear that the last time you were at Aunt Lettice's?"

"What does that signify?" replied Pandora, undoing the buttons on Lizzy's dress.

"It is only that I feel so very guilty wearing a new gown while you must wear your old sarsnet."

"It is not so old as that."

"But Mr. Underwood will be there."

"Good heavens, Lizzy, why are you forever harping on Mr. Underwood? You know that I do not care one fig for that gentleman. Indeed, I do not even like him."

"But he seems to be a most amiable gentleman, Pan. I do admit that it is a pity that he is somewhat older than you."

"Somewhat older?" said Pandora, raising her eyebrows. "Heavens, Lizzy, I daresay he is older than Papa."

"But, Pan, he is so fond of you," said Lizzy. "And he is quite rich. Winnie told me that he has a new carriage that is slap-up to the mark."

"Indeed?" said Pandora with mock seriousness. "Then I must certainly reassess my opinion of him."

Not noting her sister's irony, Lizzy nodded. "I should hope you would, Pan."

Pandora suppressed a smile. She knew that her sister wanted her to show more consideration to Mr. Underwood. After all, Pandora was twenty-two years old and very nearly on the shelf. Lizzy did not think her elder sister took the business of finding a husband as seriously as she ought to. In Lizzy's view, Pandora was well on the way to spinsterhood.

Pandora did not dispute that finding a husband for herself had not been a priority. She had been so busy managing the family that she had had little time or inclination to consider marriage.

When Pandora's mother had died eight years ago, many responsibilities had fallen to the then fifteen-year-old Pandora. The eldest of six children, Pandora had assumed the role of lady of the house. Mr. Marsh, Pandora's father, was a kind, charming, but ineffectual man, who seemed more than happy to leave decisions to his capable daughter. It was Pandora who supervised the servants and the family finances. Between her sewing and responsibilities for the household and younger children, Pandora had little time for her own social life.

In recent months, Pandora had given no thought to her prospects for marriage. Indeed, it seemed impossible to even consider the idea of leaving her father and siblings, for everyone depended on her so completely.

Now that Lizzy was old enough to be brought out into society, Pandora was far more concerned about her sister's prospects for marriage. As her brother Winfield had told her numerous times, Lizzy's beauty should assure her of many offers of marriage.

At twenty, Winfield was eager to make his own way in society, but lack of resources seemed to hinder his ascent into the ranks of sporting gentlemen. He was hopeful that

Lizzy would marry well, for a rich, well-connected brother-in-law was a very appealing prospect.

After pulling the dress over Lizzy's head, Pandora laid it gently on the bed. "I am so excited about the gown, Pan," said Lizzy, taking up her morning dress and slipping into it. "I must write to Phoebe about it."

"Then go do so," said Pandora. "I shan't need you. I shall start hemming at once."

Lizzy smiled brightly, then hurried from her sister's bedchamber. She had been a bit worried that Pandora would expect her to hem the gown herself, for she detested sewing and was not very good at it. Pandora had long ago given up on her younger sister as a seamstress, although not without many attempts at instructing her. Lizzy never failed to make a muddle of whatever sewing she attempted, so Pandora had finally decided that she would be better off doing the work herself.

When her sister had gone, Pandora took up her sewing basket and settled herself into the chair by the bed. She had scarcely begun her work when a knock at the door made her look up.

"Lizzy said you were here, Pan." Winfield Marsh entered the room. "I must talk to you."

Pandora glanced up at her brother, then returned to her sewing. She did not like the sound of "I must talk to you," for with Winfield, that generally preceded a request for money.

Winfield walked over to her. "Lizzy said her new dress is a marvel. I can see that. By Jupiter, Pandora, it looks splendid! You are the cleverest girl!"

Pandora did not react to her brother's praise, for she knew that Winfield routinely resorted to flattery in his attempt to exact favors. Sitting down on the bed beside her, he smiled his charming smile.

A very handsome young man, Winfield closely resembled his sister Lizzy, having her dark curls and blue eyes. He was tall and well built with a masculine form well suited to the closely cut coats that were in fashion.

"I daresay Lizzy will be the best-dressed lady of all."

Pandora looked up from her needle. "Winnie, I do hope that you are not going to ask me for money. Indeed, I cannot spare one penny."

A frown appeared on Winfield's handsome countenance. "Dash it, Pan, why do you always think I am going to ask for money?"

"Because you always do so, Winnie."

"I cannot help it if I am always so short of blunt, Pan. Egad, we live like paupers."

"If you knew how paupers lived, Winfield, you would not say so," said Pandora severely.

"Yes, yes," returned Winfield. "But what is a fellow to do?"

"He must economize. You know our situation well enough. We have argued about this time and again."

"But I have truly economized. One can only do so much. A man must keep up appearances. You cannot think I enjoy coming to you, begging for money. And if you would only speak to Underwood about obtaining a position for me at Whitehall, I should have a good income of my own."

Pandora frowned. The idea of talking to Arthur Underwood about her brother was a sore subject. A wealthy banker, Underwood had a number of highly placed friends in government. A few months ago, Winfield had seized upon the idea of obtaining a post in government service, where he believed he could receive a reliable income without much exertion. He was certain that Underwood had the power to find him such a post. Since Underwood was obviously enamoured of Pandora, Winfield thought it a small thing for his sister to speak on his behalf.

As much as she would like to have her brother gainfully employed, Pandora was adamant about refusing to speak to the banker. Because she had no intention of marrying Underwood, she did not wish to encourage him.

"As I have told you countless times, Winfield, I shall

not speak to Mr. Underwood about you. You are quite capable of seeking his assistance on your own."

"But he does not appear to like me, Pan," said Winfield. "I do wish you would reconsider. One word from you and Underwood would do everything he could."

"That is quite ridiculous. Now I caution you to say nothing further on this subject. If you do, I shall consider asking Mr. Underwood to obtain a post for you—in India!"

"Perhaps that would not be a bad idea," said Winfield. He spoke so dispiritedly that Pandora was suddenly more sympathetic.

"Oh, what is the matter, Winnie? Oh, very well, how much do you need? I may be able to spare something."

"You are a darling, Pan," cried Winfield. "I need fifty pounds."

"Fifty pounds!" cried Pandora. "You know very well that we do not have such a sum."

Winfield rose from the bed. "You don't understand. This is very serious. You see, I borrowed money from a man some time ago. He is a rather disreputable fellow, I'm afraid. Oh, do not look at me so! I was quite desperate. The blackguard has been hounding me for weeks, threatening me with the most horrible fate if I do not pay him. I fear he is ready to murder me and toss my body into the Thames."

"What a great gull you are, Winnie! Papa has told you time and again never to borrow money from such persons. Toss your body into the Thames indeed! You are being overly dramatic."

"I am perfectly serious! If you saw him you would not doubt that he is a veritable cutthroat."

"Well, I do not have any way of obtaining fifty pounds, Winnie. I may find five, but we will have to nearly starve for that. You will have to try to sell some of your things. Your gold snuff box for one thing."

"My dear Pan, I parted with that some time ago."

Pandora regarded her brother in frustration. "Winfield,

you must be more sensible. You will ruin us with your carelessness."

"I pray you do not lecture me," said Winfield. "I am asking for help. I know well enough that I have been a complete fool."

Pandora hesitated a moment. "If you have learned your lesson, Winnie, perhaps it is worth fifty pounds. We will somehow pay this debt of yours. If you give this man five pounds, it may placate him for a time." She rose from her chair and went over to a desk that stood in the corner of the room. Unlocking a drawer, she took out a small wooden box and extracted a few coins from it. "Here are five pounds. That is all we have at present. Tell this cutthroat of yours that he will have the rest in time, although how we will find it is a problem."

"You are a dear, Pan," said Winfield, taking the money and then leaning down to kiss his sister's cheek. "I swear I shall never borrow another farthing." Pandora raised her eyebrows skeptically at her brother. "I do mean it, Pan," he said, grinning.

The young man happily left the room, allowing Pandora to return to her sewing. As she took up Lizzy's dress once again, she paused in reflection.

As much as she dearly loved Winfield, she knew that he could not be depended upon. Despite her continuous warnings, he was always getting into debt and seemed totally unconcerned about the precarious financial state of the family.

It was not easy to run a household in London on a small income. Her father's resources had dwindled steadily due to bad investments over the years. They had been forced to sell their beloved house in Suffolk a year ago in order to make ends meet. The income from the sale allowed them to continue a somewhat tenuous existence in a rather unfashionable neighborhood in town. It also provided for Pandora's brothers Augustus, who was at university, and Henry, who was a student at Rugby. The youngest of the Marsh children, Nicholas, was still at home, but Pandora hoped that he could join Henry at Rugby next term.

Lack of money was a source of constant worry to Pandora, who carefully watched the household expenditures. Her father did as much as he could, but Mr. Marsh seemed to have no ability to earn additional income. He had been brought up a gentleman and had never dreamed that his fortune would not be adeqaute to allow him to live in the manner to which he had been accustomed. Mr. Marsh was not in the least extravagant, living modestly and staying at home most evenings. He was a sociable gentleman, and it was a disappointment to him that he could not accept many engagements due to the unhappy fact that he could not reciprocate by entertaining at home very often.

Pandora frowned again as she made a tiny stitch in the hem of Lizzy's gown. She worried about Winfield, who was foolish and aimless and so unlike Augustus, a serious, clever lad of eighteen who was doing well at Cambridge. Augustus was determined to become a barrister, and Pandora knew he would succeed.

She thought, too, of Lizzy, who would be tossed into the choppy waters of society when the season started in a few short days. Lizzy was a delightful, good-natured girl, but she was also rather silly and immature. Pandora knew that there would be no end of young gentlemen throwing themselves at her pretty sister. She could only hope that Lizzy would find a suitable young man of respectable income who would make her happy.

"Pandora! There you are!" A childish voice caused a smile to appear on Pandora's face. Her brother Nicholas ran into the room, his face flushed with excitement. He was followed by a small terrier dog that was white with liver-colored spots. "Mr. Stubbs and I have been to the park with Martha. We had such great fun, although Mr. Stubbs was exceedingly naughty."

Pandora smiled fondly at her youngest brother. Nicholas Marsh was nearly eleven. He was a handsome, high-spirited boy with a sunny disposition, who was universally loved by everyone who met him. The servants doted on him, as did his father and brothers and sisters. "Why does it not surprise me to hear that Stubbs was naughty?" said Pandora, directing her gaze to the dog at her brother's feet. The animal looked up at Pandora, wagging his stubby tail delightedly. "What did the dastardly fellow do this time?"

"Oh, it is only that he barked quite ferociously at a very stout gentleman. Then he pulled so very hard on his lead that I lost my grip on it. Then he ran off very fast, chasing squirrels in the park. And he would not obey when I told him to come."

"Bad dog, Mr. Stubbs," said Pandora, wagging a finger at the animal. The dog only cocked his head and sat down. "You must train him better, Nicky. He is far too willful."

"I know, Pan, but training dogs is not easy, especially if they are like Mr. Stubbs." He paused, noting the dress in his sister's lap. "Are you nearly finished with Lizzy's gown?"

Pandora nodded. "Yes, but I shall put it aside for a time. I am tired of sewing for today. Let us go and see Papa. We will have him scold Stubbs. Perhaps that will help."

Nicholas grinned as Pandora rose from her chair and carefully placed Lizzy's dress on the bed. "You will regret your behavior now, Mr. Stubbs."

The dog jumped up, wagging his tail furiously. Pandora laughed at the animal and then she and her brother followed the mischievous canine from the room.

2

Although the residence of Sir Humphrey Maitland was one of a number of fashionable new townhouses that lined Wellington Square, its interior was dark and uninviting. Most of the sparse furnishings that decorated the house were old and worn, having been unwanted items taken from Sir Humphrey's two other homes.

Sir Humphrey did not frequently have visitors to his London townhouse, but those who did call were often surprised to find that the home of a very wealthy baronet was so gloomy and ill-furnished. It was not only frugality that had prevented Sir Humphrey from decorating his home in a stylish, modern fashion. The fact was that he was a gentleman who favored the old and familiar. Sir Humphrey did not approve of much that had been produced during the present century, believing that quality and workmanship had declined appallingly in recent years.

Two gentlemen appeared at the baronet's door and were admitted by Sir Humphrey's butler. The older of the two men was George Wentworth, one of London's finest jewelers. As he glanced at the entry hall, Wentworth eyed the room with disapproval. A man of taste and artistic temperament, Wentworth did not think much of the chipped plaster cast of a Roman emperor that stood on a marble pedestal to greet visitors, nor did he like the moth-eaten oriental rug beneath his feet.

"Do wait here, sir," said the butler. "I shall inform the master that you have arrived."

When the butler had gone, Wentworth turned to the burly young man who had accompanied him. "Do be careful with that case, Jessup."

"Indeed, sir," said the young man, tightening his hold on a jewelry case that was clutched tightly to his chest. "Do not fear, 'tis safe and sound with me."

"I shall be glad to be rid of it," said Wentworth. "Let us hope it meets with the old gentleman's approval."

"Oh, that it will, sir," exclaimed Jessup. "How could it be otherwise?"

Wentworth seemed pleased with the young man's enthusiastic response. Before he could say anything more, the butler returned to lead them to the drawing room, where Sir Humphrey Maitland sat upon a threadbare sofa. Seventy years of age, Sir Humphrey was stout and round-faced. He wore a striped velvet coat, yellow waistcoat, and knee breeches, garments he had owned for more than two decades.

"Good afternoon, Wentworth."

"Good afternoon, sir," returned the jeweler. "May I present Mr. Jessup?"

Sir Humphrey regarded the young man indifferently. "Sit down then, gentlemen."

"Thank you, sir." Wentworth and his associate seated themselves in chairs across from the baronet. "I have brought the necklace, sir."

"Yes, yes," said Sir Humphrey. "I should like to see it."

"Jessup, the necklace."

Rising from his chair, the young man opened the case. "Here it is, sir," he said, holding it up in front of the elderly man.

"Ah, beautiful! It is truly beautiful!" Sir Humphrey's eyes expressed his pleasure as he took the case from Jessup. Sitting on black velvet was an emerald necklace of stunning beauty. "I have never seen anything so exquisite."

Wentworth appeared pleased. He was very proud of the creation in the baronet's hands, having personally supervised every aspect of it from the design to the final execution. "You are satisfied then, sir?"

"Yes, of course. By God, I'd be an ass if I were not. You've done well, sir. Indeed, you have." As he said these words, the baronet winced as if in pain.

"Are you not well, sir?" said Wentworth.

"'Tis nothing," returned the older man. "Indigestion. I have been feeling somewhat indisposed these few days." He closed the jewelry case. "I must see that a certain lady gets this at once. I have so looked forward to giving her such a gift. She will be so surprised." Sir Humphrey put a hand to his chest. "Damned pains," he said.

"Should you not see a physician, sir?" said Wentworth, noting the baronet appeared very red in the face and decidedly unwell.

"Fool leeches," returned Sir Humphrey. "I'll have nothing to do with the charlatans. I will be better after a rest. But I must ask you to do me a favor, Wentworth."

"I should be glad to do so, sir."

"You must deliver this necklace to a lady. I should have liked to have delivered it personally, but I am feeling a bit indisposed. And I want her to have this necklace at once. She will be so pleased with me! Yes, yes, she must have it immediately. I shall write a note."

"Very good, sir," said Wentworth. "I should be happy to deliver the necklace."

Rising from his chair with some difficulty, Sir Humphrey handed the necklace back to Jessup. "Hodges! Hodges!" he shouted. The butler appeared quickly in the drawing room. "Some paper and a pen." The servant nodded and hurried to fetch the requested supplies. When he returned, Sir Humphrey scribbled a quick message. After blotting the paper, the baronet folded it, and then took up his pen again to write the address. Pausing uncertainly for a moment, he could not think of the address. "Confound it," he muttered, "it was one of the royal dukes."

"I beg your pardon, sir?" said Wentworth.

"It was nothing," said Sir Humphrey, trying to recollect the name of the street. "Clarence Place," he said finally. "Number Sixteen Clarence Place." He wrote the address on the paper and turned to Wentworth. "It is Sixteen Clarence Place. You must give it to Miss M. Into her own hands, mind you!"

"Miss M.?" said Wentworth.

"Yes. I am not at liberty to disclose the lady's name. Miss M. will suffice, sir."

"Indeed it will, sir," said Wentworth with a knowing smile. He considered himself a man of the world.

"I shall count on your discretion."

"Of course, sir," said Wentworth. "We will deliver the necklace at once." He made a slight bow and started toward the door.

"Say it is from 'her Lancelot.' There will be no need to mention my name."

"I understand, sir," said Wentworth, betraying no emotion despite his amusement at the idea of the old gentleman being called "Lancelot."

"And tell her that I shall call tomorrow."

"Very good, sir," replied the jeweler. After nodding to the baronet, he and his young assistant turned to go.

"Wentworth!"

"Sir?"

"I must have your word that you will not reveal to anyone where you have taken this necklace. The reputation of a lady is at stake."

"You may have complete confidence, sir, that I shall not disclose that information to anyone."

"May I have your word, sir?"

"Indeed, you have my word on the matter."

"And the young man?" The baronet looked at Jessup.

"You have my word as well, sir," he said.

"Good. Then be off with you. And my thanks."

Wentworth and his assistant departed, leaving the drawing room and exiting the house. "Damned nuisance having to take this necklace to the old fellow's light-skirt," said Wentworth.

"Indeed so, sir," returned Jessup, who was actually

quite eager to see the lady who was the object of the elderly gentleman's affections. "What did you say the old gentleman's name was, Mr. Wentworth?"

"His name is no concern of yours, Jessup. Discretion is of the utmost importance in such matters. There is no need for you to know the gentleman's identity."

"Of course, sir," said Jessup, rather disappointed.

Wentworth took his watch from his pocket. "Nearly two o'clock," he said. Although the jeweler was also curious about Sir Humphrey's lady, he was a busy man who had a number of appointments to keep. "You will deliver the necklace, Jessup. I must return to the shop."

"Yes, sir," said the younger man.

"But take care. Should anything happen to that necklace, I'll have your head."

"There is no need to worry," said Jessup, happy to take on the responsibility for the opportunity to have a look at a bonafide mistress. Wentworth gave instructions to the driver and the two men climbed into the carriage.

After discussing Mr. Stubbs' failings with her father and Nicholas, Pandora left them, saying that she was required elsewhere. Every Tuesday afternoon, Pandora had a conference with the cook about plans for upcoming meals.

She had scarcely sat down with the cook in the drawing room when a maid appeared. "I beg your pardon, Miss Marsh," she said, "but there is a young gentleman here. His name is Mr. Jessup and he is asking to see 'Miss M.' "

"Miss M.?" replied Pandora. "How very odd. Do you think he means me?"

"I asked if he meant Miss Marsh and he said he imagined so, miss."

"That is peculiar, Martha."

The maid nodded. "Yes, miss, but he said it is very important that he see you."

"Oh, very well, Martha," replied Pandora, rather perplexed by the caller. "I suppose I must see him in order to find out why he is calling me 'Miss M.' Please excuse me, Cook. I shall call for you as soon as I speak with this gentleman."

"Yes, miss," replied the cook, rising from her chair and taking her leave.

"Martha, show the gentleman in here."

"Yes, miss," replied the maid, who turned and left the drawing room. She returned shortly with a young man.

"Mr. Jessup?" Pandora Marsh eyed the visitor with interest. "I am Miss Marsh. You wished to see me?"

"Yes, madam," said the jeweler's assistant. "I am here to deliver a gift for you . . . from a gentleman."

Pandora's eyebrows arched slightly. "Indeed, sir? From what gentleman?"

Jessup smiled awkwardly. "I am instructed to say, from 'your Lancelot.' "

" 'My Lancelot?' " repeated Pandora. She laughed. "Indeed, sir, I cannot imagine whom you might mean by such a name."

"There is a note. And this is the gift." The young man extended the case to Pandora, who opened it.

"Good heavens!" she cried as she caught sight of the gleaming necklace.

Gratified by Pandora's astonishment and obvious appreciation of the jewels, Jessup was emboldened to remark. "I can see why the gentleman chose emeralds, madam. If I may say so, they are perfect for a lady of your coloring."

Pandora hardly heard his words, so astonished was she at the sight of the necklace. She studied the emeralds in stunned silence for a time. "Surely there is some mistake," she said finally.

"Here is the note," said Jessup.

Pandora took the piece of paper from his hand. She noticed that the words "Miss M. 16 Clarence Place" were written prominently on it. Unfolding the missive, she read the message inside. "My dearest Miss M.," it said. "This is but a small token of my affection. Your

Lancelot." Pandora looked from the paper to Jessup. "What is the name of the gentleman who sent this?"

The jeweler looked rather surprised. Could the lady have other paramours in addition to the old gentleman? He paused awkwardly. "He did not think it necessary to mention his name, and, in truth, I do not know it," he replied. "The gentleman said that 'your Lancelot' would suffice."

"My Lancelot," repeated Pandora. "I admit to you that I am thoroughly mystified." Reading the note once again, she frowned. She could not imagine anyone sending her such a gift. Unless . . . Pandora knitted her eyes in concentration. Of late, Arthur Underwood had become a good deal more definite in his expressions of admiration and affection. He was a wealthy gentleman, one that could afford expensive gifts.

Pandora continued to ponder the matter. She suddenly recalled that once, some months ago, after Underwood had had a few too many glasses of rum punch at a party, he had spoken some nonsense about being her gallant knight. However, she did not remember him saying a word about Sir Lancelot.

"The gentleman said he would call upon you tomorrow," said Jessup. "He was sorely disappointed that he could not deliver the necklace himself, but a slight indisposition prevented him from doing so."

"Did you see this gentleman?"

"Indeed, yes, ma'am."

"What did he look like?"

Jessup hesitated. How did one describe the elderly man? "He is an older gentleman. And rather stout."

Pandora frowned. That did sound like Arthur Underwood, who was nearly sixty and portly. "Mr. Jessup, I cannot accept such a gift as this. Do take it back to the gentleman."

"Oh, I could not do so," said Jessup. "Indeed, madam, could you not return it to the gentleman when he calls tomorrow? I do think that would be best."

Pandora considered the matter. "Very well, I shall discuss the matter with the gentleman when he calls."

"Very good, madam," said Jessup, relieved that the lady was not going to force him to take the necklace back. He was eager to be rid of it. "I must take my leave then, ma'am."

When he had gone, Pandora sat down upon the sofa and stared at the emeralds. Finally taking the necklace from its case, she could not resist fastening it around her neck and hurrying to the mirror that hung in the entry hall.

The brilliant green stones gleamed with an almost unearthly light, and the gold glittered irresistibly. It was undoubtedly the most magnificent necklace she had ever seen. She continued to stare into the mirror, studying the fabulous jewels.

"What are you doing, Pan?" A masculine voice made Pandora turn from the mirror. Her brother saw the necklace immediately. "By all the gods, Pan, what is that you are wearing?"

"It is a gift. A man just brought it."

"Egad, Pan. If that is genuine, it is worth a king's ransom. Underwood must be very serious about you."

"Can you imagine Mr. Underwood sending me such a necklace?" said Pandora, continuing to study the emeralds in the mirror. "A young man brought it, but it was rather mysterious. He did not even know the name of the gentleman who sent it. He said it was from 'my Lancelot.' "

Winfield grinned. "Old Underwood your Lancelot? That is too funny, Pan. By God, I'd thought him too tight-fisted by half to send you such a gift. You must have bewitched him."

"There is a note." She handed it to him.

"Is this Underwood's hand?"

"I cannot say. I don't think he has ever written me a letter. But the young man said that 'my Lancelot' will call upon me tomorrow."

"Egad, Underwood must have finally decided to ask

for your hand. He may have thought a gift such as that might influence you." Winfield smiled again. "I must say that were I a woman, such a gift would influence me."

Pandora laughed. "I daresay I do not know what I shall tell Papa. And Lizzy will take one look at this necklace and decide that I must marry Mr. Underwood at once."

"Indeed, Pan," said Winfield, "when Lizzy sees that necklace, she will decide that she will marry Underwood."

Pandora laughed again and then accompanied her brother into the drawing room.

3

Robert Despencer, the fourth Viscount Sarsbrook, walked quickly through Hyde Park. It was a bright sunny day in late April, and the park was filled with Londoners eager to take advantage of the fine weather. There were fashionable ladies and gentlemen riding in gleaming phaetons as well as all manner of people strolling through the spacious green park.

It had long been Lord Sarsbrook's custom to take a brisk walk each morning, rain or shine. These walks afforded the viscount necessary exercise as well as time for reflection.

His lordship was a creature of very regular habits, whose well-ordered life afforded few surprises. The viscount's residence in London was Sarsbrook House, an impressive mansion built in Queen Anne's time. He lived there alone, entertaining few visitors and spending little time among London society.

A man of considerable wealth and illustrious ancestry, Sarsbrook lived a remarkably simple existence. Having no patience with the dandy set, his lordship dressed plainly, paying more attention to his comfort than to the dictates of fashion. He was a rare individual in that he cared nothing for what others thought of him. Therefore, he was free to do as he pleased and live as he wished.

While it was commonplace for gentlemen of his station to spend much of their time at sporting pursuits, Sarsbrook had little interest in such amusements. He did not enjoy hunting or shooting and cared nothing for horseracing. Nor did he emulate his fellow noblemen in the pursuit of women of the demimonde.

The viscount also disdained society functions, disliking the incessant chatter of young ladies hoping to impress him. Due to his rank and fortune, Sarsbrook was considered an excellent catch, but he was extremely reluctant to allow himself to be caught.

His lordship did not have a very high opinion of the female sex, but to call him a misogynist was not quite accurate, since his general opinion of the male sex was equally as bad. At twenty-six, Sarsbrook's observations of the human race had given him a very dim view of it. He was unusually cynical and inclined to dislike most people. In turn, most who met the viscount proclaimed him proud, rude, and entirely unlikable.

That he met with society's disapproval did not bother him in the least. He preferred instead the company of his books and a few close friends.

Anyone observing Sarsbrook striding across the park would have noted a tall young man dressed in a respectable-looking coat and pantaloons with a beaver hat atop his head. There was a thoughtful expression on the viscount's lean, angular countenance for he was considering a number of esoteric matters of Greek philosophy.

Devoted to intellectual pursuits since childhood, the viscount had a passionate interest in classical studies. He had possessed such a talent for Latin and Greek that his teachers at Eton had been amazed. Scholars among the nobility were rare. In fact, serious devotion to study was regarded as suspect among most society members. Yet nothing had deterred Sarsbrook, who had been a stubborn boy of surprising self-assurance. At Eton he had made friends with the more studious boys, whether or not their families passed muster with the rest of the aristocracy.

At the death of his father four years ago, Sarsbrook had inherited his father's lands and title. His sense of duty and responsibility had made him very conscientious in his stewardship of the Sarsbrook estates.

The viscount's interest in managing his many properties as well as his continuing enthusiasm for studying the worlds of the ancient Greeks and Romans kept him well occupied. At present, he was spending considerable time making a new translation of Homer's *Iliad*.

Leaving the park, the viscount walked on toward Sarsbrook House. When he arrived at his residence, he was greeted by the butler. "My lord."

"Archer," he said, handing his hat and gloves to the servant.

"Mr. Hunt is here to see you. He is waiting in the drawing room."

"Mr. Hunt? Very well. I shall see him." Sarsbrook frowned, wondering what his visitor could want. Hunt was a solicitor, and handled the affairs of Sarsbrook's uncle, Sir Humphrey Maitland.

When his lordship entered the room, the lawyer hurried to his feet. "Lord Sarsbrook," he said, bowing slightly.

"Hunt," returned the viscount, noting the man's solemn expression. "Is something amiss?"

"I fear so, my lord. I have very bad news."

"My uncle? Is he ill?"

"I am very sorry to bear such tidings, my lord, but Sir Humphrey died last night."

"Good God! But I saw him only last week. He seemed well enough."

"Indeed, my lord, I met with your uncle but two days ago. Dr. Evans believes it was his heart. You have my sympathy, my lord. Your uncle was a good man. He will be sorely missed."

Sarsbrook nodded, trying to accept what he had heard. The news of his uncle's death was a terrible shock. He had been fond of Sir Humphrey. Indeed, he was one of a handful of individuals for whom the viscount had affection. The baronet had been the one relation on whom Sarsbrook had relied. The viscount kept his composure with some difficulty. "Your pardon, Hunt, this news is so unexpected."

"Yes, my lord. Do sit down." Sarsbrook lowered himself onto the sofa. Hunt continued, speaking about funeral arrangements, but the viscount scarcely listened. He found himself thinking of Sir Humphrey. The baronet had been a man of kindness and good humor as well as eccentricity. He had had great affection for his nephew Robert, who always took his part. As the solicitor droned on, Sarsbrook stared grimly ahead, wishing there'd been a chance to say farewell to his favorite relative.

The afternoon after Pandora received the emerald necklace, she stayed at home dreading Underwood's visit. She had spent the morning in somber reflection, wondering if she were foolish in rejecting such a wealthy man. After all, the family was at present under severe financial strain. Certainly a wealthy man like Arthur Underwood could assist them. If she married him, he would have an obligation to do so.

Mr. Marsh was adamant that Pandora refuse Underwood, saying that such a marriage would make her miserable. He had told her more than once that he had no desire to see her wed to a man older than himself, especially when the man was Arthur Underwood.

When Mr. Marsh had seen the emerald necklace, he had been even more astonished than Pandora had been. A mild-mannered gentleman, Mr. Marsh was nonetheless very much annoyed at Underwood's impudence. Sending a present such as the necklace to a young lady before any understanding had been reached concerning marriage was unthinkable, he told Pandora.

Lizzy had not shared her father's irritation at Pandora's gift. The younger Marsh sister had squealed with delight at seeing the emeralds. Having always dreamed of owning jewels, Lizzy had insisted on trying on the necklace. When her father had commanded that she take it off at once, Lizzy had nearly cried.

Lizzy's opinion of Mr. Underwood had escalated sharply after seeing his unexpected generosity. The following morning she had suggested Pandora reconsider her opposition to accepting Underwood. Yes, it was a pity that he was not younger, she admitted, or more handsome or personable, but he was quite rich. And if he would provide his wife with jewels and clothes, what did such failings matter?

As one might have expected, Lizzy's comments had not endeared her to her sister that morning. Mr. Marsh, frustrated with his younger daughter, had sent her off in the company of Winfield to call upon their Aunt Lettice.

That afternoon, as she waited for Underwood to appear, Pandora sat in her sitting room, finishing Lizzy's dress. When she was done, she took up a book and tried to read, but it was hard to concentrate. She kept looking at the clock, wishing Underwood would appear so she could return the necklace and refuse him when he offered to marry her.

Finally giving up on her book, Pandora went to the drawing room. There she found her father sitting upon the sofa reading the newspaper. "Papa," said Pandora, coming in to sit beside him. "It grows late and 'my Lancelot' has not called."

A slight smile appeared on Mr. Marsh's face. At fifty years of age, he was a handsome, distinguished-looking man with gray hair and bright blue eyes. "I cannot believe the audacity of the man, sending such a necklace to you. I shall tell him in no uncertain terms that his behavior is not becoming to a gentleman."

"Now, Papa, do not fly into the boughs. I think it best to attempt to stay on good terms with Underwood."

"Indeed? My dear girl, I do not think that may be possible. Evidently he is very much enamored of you to send such a gift. When you refuse him, I daresay he will be crushed."

"I don't know, Papa. While I think he does like me, I hardly think I inspire a grand passion in Mr. Underwood. No, indeed, I cannot explain his odd behavior in sending me such an expensive necklace." Pandora paused. "What would one pay for emeralds such as those?"

" 'Pon my honor, I would have no idea." He smiled. "I

have not bought many jewels in my time. However, it appears very costly. Indeed, I am nervous having it in the house and I shall be happier when you send Underwood and his emeralds packing."

"But, Papa, are you not in the least interested in having Mr. Underwood for a son-in-law? Lizzy thinks I am passing up a golden opportunity for a wealthy husband."

"Don't be ridiculous. I'll not have him for a son-in-law."

Pandora smiled. "Winfield has been badgering me to ask Mr. Underwood if he might help him obtain a position. I have been reluctant to do so, but perhaps I have been remiss. He might have recommended Winnie for a government post. Now I don't know how I can ever ask him."

"Do not worry about that, my dear. I doubt Underwood would have exerted himself on your brother's behalf." Mr. Marsh looked at the mantel clock. "Four o'clock. I thought the man would have called by now. He is inexcusably tardy for a man so in love."

"Oh, Papa!"

Her father laughed. "Would you like a game of chess to pass the time?"

"Yes, that would be a very good idea," said Pandora. She and her father were avid players and spent many hours matching wits over the chessboard.

"It will take your mind off Underwood," said Mr. Marsh.

Pandora nodded, thinking anything that would take her mind off that gentleman a very good idea. They rose from the sofa to take their places at the table across the room on which the chessboard sat, always ready. Soon Pandora and her father were engrossed in the game.

An hour later, Mr. Marsh triumphantly checkmated his daughter. "I've got you, my girl. 'Tis clear your mind was elsewhere." He looked at the clock again. "And Underwood is still not here. The afternoon is all but gone. Is that a carriage I hear?"

Father and daughter rose from the chess table to hurry

to the window where they could view the street. A carriage was stopping in front of the house, but it was not Underwood's stylish equipage of which Lizzy had spoken so highly, but Aunt Lettice's unglamorous chaise. "Aunt Lettice has sent them home in her carriage," said Pandora, watching her brother and sister climb down from the vehicle.

"Doubtless your sister claimed she was too tired to walk," said Mr. Marsh. When Lizzy and Winfield entered the drawing room, they were very eager to hear about Underwood's visit. Both were very surprised and disappointed to find that the gentleman had not called.

Soon it was time for dinner. The four of them were joined in the dining room by young Nicholas, who had spent the afternoon agonizing over Latin declensions with his tutor.

Conversation at table passed from the subject of Mr. Underwood to the gossip Lizzy and Winfield had heard at the home of their Aunt Lettice, who was known formally as Mrs. Paget. Since Mr. Marsh's sister was what uncharitable souls might call a tattlemonger, Winfield and Lizzy were filled with all kinds of interesting tidbits. Mrs. Paget was always able to relate the most fascinating stories about persons of their acquaintance as well as high-ranking members of society they had never met.

When dinner was finished, the family retired to the drawing room, where Lizzy continued to discuss what she had heard from her aunt. "I daresay you listened to a good many tales for one afternoon," said Mr. Marsh.

"But I had not seen my aunt for nearly a week, Papa," said Lizzy. "And it was so hard not being able to tell Aunt Lettice about Pandora's necklace." Lizzy regarded her father with a long-suffering look. The elder Marsh had sternly warned his daughter to say nothing about Underwood or the emeralds. Knowing what a gossip his sister was, Mr. Marsh had not wanted Lettice Paget spreading the story all over town.

"I think it dashed odd that Mr. Underwood did not call," said Winfield.

"Perhaps he is ill," suggested Lizzy.

"Ill or not, he might have sent word," said Winfield.

Pandora frowned. It *was* strange that she had heard nothing from Underwood. "I shall not sit about here tomorrow waiting for him. Papa, will you go with me in the morning to bring the necklace back to him?"

"That is a good idea," returned Mr. Marsh. "I shall be happy to do so. The sooner we see the last of that necklace, the happier I'll be."

Pandora nodded, but Lizzy reflected that she was not at all eager to be rid of the spectacular gems.

4

Midmorning on the following day, Pandora and her father walked the mile from their home to the residence of Arthur Underwood. The weather had turned cooler, but it was a fine day for morning exercise. Pandora enjoyed the walk with her father, although Mr. Marsh was a trifle apprehensive about carrying the emeralds. Having wrapped the jewelry case in brown paper to make it look less appealing to footpads, he clutched it firmly against him as they walked along the residential streets.

When they arrived at Underwood's home, they were greeted by his butler. "I am sorry, sir and miss," said the servant in response to their inquiry if Mr. Underwood was at home. "My master is not here. Mr. Underwood has gone to Brighton."

"Brighton?" said Mr. Marsh. He turned to Pandora. "This is dashed peculiar."

"When did he leave?" asked Pandora.

"Three days ago," replied the butler. "And I do not expect him to return for a fortnight."

"A fortnight!" exclaimed Mr. Marsh.

Pandora found this troubling. Why would Underwood have given her a gift and then left the city? And he had departed three days ago, well before the necklace was delivered. A strange feeling came over Pandora. Perhaps Underwood had not sent the necklace. But if he had not done so, who else would it be? She heard her father ask the butler about Underwood's address in Brighton. The servant obligingly provided the name of his hotel.

As they walked back to the house, Mr. Marsh shook his head. He was still clutching the paper-wrapped jewelry case. "I was hoping to settle this matter. What business does Underwood have in leaving town?"

"I cannot imagine why he would do so," said Pandora, regarding her father thoughtfully.

"Unless he was so certain that you would refuse him. He left so that you would have time to consider."

"Oh, I can hardly believe that," said Pandora.

Mr. Marsh smiled. "Why not? He might fancy that you would become so fond of the necklace in the time he is gone that you will decide to marry him in order to keep it."

Pandora laughed, and the two of them continued on toward their home.

The week following his uncle's death was a difficult one for Sarsbrook. Sir Humphrey had left instructions that he wished to be laid to rest in the village churchyard at Hedgewyck, a small community thirty miles from London that was the ancestral home of the viscount's mother's family. The viscount traveled to Hedgewyck with his sister Isabelle, who seemed very unhappy to be forced to leave town for even a short time.

The funeral was a somber affair attended by a handful of mourners. Sarsbrook and Isabelle represented the family. There were two elderly gentlemen who had known Sir Humphrey as fellow officers in the army many years ago. Three of the baronet's servants were also in attendance as well as a veiled lady, who sat in the back of the church and left before the end of the obsequies.

The viscount and his sister had to stay overnight in Hedgewyck, a necessity that neither relished. Sarsbrook was too accustomed to his own comfortable home and hearth to enjoy spending a night in a shabby public inn. Isabelle, Lady Verdon, was horrified at the accommodations and complained incessantly to her brother, much to Sarsbrook's annoyance.

Sarsbrook and his sister seldom spent time together despite the fact that during the season, Isabelle resided in London not far from Sarsbrook House. Although the viscount had a good deal of affection for his sister, they got along much better when they saw little of each other.

Ten years older than her brother, Isabelle oftentimes regarded the viscount with a disapproving maternal air. A highly regarded lady of fashion, Isabelle did not think that her brother paid enough attention to his appearance. She was also very unhappy about his avoidance of society and the fact that he did not seem to be at all interested in the very serious matter of selecting someone as his viscountess.

Isabelle had married at seventeen. The most sought-after young lady of her day, she had chosen Lord Verdon, a dashing baron who was then an intimate of the Prince of Wales. Verdon had long since fallen out of favor with the Prince Regent, but he still cut an impressive figure in society. He was considered to be one of the handsomest and best-dressed gentlemen in town.

Isabelle had been happy in her marriage, most of the time. She had had some bad moments years ago, before she had reconciled herself to her husband's infidelities. They had subsequently reached an understanding that allowed them to live peacefully together. Isabelle had three very handsome children, whom she adored. All in all, she thought herself a very fortunate woman.

Sarsbrook did not enjoy spending time with his sister or her family. He did not like his brother-in-law, judging him to be an "addle-pated dandy." Having no tolerance for children, the viscount did not much care for his two nephews and niece, whom he considered spoiled and ill-mannered.

Most times when brother and sister found themselves together, it was not long before they quarreled. The journey to Hedgewyck had been no exception. They had traveled from town together and had hardly left the city when Isabelle had brought up the topic of the new season and her brother's obligation to cease hiding himself away at Sarsbrook House. The viscount had very forcefully replied that what he did was no concern of hers, and that if she were to continue her prattling on about the subject, he would have his driver stop the carriage and deposit Isabelle and her lady's maid on the road.

Since Isabelle had not doubted that her brother was capable of carrying out such a threat, she had spent the rest of the journey in silence, glaring across at him. When they arrived at Hedgewyck, Isabelle had broken her apparent vow of silence to express a most unfavorable opinion of the village.

Sarsbrook had been glad when he had returned to town the day after the funeral. He had happily deposited his sister at her residence, expressing his regret that he had no time to come in to see the children.

Once back at Sarsbrook House, the viscount retreated to his library, where he took up his Greek texts while sipping a glass of sherry.

"Your pardon, my lord," said the butler, entering the room with some trepidation. His master did not like being disturbed while at work in the library and Archer had more than once received a spirited tongue-lashing for daring to enter his lordship's inner sanctum.

"What is it?" said Sarsbrook a trifle impatiently.

"Mr. Tucker is here, my lord. Will you receive him?"

"Yes, of course, do send him in."

The butler nodded, relieved. Since Tucker was the viscount's closest friend, Archer had suspected that his master would not be unhappy at being disturbed. However, with Sarsbrook, one never knew, for his lordship had a mercurial temperament that made it difficult to know how he would react.

"Robin, I am so glad to find you at home." The visitor entered the room. He was a tall, burly young man with a broad, boyish countenance and unruly black hair. An affable, cheerful man, Tucker smiled at his friend. "I do hope your journey to Hedgewyck was not too trying."

"Tuck," said the viscount, rising from his desk. "How good of you to come. Do sit down. Will you have some sherry?" Tucker was only too happy to indulge, and seated himself in an armchair as the viscount poured the sherry. Sitting down across from his friend, Sarsbrook took a long sip from his own glass. "My journey was damned trying, Tuck. I should not wish it upon anyone to be closeted with my sister on the bumpy road to Hedgewyck."

"But your sister is charming."

"Is she?" Sarsbrook regarded his friend in some surprise. "Do you think so? You would change your mind if you knew what she thought of you."

Tucker laughed. "I know what she thinks of me—that I'm a low-born nobody who dirties his hands in trade. But she cannot help it. She was raised to think in such a way."

"Good God, Tuck, your unbounded tolerance is altogether absurd."

"But that's how I tolerate you, Robin," said Tucker with a grin.

Sarsbrook smiled. He was very fond of his friend. Having met at Oxford, as students they had become inseparable companions. The friendship continued after they had left university and the two of them saw one another frequently.

Tucker's father was a wealthy textile mill owner who had risen from humble beginnings to great financial success. Although his lowly origins made London's society matrons view him with little enthusiasm, Tucker was a popular young man with a wide circle of friends of all ranks and stations.

"So, my friend," continued Tucker, "was Lady Verdon doing her best to vex you?"

The viscount nodded. "Like most of her sex, she is very good at irritating a man."

"You are too hard on women, Robin."

"Oh, yes, you are always championing them. But now that you are a married man, I daresay it will not be long before even gallant Tuck realizes how intolerable females can be."

Smiling, Tucker shook his head. "What a knothead you are, Robin. I must say marriage is a wonderful institution. Fanny and I are blissfully happy."

"Perhaps you are, but then you are one in a million."

"Nonsense. I only wish that you will one day know the same happiness. Indeed, you should think of marriage."

"Beware, Tuck, you tread on dangerous ground. I nearly came to blows with Isabelle on the same topic. It was my obligation to the family, she said, to provide an heir. Well, I am far too young to shackle myself to some bird-witted creature."

Tucker appeared amused. "I only hope that Cupid's arrow will find that black heart of yours one day."

The viscount's eyebrows arched slightly. "What a cruel thing to say, Tuck." Both of them laughed heartily at this comment. Then Sarsbrook began to tell his friend about his journey to Hedgewyck and his uncle's funeral.

After a time, the butler once again entered the library. "My lord, Mr. Hunt is here. He wishes to speak to your lordship."

Sarsbrook frowned. "He is my late uncle's solicitor," he said, turning to Tucker. "Show him in here, Archer."

"I will be going then," said Tucker, rising from his chair.

"No, do wait, Tuck. Hunt will not be long. You must stay for tea."

"Very well," replied Tucker.

The solicitor entered the room, looking appropriately solemn. "Lord Sarsbrook," he said.

"Hunt. May I present Mr. Tucker?"

"Your servant, sir," said Hunt, nodding to Tucker. He then looked at the viscount. "I shall not disturb you long, my lord. I have been going over your uncle's papers. His affairs are, in most regards, in order. As Sir Humphrey was a remarkably frugal man, it appears that there are few debts to settle. Of course, it will be some time before everything is sorted out.

"What I wished to tell you was that your uncle left

specific instructions that your lordship was to see to his private papers. I was to give you this key, which unlocks the desk in his library. The reading of the will has been scheduled for Tuesday next at eleven o'clock, if that will suit you."

"Yes, I suppose so," said Sarsbrook.

"Very good, my lord. Should you have any questions, do not hesitate to send word to me." After the solicitor took his leave of the viscount, Tucker and he returned to their sherry.

Sarsbrook looked down at the key in his hand. "My uncle's personal papers? What a dreary business."

"I imagine it will be very sad reading old letters and that sort of thing."

The viscount shrugged. "I expect so. By God, I do not relish the job." He appeared to suddenly have an idea. "You must help me, Tuck."

"Really, Robin, I shall be extremely busy for the next few days."

"But what about now?"

"Now?"

"Yes. Let us go there now."

Tucker was slightly taken aback by the suggestion, despite the fact that Sarsbrook often got an idea in his head and acted upon it at once. He had never been one to procrastinate. "Why, yes, I suppose I could go now."

"Good. Let's be off then." Without further discussion, the two men rose from their chairs and left the library.

5

When, after three days, there had been no word from Arthur Underwood, Pandora had written him a letter. She had spent a long time trying to decide what to say and it had taken three drafts before she was satisfied. Having thought it best not to directly mention the necklace, Pandora had asked whether he had sent, "the interesting parcel" she had received. By the time she had posted the letter, she had begun to think that perhaps Arthur Underwood had nothing to do with it.

The emeralds had been carefully secreted in the family safe although they were often taken out so Lizzy could admire them. Pandora had been glad when the day of Aunt Lettice's soiree arrived to provide a distraction.

Lizzy's first foray into society had been a great success. She had looked exquisite in the gown Pandora fashioned for her. As expected, Lizzy had excited a good deal of masculine attention, but when they had returned home, the younger of the Marsh sisters had expressed great disappointment that her aunt's company had seemed dull and commonplace. The gentlemen had been neither witty nor handsome enough to interest her, and Lizzy had lamented that they were outside the first circles of society.

Evidently having far lower standards, Pandora had enjoyed herself at her aunt's. Although she had first felt hopelessly dowdy beside her glamorous sister, Pandora had been happy to see a number of friends and acquaintances.

Upon returning home, Pandora had realized why she

had enjoyed herself so much that evening—Arthur Underwood had not been there. Whenever he was in attendance at functions, he so monopolized her company that she felt as though she could scarcely breathe.

Two days after Aunt Lettice's soiree, Pandora was in her sitting room, working on another gown for Lizzy. Her brother Nicholas dashed into the room, Mr. Stubbs at his heels. "Pandora! A letter has come for you. I knew you would wish to see it. Perhaps it is from Mr. Underwood."

Pandora took the missive from her eager young brother. "Thank you, Nicky." Breaking the seal, she opened the envelope while Nicholas sat down on the chair next to her. "It *is* from Mr. Underwood. At last I shall have some answers."

Nicky swung his legs back and forth as he watched his sister read the letter. He had been nearly as excited as Lizzy about the necklace, thinking it a very great pity that anything so beautiful would have to be sent back. Of course, unlike Lizzy, Nicholas thought the idea of Pandora marrying Underwood quite unthinkable. He had met that gentleman three times, and upon each occasion Underwood had roughly tousled his hair and called him a "fine little fellow." This form of greeting left Nicholas reluctant to make Underwood's acquaintance again.

"What does he say, Pan?"

Pandora looked up from the letter. "Do allow me to finish, Nicky." She turned the paper over and quickly scanned the rest of it. "Here it is. 'And, my dear Miss Marsh, as to your question concerning an interesting parcel, I fear I know nothing of that. I sent nothing.' "

"But, Pan, if he did not send the necklace, who did?"

Pandora frowned. "That," she said, "is a very good question."

While Pandora was reading Underwood's letter, Sarsbrook and Tucker arrived at the home of Sir Humphrey Maitland. The house was dark and covers had been placed over some of the furniture. Sir Humphrey's butler appeared forlorn as he admitted his late master's nephew and his friend.

They were ushered into the baronet's library. The curtains were drawn over the windows and the room was very dark. When the butler pulled the drapes open, bright light entered the room, illuminating the bookshelves and heavy oak furniture that adorned the library. "Good heavens," said Tucker, glancing about and catching sight of the one painting that hung in the room. It was a portrait of a very grim-looking ancestor from the sixteenth century. "Who is that?"

"That is Sir Richard Maitland. He was beheaded by Henry the Eighth."

"Then he has reason to be unhappy," said Tucker with an amused expression. "It appears your uncle had a great many books."

"They were his one extravagance," said Sarsbrook. Moving to the desk, he took from his waistcoat pocket the key Hunt had given him. Unlocking the drawer, he pulled it open. There was a box stuffed with what appeared to be letters. "Tuck, would you look through the papers on the desk? See if they are anything important. I shall look through this box of letters."

Tucker nodded as he took up a stack of papers from the desk. "They appear to be receipts," he said, examining them one by one. The viscount did not seem to be attending, for he was reading one of the letters he had taken from the box. Tucker continued to study the receipts. They were household expenses, for the most part. Noting the dates on the sheets of paper, Tucker nodded thoughtfully. "It appears your uncle was very regular in his payment of bills. I can imagine that he was much beloved by the butcher, the baker, and the candlestick maker."

Sarsbrook looked up. "Yes, I do not doubt it. These letters appear to be mostly from my mother. They are quite old. I should like to read them. I daresay Isabelle will be very interested as well."

Tucker nodded absently as he began looking over another receipt. "But what is this?" he said suddenly.

"What?"

Tucker regarded his friend with interest. "It appears books were not your uncle's only extravagance." He handed the piece of paper to Sarsbrook.

"What the devil!" exclaimed the viscount. "Wentworth and Johnson, Jewelers. One thousand pounds for an emerald necklace! And it is dated the day he died. This is very peculiar, Tuck."

"Indeed," returned the other gentleman. "I did not think your uncle left a widow."

"He was a lifetime bachelor. I had thought he lived the life of a monk. You cannot think he bought this necklace for some woman?"

"My dear Robin, for whom else does one buy jewels?"

Sarsbrook continued to stare at the receipt. "Perhaps there will be some clue among his letters. Surely if there was a woman, there would be some correspondence."

"In all probability. Then we must look for the billets-doux. Perhaps there is a secret panel under a drawer where Sir Humphrey hid them."

"Do not be absurd," said Sarsbrook.

Tucker burst out laughing. "It is not so incredible, Robin. Do look in the rest of the desk."

The viscount opened the other drawers. There he found sheets of stationery, sealing wax, pen nibs, scraps of paper with scribbles on them, but no perfumed letters carefully bundled. "There is nothing."

"Let me see," said Tucker, walking to the other side of the desk where he could peer into the drawers. "My father had a desk much like this one and there was a secret drawer."

"Secret drawers," scoffed Sarsbrook. "You have read too many romantic novels."

"Perhaps so," replied Tucker, continuing to study the desk. Pulling the drawers open slowly, he tapped lightly on the bottom of each one. While this search appeared fruitless, Tucker remained undeterred. "Would you please move, Robin? You are in my way."

"Of course," growled Sarsbrook, rising from the chair and moving away from the desk. Pulling the chair away, Tucker got down on his knees and climbed under the desk. The viscount heard him tapping underneath. "What in blazes are you doing?" he demanded.

"Wait a moment," said Tucker, continuing to crawl about. "I think I've found it!"

"What!"

"Yes, there is a drawer under here. "I'm not sure how to open it." There was a pause while Tucker worked to release the latch on the hidden drawer. "*Voilà!*" he shouted finally. Coming out from beneath the desk, he appeared very pleased with himself. "Look, there was something there. A book of some kind."

Sarsbrook took the volume from his friend. "It looks like a diary."

"Wonderful. Perhaps your uncle will mention the fortunate lady who received the emerald necklace."

Sitting back down at the desk, the viscount opened the book. Tucker pulled an armchair up beside him. "It *is* a diary. The first entries are from February of 1814."

"Scarcely more than two years ago. Does he mention a lady?"

Sarsbrook scanned the first page. "I do not know whether my uncle would have wished me to read his diary. Perhaps the honorable thing to do would be to toss it into the fire."

"You may toss it after you discover something of the necklace. I am consumed with curiosity."

The viscount did not reply. He turned the page of the diary, reading with rapt attention. "Good God!" he muttered.

"What is it, Robin?"

"Do wait a moment, Tuck," said Sarsbrook, continuing to read. Tucker sat watching him with interest. The viscount found the narrative he was reading as compelling as it was shocking. Having thought his elderly uncle a reclusive old man with no knowledge of women, it was an unsettling revelation to find that Sir Humphrey's diary was a detailed account of his amorous relationship with a certain "Miss M."

Miss M. was, in the baronet's words, "a goddess who brought to him the joys of Venus." While the viscount did not consider himself a prude, he was not prepared to find such vivid descriptions of the lady's charms. Sir Humphrey began innocently enough, expounding upon his love's "milk-white neck and shoulders," and then proceeding to her "two perfect breasts, the soft and delicious orbs that I made free with" and her "rounded thighs that quiver at my touch." Further descriptions made Sarsbrook's face grow quite hot.

"Dammit, Robin, are you going to tell me what it says?" said Tucker, seeing his friend's expression and growing impatient.

"In a moment, Tuck," said Sarsbrook, leafing through the pages. His eyes stopped on one paragraph. "There I found her in her bedchamber, lying upon the bed with her nightclothes fallen from her shoulders. Her red hair was spread about the pillow and her lovely face was flushed with wantonness." The narrative continued on, describing the bawdy revels that followed. As he read this account, Sarsbrook felt his body stir involuntarily. Shutting the book abruptly, he regained his composure with some difficulty.

"Whatever has he written?" said Tucker.

The viscount frowned, and then handed the diary to his friend. "You must swear you will tell no one about this."

"Upon my honor," said Tucker, taking up the book.

Sarsbrook watched his friend's eyes grow wide as he began to read. "By God, your uncle wrote this? And you thought that he lived like a monk. But then I suppose there were some very lecherous monks, were there not?" He continued reading. "My heavens, I should like to meet this Miss M."

"You are a married man, Tuck."

"Thank God. After reading this, I am very glad that I have a lovely girl sharing my bed tonight."

"Give that back to me," said Sarsbrook testily, grabbing the diary away from his friend. "And cease that smirking. I do not see that this is amusing in the least."

"No, of course not," said Tucker, trying hard to refrain from bursting into laughter. "But did he mention the emeralds?"

Opening the diary once again, the viscount turned to the last page. He read aloud, " 'I have commissioned a necklace for my dearest Miss M., to be made with emeralds said to be from the crown of an ancient queen. How splendid they will look with her wondrous red hair.' " He scanned the next few pages and then continued. " 'I had the necklace delivered to her today. I did not feel well enough to go to her myself. My dearest Miss M. has been so eager to see it. I only wish that I might have been there to behold her as she first cast her eyes upon it. I know I must change my will to protect my darling girl should anything happen to me. I shall send word to Hunt at once. And I must write to Sarsbrook. He is a good lad. I will entrust my dearest Miss M. to his care. He will not fail me."

"He changed his will?" said Tucker. "I daresay you will soon know the identity of this Miss M."

"I am not so sure of that, Tuck," said the viscount. "This entry is dated the day he died." Sarsbrook frowned again and closed the diary.

6

Pandora's father advised her to wait a few days before dealing with the problem of the emerald necklace. Although his daughter insisted she knew no other candidate for "Lancelot," Mr. Marsh thought that Pandora might have a secret admirer. This mysterious gentleman could still reveal himself, suggested Mr. Marsh.

The idea greatly amused Winfield and Lizzy, who delighted in suggesting possibilities no matter how preposterous. Pandora did not find the situation very amusing. Knowing that some kind of mistake had been made and that she had not been the intended recipient of the jewels, Pandora was eager to clear up the matter and find the rightful owner of the necklace.

Finally, at Pandora's insistence, Mr. Marsh sent Winfield on the mission of visiting jewelers and inquiring whether they knew of an emerald necklace that had been sent to a Miss M. Winfield returned some time later, saying that after exhausting himself by visiting every jeweler in the entire city, he could find no one who knew anything about the jewels.

While Winfield spoke very convincingly about the various shops he had visited, in truth, he had actually gone to but one jeweler. When he had received a negative reply at this establishment, Pandora's brother had begun to think seriously about what he was doing.

Having diverted himself to a public house where he could ponder the matter over a pint of ale, Winfield had reflected that if he found the jewelry shop that knew about the necklace, the matter would doubtless be straightened out very quickly. Pandora would return the necklace and that would be the end of it.

It seemed a very great pity to Winfield that an emerald necklace that very possibly was worth a fortune would be taken from the Marsh family. If they were to sell the jewels, there would be enough money to pay his debts as well as cover the family's expenses for a long time to come.

Although aware that the idea of keeping and selling the necklace was certainly unethical, it had seemed a very practical solution to a good many problems. After all, life was becoming increasingly difficult for Winfield, who had been forced to borrow money from disreputable lenders at ururious rates. In recent weeks, these lenders had been making it very clear that they wanted payment soon.

Pandora was disappointed that her brother was unsuccessful in finding out anything about the necklace. She insisted that he must have missed a few establishments, and asked him to try again the next day. Winfield promised he would, and that he would not rest until the mystery was solved.

The following afternoon Arthur Underwood appeared at Pandora's home, carrying a bunch of daffodils. As Underwood entered the drawing room where she sat with Lizzy and her father, Pandora suppressed a sigh. However, she managed a gracious smile when her suitor handed her the flowers.

Underwood was not a handsome man. Very stout and balding, he had a round face with a double chin and a bulbous reddish nose. Underwood tried to disguise his badly receding hair line by combing longer hair forward from the back of his head. The result was not very successful.

Thinking himself a man of fashion, Underwood tried very hard to dress in the manner of the dandies. However, the tight-fitting coats and pantaloons that were in style were entirely unsuited for his corpulent frame. Yet with the help of whalebone stays, Underwood managed to squeeze himself into a coat of dove-gray superfine, so tight that it made Pandora think of a sausage in its casing.

Mr. Marsh rose when their visitor entered. Although he had no wish to encourage Underwood, Mr. Marsh very civilly invited him to be seated. This Underwood did rather gingerly due to the tightness of his coat and pantaloons. When he finally settled himself into the armchair, he smiled brightly at Mr. Marsh and Lizzy before settling his admiring gaze on Pandora.

"You cannot know how glad I am to be back in town," said Underwood happily. "I sorely missed the company." He directed a meaningful look at Pandora. "What a delightful surprise receiving a letter from Miss Marsh."

Pandora frowned slightly. If only she had not had to write to him. Always careful to appear indifferent to his attentions, she had unintentionally encouraged him very much by her letter. "I hope you enjoyed Brighton, Mr. Underwood," said Pandora, hoping to deflect attention from the unfortunate missive.

"I had business there, Miss Marsh. It was rather dull for the most part. But the Prince Regent was there."

"Did you see His Royal Highness?" asked Lizzy, quite interested.

"Indeed I did, Miss Lizzy. And the prince nodded very civilly to me when I passed him on the promenade. I was quite astonished to find him looking directly at me. He nodded thus." Underwood demonstrated by nodding his head in a regal manner.

"Oh, how very exciting," cried Lizzy. "How I should love to see him. What a memorable day, Mr. Underwood."

"Yes, indeed," said Underwood, smiling broadly. "My cousin, Lady Shelbourne, is well acquainted with His Royal Highness. She has upon more than one occasion spoken with him."

"How wonderful for her," said Pandora, hoping her remark did not sound sarcastic. Unlike her sister, Pandora did not go into raptures at the idea of meeting royalty. Underwood was fond of mentioning his cousin Lady Shelbourne, who was married to an earl. This illustrious connection was a source of great pride to the banker, who scarcely allowed an hour to go by without reminding his listeners that he was related to a titled lady.

"I do wish I might meet Lady Shelbourne," said Lizzy wistfully.

"Why, perhaps you will," said Underwood. "Indeed, I am in hopes that my cousin will accept an invitation to dine with me soon and I shall certainly invite you all."

While Lizzy expressed great enthusiasm at the idea of meeting the great Lady Shelbourne, Pandora attempted to hide her irritation. She was very tired of hearing about the Countess of Shelbourne, especially since Pandora knew very well that the lady had nothing to do with Arthur Underwood. Lady Shelbourne had made an advantageous marriage that had propelled her into the first circles of society. According to a number of Pandora's acquaintances, her ladyship had been very quick to abandon her more ordinary relatives.

"And so, Miss Marsh," said Underwood, turning to Pandora, "did you ever find the answer to your question about the item you received? I was quite intrigued about that when you mentioned it in your letter. You did not say what sort of item it was."

"No, I did not," said Pandora. "Really, sir, it is of no consequence. Just a silly misunderstanding. I should not have troubled you with it."

"You did not trouble me at all, Miss Marsh. Indeed, you must feel free to ask me what you will."

"You are very kind, Mr. Underwood," returned Pandora politely.

"Do tell us more about Brighton, Mr. Underwood," said Lizzy, eager to return the conversation to the subject of the Prince Regent. "You did not say who was with the prince or what His Royal Highness was wearing."

Underwood was only too happy to fill in the details, chatting for some time about Royal George. Pandora, although not uninterested in her country's first gentleman, found herself hoping that Underwood would soon take his leave. When he finally did so, Lizzy looked at her sister. "Why did you not tell Mr. Underwood about the necklace, Pan?"

"My heavens, Lizzy," said Mr. Marsh. "Don't be a goose. Underwood is nearly as big a gabblemonger as your Aunt Lettice. No, indeed, Pandora was very wise to say nothing of it."

"Papa," said Lizzy thoughtfully. "If we cannot discover who owns the necklace, Pandora would be able to keep it, would she not? After all, she is a 'Miss M.' What else could one do?"

"I daresay one must contact the proper authorities," said Mr. Marsh. "You must rid yourself of the idea of Pandora keeping those jewels, Lizzy. It is out of the question."

"Indeed so," said Pandora, but in truth, lately she had been thinking how wonderful it would be if she were indeed the "Miss M." for whom the emeralds were intended.

7

When Sir Humphrey Maitland's will was read, no one was surprised to find that Lord Sarsbrook was the primary beneficiary. The baronet had had few close relatives. The eldest of three children, Sir Humphrey had had two sisters, one of whom had been Sarsbrook's mother. The other sister, Anne, had married against her family's wishes, eloping with the ne'er-do-well younger son of a country squire. Sir Humphrey's parents had disowned their willful offspring. The baronet had agreed with his parents and, for the rest of his life, had refused to have any contact with her.

In recent years, Sir Humphrey had relented enough to receive his sister's younger son, Miles Brackley. Yet after meeting with his nephew a few times, the baronet had taken a distinct dislike to him. The aversion had been primarily the result of young Mr. Brackley's brazenness in asking for financial assistance from his rich uncle.

Both Miles Brackley and his mother attended the reading of Sir Humphrey's will. Despite the unfortunate family situation, the Brackleys had some hope of the baronet having a last-minute change of heart. However, Mrs. Brackley and her son were sorely disappointed when they heard that Sir Humphrey had left his sister Anne the modest sum of one hundred pounds. To his nephew Miles he left the pitiful amount of ten pounds.

Sarsbrook's sister and her family fared much better, with Isabelle receiving ten thousand pounds and each of her children five thousand. There were a few other be-

quests to longtime servants, but the rest of Sir Humphrey's wealth went to Sarsbrook. Since the baronet had
lived frugally, increasing his fortune over the years with
prudent investments and the purchase of profitable land,
his estate was enormous.

The exact worth of it was difficult to calculate, but
knowledgeable persons judged that Sarsbrook's inheritence could be worth well over a million pounds. Since
he was already a man of considerable property, the viscount would soon find himself one of the richest men in
England.

Sarsbrook had expected to be the principal legatee of
his uncle's estate, since he knew very well that Sir
Humphrey had never made peace with his sister Anne.
However, he did have some sympathy for his cousin and
aunt when he heard the paltry sum that was to be settled
upon them.

After the reading of the will, Miles Brackley directed
an icy look at the viscount, while his mother held a
handkerchief to her eyes. Sarsbrook ignored them both,
adopting the supercilious look he reserved for persons he
actively disliked. While he had met Miles Brackley upon
only four occasions, that had been sufficient to form a
most unfavorable opinion of his cousin. The viscount
and Isabelle did not speak to Brackley or his mother, but
walked past them as if they did not exist.

After the reading of the will, the viscount reluctantly
agreed to join his sister and her husband for tea. When
they sat in Isabelle's drawing room, the conversation
was understandably about the will. "I must say I had not
expected the old fellow to do so well by me," said Isabelle's husband as he took up his teacup. "He hardly
knew us."

"He was an odd one," said Isabelle. "He never saw
anyone except Robert. I was terrified of him."

"That is ridiculous," said Sarsbrook.

"He was something of a recluse," said Lord Verdon. "I
believe I only met him once. He scarcely afforded me a
'How do you do?' But I think better of him now."

"And so do I," said Isabelle. "But did you see how that odious Miles Brackley looked at us? The audacity of the man. Why should he think that Uncle Humphrey would leave him anything? After all, when Aunt Anne ran off with his father, it nearly killed our grandmother. From what I have heard of my aunt and cousin, they are hardly worthy of any consideration."

"I so love a family feud," said Verdon. "In my family we all get on so famously. I should like a bit of a fuss."

Sarsbrook looked over at his brother-in-law, thinking him a great blockhead. He considered that he would not mind a family feud that kept him from speaking to Verdon. "I feel rather sorry for them," he said finally.

"Oh, come now, Robert," said Isabelle. "You cannot mean you think they deserved more from Uncle."

The viscount shrugged. "I doubt that most anyone deserves anything. But Brackley and his mother were left virtually nothing. They are as closely related by blood as we are."

"Well, you are too kind-hearted, Sarsbrook," said Verdon. "I have heard so many stories about your cousin Brackley—none of them complimentary."

"Indeed," said Isabelle, "he is nothing but a scheming fortune hunter."

"I do not doubt it," said the viscount, "but then so are half of those who inhabit the finest drawing rooms in London. There is certainly no shortage of fortune hunters, male and female."

"You are so cynical, Robert," said Isabelle, directing a disapproving frown at her brother.

"If anyone can live in this world and not be a cynic," replied Sarsbrook, "he is a fool."

"Come, come, that is nonsense," said Verdon. "I am no cynic, not in the least."

The viscount was tempted to remark that his brother-in-law's comment was proof of his theory, for he thought Verdon a great fool indeed. Exerting laudable self-control, he only raised his eyebrows slightly. "I fear I must return to Sarsbrook House. You must excuse me."

"But will you come to dinner on Friday, Robert? There will be a small gathering. Do say you will come."

"I could not possibly do so, Isabelle," replied Sarsbrook. "You know I detest dinner parties."

"Do you mean to refuse every invitation from me?"

"Most probably."

"You cannot intend to hide yourself away from society all season."

"I think that an excellent idea," returned Sarsbrook. "Now you must excuse me. I must take my leave."

Rather vexed with her brother, Isabelle was not displeased to see him go. When he had left the drawing room, she shook her head. "My brother grows more eccentric each year. Very soon he will be as reclusive as my uncle Humphrey was."

Verdon nodded. "Your brother dislikes me."

"He dislikes everyone."

Somewhat placated by knowing that he was not the only one in disfavor with the wealthy viscount, Verdon smiled. "My dear Isabelle, I don't believe I told you what Mrs. Fitzherbert said to Lady Westmont." Apparently forgetting all about his difficult brother-in-law, the baron launched into the latest bit of gossip.

The following morning the viscount rose early as was his custom. After completing his usual vigorous walk in Hyde Park, he ate a light breakfast before retreating to the library to work on his translation of Homer. Sarsbrook worked diligently for a time, but he found that he was having some difficulty concentrating. Try as he might, he could not prevent his mind from wandering to his late Uncle Humphrey and the baronet's extraordinary diary.

Sarsbrook attempted a particularly difficult passage for a time, but soon he laid it aside. Then, unlocking the drawer of his desk, he took Sir Humphrey's diary from its new hiding place. Since bringing it home, he had read it completely. Although Sarsbrook felt rather ashamed of his voyeuristic interest in his uncle's risque revelations, the book was irresistible.

After rereading the first section of the diary again, the viscount closed it. It would not do to dwell on the prurient document, he told himself sternly. He had always been a firm believer that a man must control his passions. His classical Greek studies had firmly committed him to the idea that logic and reasoning must keep the baser instincts in check.

He frowned, reflecting that the baser instincts had seemed easier to keep in check before he had read about Miss M. Since learning of his uncle's mistress, he had found himself wondering about that lady with alarming frequency. Of course, she was hardly a lady, considered the viscount.

Sarsbrook turned his thoughts to his uncle's final concerns for Miss M. He had expected that his nephew would see to her care. The viscount frowned. What was he to do about it? How did one provide for an uncle's mistress? In all probability, Sir Humphrey had showered her with gifts and money already. After all, there was the evidence of the emerald necklace.

The viscount pulled out the receipt for the jewels, which he had placed inside the diary. If he wished to find out the identity of Miss M., all he had to do was visit Wentworth and Johnson on the Strand.

After staring pensively at the receipt for a time, Sarsbrook tucked the paper into his pocket. Returning the diary to the locked drawer, he rose from his desk and called for his carriage.

It was not long before the viscount arrived at the jeweler's shop. Mr. Wentworth greeted Sarsbrook in the polite and dignified way he always greeted potential customers. When the tall young gentleman produced the receipt for the emerald necklace and handed it to the jeweler, Wentworth regarded him curiously.

"I wish to know to whom this necklace was sent," said Sarsbrook.

"I am afraid, sir, that that is confidential. May I ask your name, sir, and why you wish this information?"

"My name is Sarsbrook," replied the viscount, "and I shall keep my reasons my own."

"Lord Sarsbrook? Then you are the late Sir Humphrey's nephew. My profound condolences to you, my lord."

"Yes, yes," said the viscount impatiently. "Now what is the name and address of the person to whom this necklace was sent?"

"Of course, my lord," said Wentworth. "You must pardon me, I did not know who your lordship was. Do excuse me. I shall get that information at once." He hastened off, returning in a moment with a piece of paper, which he handed to Sarsbrook. "This is the name and address of the lady to whom the necklace was delivered."

The viscount glanced down at it. "Miss Marsh. 16 Clarence Place," it said. "Thank you," said Sarsbrook.

"Oh, it was my very great pleasure, my lord," said the jeweler.

Responding to this remark with an imperious nod, Sarsbrook left the jeweler's shop. Directing his driver to go to the address Wentworth had given him, the viscount sat back into the plush leather seats of his carriage. So her name was Miss Marsh, he said to himself. It was an ordinary enough name, not in the least flamboyant. He stared out the window as the carriage passed through the bustling London street. With luck, he reflected, he would very soon behold the amorous Miss M.

Pandora returned to the house in an excellent mood, having just completed a walk in the park with Nicholas and Mr. Stubbs. The weather had been cool and the walk invigorating. Pandora had enjoyed Nicholas's joyful chatter and Mr. Stubb's energetic enthusiasm when he saw squirrels and other fascinating creatures in the park.

Returning inside, Pandora deposited her straw bonnet on one of the chairs in the drawing room. She then took up the morning post and sat down on the sofa. Nicholas, having paused to give his hat to the maid in the entry hall, bounded into the room, Mr. Stubbs at his heels. "Martha said that Father has taken Lizzy to the glovemaker's," he said.

"Where is Winnie?"

"Martha said he has gone to see Mr. Aldrich."

"Oh," said Pandora. Mr. Aldrich was one of Winfield's closest friends. While Pandora liked him very much, she thought Mr. Aldrich an irresponsible young man who encouraged her brother's bad habits. Pandora looked at the mantel clock. "Why, it is nearly ten o'clock. Your tutor will be here at ten-thirty. Are you prepared for your lesson?"

"I am never prepared," said Nicholas. "And Mr. Mawson is so very ill-tempered."

"If you would study your lessons, he would be not so ill-tempered. You had best go and study before he arrives."

"Yes, Pan," said Nicholas gloomily. "Come, Mr. Stubbs." The little dog followed his reluctant master from the drawing room.

Pandora began sorting through the mail. There were several letters and a good many pieces of mail that Pandora knew would be tradesmen's bills. Recognizing the handwriting of a dear friend on one letter, Pandora opened it eagerly. She had just begun reading when her brother came into the room again with a book in his hand.

"Nicky, you should be studying."

"But I don't understand it in the least. What does it say?" Thrusting the book into his sister's hands, he pointed at a passage.

Pandora looked down at it. "In the words of Shakespeare, 'It was Greek to me.' " She smiled. "You know very well that I learned only a smattering of Greek. Father always said the study of Greek should be reserved for gentlemen."

"I do not know why ladies should be so fortunate,"

muttered Nicholas. "Can you not make anything out of it?"

Pandora shook her head. "Not much, I fear."

"Excuse me, miss." The maid entered the drawing room. "There is a gentleman to see you."

Pandora looked surprised. It was not an hour when one expected callers. "Who is it, Martha?"

"He gave me his card, miss." The servant extended the calling card to her mistress.

Taking the card, Pandora regarded it curiously. On it was written "The Viscount Sarsbrook." Pandora looked at the maid in some surprise. "The Viscount Sarsbrook?"

"He is waiting in the hall, miss. What shall I do?"

"I don't know," said Pandora, somewhat taken aback. Who was this Viscount Sarsbrook and why would he wish to see her? Suddenly a flash of insight came to her. The necklace! Perhaps it was about the emeralds. "I shall see him, Martha. Show him in." The maid nodded and hurried to return to her titled visitor.

"Who is it, Pandora?" said Nicholas.

"A gentleman is paying a call. Do mind your manners, Nicky," said Pandora, rising from her seat on the sofa and looking expectantly at the door. A moment later, a gentleman entered the room. Catching sight of Pandora and Nicky, he stopped and stared. On his face was an odd expression that was akin to bewilderment.

"Lord Sarsbrook?" said Pandora, noting the visitor's perplexed look. "I am Miss Marsh. And this is my brother, Nicholas."

Eager to display his good manners, Nicholas bowed gravely. "Your servant, sir," he said.

The viscount was aware that he was staring, but he had been completely surprised by the appearance of Miss M. She was very pretty, he thought, but far younger than he had imagined. Yet, there was the coppery red hair that his uncle had rhapsodized about. His eyes took in Pandora's excellent figure with keen interest, noting the voluptuous curve of her bosom beneath the modest, high-necked muslin dress she was wearing.

So this was the wild and passionate Miss M.! How proper and respectable she appeared, thought the viscount. Yet looking into her face, Sarsbrook thought he could detect a glimmer of her sensuous nature in her attractively full lips and expressive eyes.

"Is something wrong, my lord?"

"Wrong?" said Sarsbrook. "No, nothing."

Pandora looked expectantly at the viscount, who continued to regard her with such intensity that she felt rather embarrassed. Although rather discomfitted by her visitor, Pandora managed to return his gaze. There was something about him, she thought, that was rather attractive.

Pandora knew that Lizzy would not pronounce the viscount at all dashing, for he was dressed rather plainly and was not exceptionally handsome. His face was lean and his features too angular. Yet there was an intensity in his brown eyes that made Pandora's pulse quicken.

"Would you like to be seated, Lord Sarsbrook?" said Pandora finally, hoping her voice did not betray the fact that she was finding her caller rather disconcerting.

"Yes, thank you."

The viscount politely waited for Pandora to sit down before taking a seat across from her. Nicholas, utterly fascinated by the titled visitor, hurried to sit down as well. His lordship eyed him with disfavor. "I believe, Miss Marsh, that I should prefer to have a private discussion with you."

"Yes, of course. Nicholas, do go to your room. You must study your Greek before Mr. Hawson arrives."

"Very well," he said, reluctantly rising from his chair. He started to turn to go, but then paused. Looking at the viscount for a moment, the boy hesitated. "Do you know Greek, my lord?"

"Greek?" The unexpected question diverted Sarsbrook from his attention to Pandora. "Yes, I do."

"Oh, good. Would you look at this for a moment, sir? I cannot understand this part at all. Mr. Mawson will be furious with me. He has such a temper. Pandora is no

help, for ladies seldom know Greek, do they, sir?"
Nicholas hurriedly paged through the book until he
found the passage he was looking for. He pointed his finger to it. "Here, sir."

The viscount glanced at the text. " 'The Persians are
accustomed to deliberate on matters of the highest moment when warm with wine but whatever they in this situation may determine is again proposed to them on the
morrow in their cooler moments. Whatever also they
discuss when sober, is always a second time examined
after they have been drinking.' " Sarsbrook turned to the
boy. "Herodotus."

Nicholas viewed him with undisguised admiration.
"Why, thank you, my lord. I expect you know Greek
nearly as well as Mr. Mawson."

"Indeed," returned Sarsbrook, allowing a slight smile
to appear on his lips. "And I suggest you work harder at
it, sir."

"Do listen to Lord Sarsbrook, Nicholas," said Pandora. "I can imagine that he studied very hard when he
was your age. Now do go on. Lord Sarsbrook wishes to
speak to me."

"Thank you again, sir," said Nicholas before he reluctantly took his leave.

When he was gone, Pandora found herself feeling a
trifle uneasy being alone with the viscount. "It appears
you are a scholar, Lord Sarsbrook," said Pandora.

"I have devoted considerable time to the study of
Greek," he said, continuing to regard her with keen interest.

"Indeed," said Pandora. She looked down at her hands
and then back up at him. "Perhaps it might be best, my
lord, if you would state the purpose of your visit."

"The purpose of my visit?" Sarsbrook appeared mo-
mentarily confused. "Yes, of course," he said. "Forgive
me. You must be wondering why I have come here."

"Indeed I am, my lord."

"Very well, I shall get to the point. I am Sir Humphrey
Maitland's nephew." The viscount expected this pro-

nouncement to provoke some response in his listener, but Pandora only continued to regard his expectantly. He continued, "And it was my uncle's wish that you be taken care of. You must not worry. I shall do as my uncle wishes and you will be well looked-after."

"I am sorry, Lord Sarsbrook," said Pandora, regarding him with a confused look. "I do not understand what you are talking about. I do not know Sir Humphrey Maitland. I fear you mistake me for someone else. I am Pandora Marsh. Surely you are looking for some other lady."

"Pandora," said Sarsbrook. "She who released all the evils into the world."

"It is a ridiculous story," said Pandora. "An excuse for men to blame women for everything."

"Perhaps," said Sarsbrook, thinking "Pandora" a very fitting name for Miss M. "But Miss Marsh, I assure you that there is no need for you to pretend that you did not know my uncle."

"I am not pretending anything. I have never met Sir Humphrey Maitland."

"Then you did not accept a certain emerald necklace given to you by my uncle?"

"The necklace! Oh, yes, I did receive the necklace, but it was a mistake. It must have been delivered to the wrong address."

"And you are in the habit of keeping emerald necklaces that arrive from complete strangers?"

"I did not know who sent it," said Pandora. "I was trying to discover who did so. I would have returned it. Indeed, I shall fetch it at once."

"No, that will not be necessary. My uncle wished you to have it. It was one of the last things he did before he died."

"Before he died?" said Pandora.

"Didn't you know?"

"No, I did not. But why would I? I had never met him."

"Really, Miss Marsh, there is no need to deny it. Oh, perhaps I can understand your reluctance. It appears that you have been careful to maintain an appearance of respectibility. But you have my word that no one will know that you were my uncle's mistress."

"His mistress?" Pandora regarded him in utter amazement. Suddenly she felt as though she were having a bad dream. "I must ask you to leave this house, sir. I have been no one's mistress. You are making a very serious mistake." She rose from the chair and Sarsbrook followed suit. "This is quite preposterous. I should laugh if I were not so insulted. Indeed, I must ask you to leave at once, my lord. I shall get the necklace for you."

"That is not necessary, Miss Marsh. I wish you to have the neckalce. And I shall not distress you further. I do not doubt that the news of my uncle's death is most upsetting."

"I did not know your uncle!" cried Pandora in exasperation.

"As you wish, Miss Marsh," returned the viscount. He nodded to her and then turned to go. Pausing, he turned back to face her once again. "In accordance with my uncle's wishes, I have decided to settle one thousand pounds upon you immediately. You will receive the sum of five hundred pounds per year thereafter. I think that will be more than sufficient."

"That is utterly absurd! Why do you refuse to believe that I was never your uncle's mistress?"

Sarsbrook regarded her solemnly. "Because you are exactly as he described you. Now I must take my leave of you. Good day, Miss M. You may expect your money very soon."

"I shall not accept it," said Pandora.

"As you wish," said the viscount, leaving the room.

When he was gone, Pandora sat down in the chair once again. She picked up the calling card that she had dropped there. Was this Lord Sarsbrook mad? He was going to settle one thousand pounds on her because he thought she had been his uncle's mistress despite the fact that she vehemently denied it! It was too ridiculous.

At least the mystery of the necklace had been solved,

Pandora decided. She frowned to think of the jewels. At least now she knew to whom she could return them. She resolved to have Winfield do so at once.

Pandora sat with her arms folded, remembering the absurd scene she had just been part of. She wondered about Sir Humphrey's real mistress. Where was she? Had she been expecting to receive an emerald necklace? Pandora appeared thoughtful. Perhaps Sir Humphrey's actual mistress would appear. Perhaps she would call upon the viscount and explain who she was. How humiliated Lord Sarsbrook would be to find that he had made such a fool of himself. Smiling at the idea, Pandora devoutly hoped that the real Miss M. would reveal herself.

8

When Winfield came home, he entered the drawing room to find Pandora paging through fashion magazines. "Winnie!" cried Pandora, tossing the magazines aside. "You are back early."

Winfield shrugged. "Aldrich was indisposed. We were to go see a new horse he was thinking of buying, but he had a frightful headache and did not wish to go."

While normally Pandora would have suggested that her brother's friend was doubtlessly suffering the effects of his previous night's inebriation, she was at that moment unconcerned about Aldrich. "Thank heavens you are here, Winnie. I must tell you what happened."

"Is something the matter?"

"Not really. Or perhaps it is. Oh, Winnie, it was the most absurd thing. I daresay I do not know what I shall tell Papa."

Winfield sat down in a chair across from Pandora. "Then do tell me what has put you in the high fidgets."

"Scarcely an hour ago, a gentleman came here in regard to the emerald necklace."

"Good God, I hope you did not give it to him without proof that it was his."

"He would not take it although I was very eager to give it to him. His name was Sarsbrook."

"Not Viscount Sarsbrook?"

"You have heard of him?"

"Of course. Why, he is a very rich fellow. In fact, there was talk he had just inherited another fortune from his uncle. Can you imagine? A man who is already rich as Croesus receiving even more? There is no justice. But you mean that he sent the necklace?"

"No, it was his uncle. His late uncle, I should say."

"The one who left him the fortune?"

"I don't know," said Pandora. "His name was Sir Humphrey Maitland."

"Yes, I think that is the name."

"But, Winnie, I could not convince him that it was all a mistake. You will never guess what he thinks."

"What do you mean?"

Pandora paused for effect. "This Viscount Sarsbrook thinks that I was his uncle's mistress."

Winfield looked at his sister's indignant face for a moment before bursting into laughter. "Oh, Pan, that is too funny."

"Funny!" cried Pandora. "I should think you would be furious."

"But it is so ridiculous! That you are someone's mistress!" said Winfield, laughing again.

Pandora found herself rather insulted. She frowned. "Winfield Marsh, I am glad you find this so amusing."

"I am sorry, Pan. It is just that it was rather unexpected. Indeed, I shall summon up the appropriate righteous indignation." He stopped, and then continued in a melodramatic fashion. "How dare the man cast such aspersions upon the character of my sister!"

Pandora had to laugh. "Oh, very well, it is absurd. I have said so."

"But tell me exactly what Sarsbrook said."

"He said it was his uncle's wish that I be taken care of. That he would see to it that I was well looked-after.

"I told him he had mistaken me for someone else, for I did not know his uncle. He seemed unwilling to believe me, saying that I was trying to keep up a pretense of respectability. And then he said I was not to worry. He would tell no one that I was his uncle's mistress!"

"Good God," said Winfield. "This is damnably odd. And when you denied that you were Sir Humphrey's mistress, he refused to believe you?"

Pandora nodded. "He said I was exactly as his uncle had described me."

"By heaven, this is all very curious," said Winfield.

"You will be much astonished at this, Winnie. Sarsbrook then informed me that he would settle one thousand pounds on me immediately. Then I would receive five hundred pounds per year."

"Egad!" cried Winfield. "One thousand pounds! I must say this Sarsbrook is no lickpenny."

"And then when I wished to give him the necklace, he said he would not take it."

"One thousand pounds," said Winfield again. He shook his head. "Why, I should almost wish you *had* been the fellow's mistress, Pan."

"Winfield!"

"Oh, I am only quizzing you, Pan. Yes, I can see why this interview was most disturbing to you."

"What am I to do? What shall I tell Papa?"

Winfield appeared thoughtful. "Perhaps it would be wise to say nothing to him about Sarsbrook's thinking you were his uncle's mistress. He may be very upset. Family honor and all that. One doesn't know. Yes, I should think it better to say little to him."

"Perhaps you are right, Winnie. I think that the best thing to do would be to return the emerald necklace to Sarsbrook. You and I could go to him."

"I think it best that I return the necklace to Sarsbrook," said Winfield. "It would not do for you to go. Indeed, this is something better done by a man."

"Perhaps so, Winnie. Could you take the necklace immediately? I should like the matter settled before Papa returns home."

"Certainly, Pan. I shall go at once to this Sarsbrook. I daresay it will be a simple matter to find out where he lives. I shall take the emeralds and then we will be rid of them."

"Good," said Pandora, rising from her chair. "I shall fetch the necklace."

After his sister left the drawing room, Winfield folded

his arms across his chest. So this viscount was going to give Pandora a thousand pounds and then five hundred a year thereafter? The cogs in Winfield's fertile brain began turning rapidly as he considered what a difference that money could make to him. His financial difficulties were becoming more serious with each passing week. He really had no idea what he would do if he did not get some money to pay off his most pressing debts.

And now Pandora informed him that a wealthy lord was offering to settle a tidy sum upon her. A smile crossed Winfield's handsome countenance as he considered the irony. Perhaps it *was* a pity that Pandora hadn't actually been the old man's mistress.

After chiding himself for thinking such a thing, Winfield considered the matter further, wondering if there would be a way to profit from Sarsbrook's mistake. He half-wished that his sister was not such an honorable lady. Were she as unprincipled as he, they could extract a tidy sum from this viscount by accepting his offer of support. Still, reflected Winfield, perhaps there might be a way to keep the necklace. He continued to ponder the matter until Pandora returned to the drawing room.

Entering his library, Sarsbrook sat down at his desk and stared into the fire that burned brightly in the massive fireplace. Since leaving the home of Miss Pandora Marsh, he had replayed their meeting over and over in his mind.

How different she was than he had imagined, he thought. And how admirable of her to deny that she knew his uncle. Most women in her position would have been all too eager to accept money from him.

And she was damned attractive, reflected the viscount, thinking of Pandora seated in her drawing room. She had an almost regal dignity that he found very appealing. Having always prided himself on his ability to withstand the appeal of the various females who threw themselves in his direction, Sarsbrook had never lost his head, let alone his heart, over a pretty girl. Yet Pandora had exerted a strange, unsettling influence on him.

"I beg your pardon, my lord." His butler's words made the viscount look up in some surprise. "Mr. Miles Brackley is here to see you. Shall I tell him you are not receiving anyone?"

"Brackley?" said the viscount. "Damnation," he muttered to himself. "No, Archer, I shall see him. Show him in."

The servant bowed and retreated. He returned a short time later with a young man. Miles Brackley was a very handsome gentleman who dressed in the height of fashion. Of average height, he was blond, broad-shouldered, and solidly built. Feminine observers were always noting how his well-muscled calves and thighs filled out his tight-fitting pantaloons. His many admirer's thought his manly countenance particularly attractive. Brackley's aristocratic nose, pale-blue eyes, and square jaw set many feminine hearts aflutter.

"Sarsbrook." Brackley stood before his cousin, regarding him with a cool, disdainful expression.

The viscount did not rise from his chair, nor did he offer Brackley a seat. "Brackley," he said.

"I shall not take up much of your time, Cousin. I only wish to say that I believe a great injustice has been done to me and to my mother."

"Indeed?" said the viscount, regarding Brackley with disfavor. Although he had been sympathetic to his cousin at the reading of the will, seeing Brackley standing before him reminded Sarsbrook that he had little liking for him.

"I feel that Sir Humphrey treated me and my mother in an unspeakably shabby manner. I shall expect you, sir, to set matters right."

"And how do you propose I do so?"

"Why, by releasing our rightful inheritence to us."

"And what is your rightful inheritence?"

"Your sister received ten thousand pounds. I should

expect a like sum for my mother and also for myself. I would consider that fair."

"Would you?" returned the viscount. "I would think that rather excessive in light of the fact that it was clearly my uncle's wish that you be excluded. I am under an obligation to take his intentions into account."

Brackley frowned. He was growing increasingly aggravated with his cousin, who sat there looking up at him with obvious disfavor. Although they were hardly acquainted, Brackley had a deep-seated hatred for the viscount. He had grown up hearing his mother's stories of her family's iniquitous behavior toward her. Throughout the years, the thought of Sarsbrook's vast wealth while they lived in what Brackley considered to be near-poverty, irritated him like a festering sore.

The fact that Sarsbrook had aided his cousin upon each of the occasions he had asked for money only seemed to make matters worse. A proud young man, Brackley did not enjoy going to his wealthy relation hat in hand. He resented Sarsbrook's grudging generosity and coolness toward him.

"Does this mean that you have no intention of giving us what is our due?"

"Good heavens, Brackley, don't speak like a simpleton," said the viscount. "I have every intention of making some provision for you and your mother. I shall discuss the matter with my solicitor."

"Oh, yes," said Brackley, "you will discuss this with your solicitor and then settle some tiny allowance on us to salve your conscience."

Sarsbrook's brown eyes narrowed ominously. "I have no need to salve my conscience, Brackley. I suggest you get out of my sight before I decide to give you nothing. And I also suggest that should any further communications with me be necessary, you send a letter."

"Very well," replied Brackley. "Good day to you . . . Cousin." The last word was said with such vitriol that the viscount was rather taken aback. Before he had time to reply, his cousin had turned and stalked off.

"Idiot," muttered Sarsbrook. He considered Brackley a hotheaded fool. Had the man any sense, reflected his lordship, he would have sent a very civil, conciliatory letter, rather than appear before him resentful and ill-tempered.

The viscount rose from his chair to look out the window. He saw his cousin hop up into a stylish curricule pulled by two perfectly matched grays. Taking up the reins, Brackley directed an impatient blow with his whip to one of the animals. As Sarsbrook watched him drive recklessly away, the viscount shook his head disgustedly.

He then returned to his desk where he tried to forget both Miles Brackley and Pandora Marsh as he took up his translation of Homer. After some further musing about Pandora, the viscount was able to concentrate on his work. He was making good progress when the butler once again interrupted him.

"God in heaven, Archer," said Sarsbrook, "I want no more interruptions."

"But, my lord," said the servant, "there is a young gentleman here who says it is very urgent. He wished me to give your lordship this."

"What is it?" snapped the viscount. The butler walked over to the desk and placed a small jewelry case upon it. Sarsbrook opened the case to see Pandora's necklace. The emeralds glimmered seductively in their bed of velvet. His lordship looked up at the butler. "Send this young man in, Archer."

Winfield Marsh entered the library with some trepidation. Although he was a self-confident young man, he was not accustomed to visiting persons of rank and wealth like the Viscount Sarsbrook. While following the butler into the library, Winfield had not failed to note the grandeur of Sarsbrook House.

Catching sight of the viscount seated at his desk, Winfield saw a young man not much older than himself. He had expected someone of more advanced years and more grand looking. Winfield noted that the viscount was dressed in an unexceptional coat and that his lordhip's

cravat was very simply tied. It surprised Winfield, who
cared so much for the cut of his own clothes, that a man
of his lordship's wealth could be so indifferent to fashion.

As he approached the viscount, Winfield thought there
was something rather formidable about the man sitting at
the desk. Sarsbrook's demeanor was icy and his gaze intense.

Winfield bowed slightly. "My lord. I am Winfield
Marsh. Pandora is my sister."

"I see," said Sarsbrook. He pointed to an armchair
near the desk. "Sit down."

"Thank you, my lord," replied Winfield, seating himself. "You are very good to see me. My sister has told
me all about your visit with her. She insisted that I bring
the emeralds to you immediately. She did not want
them."

Sarsbrook looked from the glittering jewels to Winfield. "And you know of my conversation with Miss
Marsh?"

"Yes, my lord."

"And do you, too, wish to deny that your sister knew
my uncle, Sir Humphrey Maitland?"

Winfield paused before answering. He had given a
good deal of thought to what he would say when he met
the viscount. "I fear I cannot deny it, sir," he said.

"Then why would your sister do so?"

Winfield adopted a pained look. "I hope that you will
understand the sensitivities of my sister. Pandora
is ... or was a respectable young lady before she made
the acquaintance of your uncle." Sarsbrook raised an
eyebrow at this remark, but said nothing. Winfield continued, warming to his story. "We are not wealthy, Lord
Sarsbrook, but my family is an old and honorable one.

"Pandora made the acquaintance of Sir Humphrey
Maitland by chance, while walking in the park. He was
quite taken with her. Although she did not encourage
him, Sir Humphrey pursued her tenaciously. I fear he
contrived to seduce her." Winfield lowered his head and

placed his hand on his brow, hoping to look appropriately tragic. "He took advantage of a young, innocent girl whose confidence he had gained."

Sarsbrook frowned. He could scarcely imagine his uncle seducing an innocent young girl. But then, he could never have imagined his uncle engaging in the frolics described in his diary. It seemed to the viscount that one actually knew very little about anyone.

"And you knew about your sister and my uncle?"

Winfield hung his head in a shamefaced manner. "Alas, Lord Sarsbrook, I did learn of it. But what could I do? Pandora begged me not to tell our father. And Sir Humphrey was very generous to Pandora. Of course, Pandora did not use the money for herself. She used it for the family. I have three brothers, sir. One is at Cambridge and one at Rugby. And the youngest is still at home."

"I have made his acquaintance," said the viscount.

"Then you know what a fine lad he is. And I have a younger sister as well who is having her first season. You see, my lord, we have very little money and a good many members of the family to provide for. I am quite ashamed of myself, Lord Sarsbrook, but I did nothing about Sir Humphrey because I so needed money myself. You cannot know what it is to live with such a thing as this." Winfield once again placed his hand over his brow.

The viscount eyed Winfield curiously, thinking that his visitor was either telling the truth or that he was a very good actor. Deciding upon the former explanation, Sarsbrook nodded. "I told your sister that I had determined to settle a sum of money on her. She said that she would not accept it."

"She is very upset, my lord. I do hope you will understand how she would feel. She has been consumed with guilt over what has transpired. She wished me to tell you that she expects nothing from you—only that you keep her secret." Winfield paused to look earnestly at Sarsbrook.

"I have told her I would tell no one. And I do not understand why she would not allow me to settle an income upon her. My uncle expected me to take care of her."

"But Pandora was very adamant about not taking any money, my lord. And she wanted me to return the necklace to you. I believe she felt that it was not . . . proper that she keep it. It would only be a reminder"—Winfield paused and directed a stricken look at Sarsbrook—"of her shame."

Sarsbrook glanced down at the emeralds. "This belongs to your sister. I do not want it. You return it to her. If she finds it painful to have it, she may sell it if she likes. If she will not accept any money, she must take the necklace. You must tell her so."

Winfield rose from his chair, delighted. The interview was going exactly as he had planned. Hiding his true feelings behind a solemn expression, he nodded. "You are very kind, my lord. I shall tell her what you have said. I shall convince her to accept he necklace."

"I'm certain you will," returned the viscount, handing him the jewelry case. He had concluded that Winfield Marsh was something of a rogue. He was obviously unscrupulous, having admitted that money was more important than his sister's honor. "You must tell your sister that if she changes her mind, she has only to notify me. I would be happy to assist her."

"I shall tell her my lord," said Winfield.

Sarsbrook frowned slightly as the young man bowed and retreated from the library. He cynically reflected that in all probability he would hear from Pandora Marsh one day. He did not doubt that her brother would try very hard to convince her of the foolishness of rejecting his offer of support.

When Winfield left Sarsbrook House, he could hardly contain his joy. Very pleased with the interview, he congratulated himself for successfully hoodwinking Sarsbrook. Winfield felt like skipping down the street, but instead he very sedately climbed into the chaise he had hired and hummed to himself as it drove off.

9

While Pandora waited somewhat anxiously for Winfield's return, her father and Lizzy returned from their visit to the glovemakers. Lizzy was particularly pleased with the kid gloves she had bought. She chattered on about the excursion to the shop and the splendidly dressed ladies of fashion they had seen there.

Mr. Marsh was his usual good-natured self. Exceptionally hungry, he sent orders to the kitchen to serve luncheon early.

Nicholas joined them as Pandora, Lizzy, and their father were taking their places at the dining room table for a meal of cold mutton and potatoes. "Good afternoon," he said, hurrying to his chair.

"Good afternoon to you, Nicholas," said Mr. Marsh. "Did you have a good lesson with Mr. Mawson?"

Nicholas shrugged. "At least he was not altogether vexed with me, thanks to the gentleman who called on Pandora this morning."

Mr. Marsh regarded his elder daughter in some surprise. "A gentleman called here this morning?"

"Yes," said Pandora, "I was just about to tell you about him."

"He was a real lord, you know," said Nicholas. "And he knew Greek. He gave me a bang-up translation. Mr. Mawson said I had done very well."

"A lord?" said Lizzy. "Why did you not say anything, Pan?"

"I did not have the opportunity," said Pandora.

"Who was he, Pan?" said Lizzy. "Do not keep us in suspense."

"The Viscount Sarsbrook."

"Sarsbrook?" said Mr. Marsh. "I've heard the name. He was here? Was it about the necklace?"

"Yes, Papa. It was Lord Sarsbrook's late uncle who had sent the necklace. It was a mistake of some kind."

"Indeed it was," said Mr. Marsh. "Did you give him the necklace?"

"He did not wish to take it with him. When Winfield came home, I asked him to take the emeralds to Lord Sarsbrook. He should be returning shortly."

"Dashed odd that the man did not take the necklace in the first place," said Mr. Marsh.

"But how lucky that he did not," said Lizzy. "Is is not much better that Winfield calls upon him? Now Winfield will make Lord Sarsbrook's acquaintance. Wouldn't it be wonderful if he would invite us to dinner or to a ball?"

"Lizzy," said Mr. Marsh, "your imagination is running away with you again. I know my son is a charming fellow, but I doubt that he will become this Sarsbrook's boon companion in an instant. No, my dear, I don't believe we will hear of the viscount again."

"But one never knows," said Lizzy hopefully. "Pandora, what was he like? How old was he? Was he very dashing?"

"I should not call him dashing, although he was not unhandsome," said Pandora. "He was fairly young, not past thirty, and he was tall, with brown eyes."

"Oh, how I wish I had been here," cried Lizzy. "Phoebe would have died of envy had I met him."

"Then it is fortunate that you were absent," said Mr. Marsh, smiling at Lizzy. Turning to Pandora he continued. "What I wish to know is how his uncle sent an expensive necklace to you in the first place."

"I fear I do not know, Papa," said Pandora, not wishing to reveal that the necklace had been intended for Sir Humphrey's mistress.

At that moment Winfield entered the dining room.

"Winnie!" cried Lizzy. "Did you see Lord Sarsbrook? Pan was telling us that he came here about the necklace. Did you see him?"

"I did indeed. He received me in his library. And I must say Sarsbrook House is very grand. But then they say that Sarsbrook is one of the richest men in England."

"You must tell us everything!" said Lizzy excitedly.

"Yes," said Pandora. "What happened?"

Winfield sat down at the table. "I brought the necklace to Lord Sarsbrook. We had a short chat and that was all."

"Was he quite civil?" said Lizzy.

"Entirely civil," said Winfield.

"Did you make a good impression on him?" said Lizzy.

Winfield grinned. "When do I not make a good impression, Lizzy?"

"Don't be odious," said Lizzy. "Do you think he liked you?"

"I could not imagine that he did not find me a perfectly delightful fellow," returned Winfield with a grin.

Pandora laughed. "Lizzy is hopeful that you so charmed the viscount that he will issue us an invitation to dine at his house."

"Oh, I am not certain that I was that charming, Lizzy," said Winfield. "I fear we did not converse very long. And Sarsbrook is not the most amiable of gentlemen."

"That is a pity," said Lizzy. "And now we will never see the necklace again."

"I am glad it is gone," said Mr. Marsh. "Did this Sarsbrook explain how it happened that the jewels were delivered here?"

Winfield shook his head. "He really said very little, Father."

"Well, the matter is closed. I fancy you will miss your grand necklace, Pandora," said Mr. Marsh.

"No, Papa," said Pandora. "I do not think emeralds suit me very well." She smiled. "I much prefer rubies and diamonds."

Lizzy sighed. "Would it not be wonderful if one were really rich like Lord Sarsbrook?"

"If we were rich," said Nicholas eagerly, "Pandora could buy that silk she saw at the linen drapers, and I could have the lead soldiers that we saw at the toy shop."

"Yes," said Lizzy, "and I could have a new hat and Papa a new coat."

"And I a coach and four!" cried Winfield. Gales of laughter greeted this pronouncement.

"You are all very silly," said Pandora.

"It does not hurt to dream, Pan," said Winfield with a grin.

"No, indeed not," said Lizzy. "But Winfield, you have not told us everything. Do tell us more about Lord Sarsbrook and his house."

Winfield was very pleased to do so. While he launched into a description of the very grand Sarsbrook House, Pandora regarded her brother thoughtfully and wished that she knew exactly what had occurred at the viscount's residence.

In the afternoon Sarsbrook was diverted by business matters concerning his estate in Somerset. His solicitor called, bringing a number of financial statements for his consideration.

Shortly after the lawyer had taken his leave, the viscount's butler announced another visitor. "Mr. Tucker is here, my lord. He is in the drawing room."

Always pleased to see his friend, Sarsbrook nodded. "I shall join him there." Entering the drawing room, the viscount found Tucker standing before a portrait of one of his lordship's ancestors, another sour-faced gentleman, in Elizabethan costume. "I am glad to see you find that painting so fascinating, Tuck."

Tucker turned to smile at the viscount. "I find all of your ancestors fascinating, Robin. They all look so fierce and formidable."

"All of the Despencers were fierce and formidable,"

replied Sarsbrook, "especially the female members of the family."

Tucker laughed. "Well, Robin, I am here to get you out of your den and into the sunlight. 'Tis a fine spring day outside, my lord. And I have a new phaeton. Come for a ride."

"I fear I am not in the mood, Tuck. Maybe another day. But do stay for tea."

"I should be happy to," said Tucker. "Your Mrs. Chambers' tea is incomparable." The amiable Mr. Tucker settled his burly form onto the sofa while the viscount rang for tea. When the servants entered with the refreshments, Tucker smiled appreciatively at the assortment of bread and tea cakes that graced the silver serving trays. "Yes, yes, Mrs. Chambers is in fine fettle, it appears."

"Yes," said Sarsbrook, taking up his teacup and a piece of bread and butter, while Tucker loaded a variety of delectable baked goods onto his plate.

"Well, Robin," said Tucker, "I heard that your uncle's will was read. You are now an even richer man."

Sarsbrook nodded. "It would appear so."

"I congratulate you on your good fortune." Tucker took a bite of cake. "But did you discover anything more about your uncle's mistress? I must say that is what interests me. I should very much like to find out who this Miss M. is."

The viscount sipped his tea. "I did find out who she is. My uncle wished that I provide for her, so I had no alternative but to discover her whereabouts. In fact, I have met her."

"You have met her! I must say you act quickly, Robin. What is she like?"

Sarsbrook tried very hard to appear indifferent. "She is not what one would expect. She appears in all ways perfectly respectable. She is very young, perhaps twenty or somewhat older. It appears my uncle led her astray."

"Very far astray if one is to believe his diary," said Tucker with a grin.

The viscount frowned. "I have tried to settle an income on her, but she has refused my assistance."

"Indeed?"

Sarsbrook nodded. "It is quite remarkable to me that a woman would fail to accept money."

"Robin, do not be so ungallant."

"I wish she would have accepted my support. I cannot help but think that I have not fulfilled my obligation to my uncle. And I feel guilty for his actions toward the young lady. He ruined her."

"Come, come, now, Robin, there is no need for you to feel any responsibility. 'Tis the way of the world, like it or not. I'm sure you attempted to treat the girl generously. I daresay it is more than most men would have done."

"But what will she do?"

"What does any woman do? Find another lover or perhaps a husband."

"A husband?" said Sarsbrook.

"Why yes, there are plenty of cast-off mistresses well-married. Perhaps you could find a husband for her, Robin. Indeed, find her a husband and make a respectable woman of her."

Although Tucker was joking, he saw that his friend appeared to be taking him seriously. The viscount took another sip of tea, a thoughtful expression on his face. For some reason, he did not like the idea of Pandora Marsh taking another lover or a husband.

Tucker noted his friend's serious expression with a mixture of surprise and amusement. It appeared that Sarsbrook was unusually interested in his late uncle's mistress. Tucker suppressed a smile and hoped that he would soon be able to have a look at the mysterious Miss M.

10

At her first opportunity Pandora asked Winfield for more details regarding his visit to Lord Sarsbrook. Winfield insisted he had set things right. He informed his sister that he had made the viscount understand his mistake, and Sarsbrook had been suitably embarrassed. Winfield noted that the matter was settled and Pandora should think nothing more about it.

Pandora, however, could not help thinking about the viscount and her brief encounter with him. It seemed very curious to Pandora that such a short meeting with a stranger had such a strong effect on her.

Pandora had never been given to romantic fancies. In fact, she had not found any of the gentlemen she had met in the past to be memorable in the least. Yet there was something about Sarsbrook that made her keep thinking about him. It was oddly vexatious.

As the week went by, Pandora thought less about Sarsbrook and more about the day-to-day matters of the household. She was making another gown for her sister, more elaborate than the last one. There were great lengths of French lace to be affixed to the skirt and bodice of the dress, which kept Pandora busy with the time-consuming work.

Winfield was gone most of the time with his friend Aldrich, a fact that did not please Pandora. She worried that her brother was gambling despite the fact that he denied it vehemently. Pandora did not know where he had gotten the money to game away, but she suspected that he was going further into debt.

Saturday morning, Pandora rose before eight. Unlike the other members of her household, she was an early riser. The house was always quiet in the morning and it was a good time to write letters or go over tradesmen's bills.

That day, however, Pandora found that she was not the only one to have risen early. She was surprised to see Nicholas in the drawing room reading a book with Mr. Stubbs at his feet.

"Nicky, you are an early bird today."

"Pan," said the boy, shutting the book. "I could not sleep. I was too excited."

"Excited?" said Pandora. "Whatever for?"

"Winfield said that he would take me to Hyde Park to fly my kite."

"Oh, that is very good of him." She looked at the clock. "I fear it is rather early for Winfield."

"I know. I shall go and see. I may have to wake him up."

"That is a good idea," said Pandora. Nicholas nodded and hurried from the room, the terrier at his heels. Pandora sat down at the desk in the corner and took out her stationery. She had a number of letters she had been meaning to write.

She had scarcely picked up her pen when Nicholas appeared again in the drawing room. "Oh, Pan, Winfield said he will not take me to the park," he said gloomily. "He said he is too tired. He got home very late and he does not wish to be disturbed. I think it quite infamous for someone to give his word and then not do as he promised."

"That is horrid of him, to be sure," said Pandora. "But Nicky, perhaps you could go some other time."

Nicholas shook his head. "Today is perfect. I went outside. It is very windy. Perfect for kites. I cannot think it will ever be better."

Seeing her youngest brother so disappointed, Pandora frowned sympathetically. "What would you think, Nicky, if I took you to the park?"

"Would you, Pan?" said Nicky, his face brightening. "That would be famous! I shall get my kite!" He sped off, with Mr. Stubbs running excitedly after him.

Pandora went to her room to fetch her bonnet and pelisse. She was wearing a fetching morning dress of sprigged muslin that she had made herself last season. She was rather proud of the close-fitting pelisse that was worn over the dress. Having copied it from a French design, Pandora had fashioned the garment from pale-blue Italian silk. It had a military look, with epaulettes and silver braid trim. Glancing in the mirror as she put on her hat, Pandora eyed her reflection with approval, thinking that she looked quite presentable that morning.

When she came downstairs, Pandora found Nicholas and his dog waiting impatiently. In her brother's hands was his kite. "Do let us go, Pan, it is growing late."

"It is not late at all, Nicky," said Pandora. "Come, give me Mr. Stubbs' lead. You must carry the kite. I will tell Martha that we are going out."

"Oh, I have told her, Pan," said Nicholas, not wanting to wait one moment longer.

"Very well," said Pandora with a smile. "Let us be off then."

Nicholas needed no further encouragement. He opened the door and politely allowed his sister to go first. Hyde Park was more than a mile from their house, but it seemed a very short way to Nicholas and Pandora, who were well accustomed to walking. The sky was overcast, but the weather was warm. To Nicholas' delight the wind blew gustily as they strolled along.

As usual, despite the early hour, there were many in the park taking advantage of the spring weather, riding or walking through the broad expanse of greenery. Pandora loved Hyde Park. Now that their circumstances forced them to live in town throughout the year, she often missed the country. Hyde Park, with its trees and vast green lawns, always made her feel much better whenever the bustle and dirt of the city seemed oppressive.

Very eager to fly his kite, Nicholas led Pandora to the area of the park he had long ago selected. No one else was there and Nicholas was particularly glad that he would have the area to himself. Mr. Stubbs was particularly happy to find himself in the park. He pulled at his leash, barking every so often with sheer happiness.

It took a good many attempts for Nicholas to get his kite airborne. At first it seemed to take off only to come crashing to earth, but finally the fragile kite was lifted into the sky where it twisted and turned and rose higher and higher. Nicholas was delighted. He released more and more string. "Do you see how high it is, Pan?" he cried. "Isn't it wonderful?"

"It is indeed," said Pandora, watching the kite's graceful movements. Mr. Stubbs appeared to watch, too. He wagged his short tail excitedly and danced about, jumping into the air from time to time as if he, too, wished to fly. When he finally tired himself out, the terrier sat down and cocked his head as he watched Nicholas.

The kite flew easily for a good long time. Finally, Pandora realized that they should get home. "Nicky, I think that you should bring the kite down. It is growing late. We should go home."

"Oh, Pan," cried Nicholas. "Could we not stay a little longer?"

"Just a few minutes then."

When the few minutes quickly passed, Nicholas was once again reminded that they would have to be going. He reluctantly began to reel in the kite. As the kite lost its altitude, it was hit by heavy winds, causing it to fly wildly downward. In a brief moment it came crashing down, coming to rest in a tree.

"No!" cried Nicholas in alarm.

Pandora had watched the unfortunate descent with nearly as much horror as her brother. "Oh, dear, Nicky. I fear that is the end of your kite."

"Oh, I do think I can get it," said Nicholas, running to the base of the tree. The flimsy object was in one of the upper branches.

"I don't see how," said Pandora as she and the dog followed her brother. She peered up into the branches. "It is hopeless."

Nicholas continued to roll up his string as he looked up into the tree. "If I climbed up there I could pull it down," he said, pointing to a branch above his head.

"That is out of the question," said Pandora. "I shall not have you risking life and limb over a kite."

"But, Pan, it is only that branch there. I could hop up here and then climb there in a trice."

"Absolutely not," said Pandora firmly.

"Oh, please, Pan, this is the best kite I have ever had!"

Pandora looked at the tree limb in question. It was not very high up and it did look fairly easy to climb. "Oh, very well, if you are careful. And you are not to go any farther than that branch. If the kite does not come down, you climb down at once."

Grinning, Nicholas jumped up to grasp the tree branch. With the agility of a monkey he swung up onto the branch and then proceeded to the next higher one. From there he pulled at the kite string. The kite did not budge at first, but finally pulled free from its perch. Nicholas uttered an exclamation of triumph as it fell to the ground.

"Now come down, Nicky!"

The boy grinned again and lowered himself to the next branch. "You see, Pandora, that was so very simple." Nicholas had scarcely uttered these words when he lost his footing on the lower branch. While his sister watched in horror, he came tumbling down, landing with a thud beside Pandora.

"Nicholas!"

"Oh, it is nothing, Pan," said the boy. "What a dashed numbskull I am. I am glad that Winfield did not see me. He would call me a clumsy oaf."

Relieved that Nicholas appeared unhurt, Pandora reached down to help him to his feet. "Ow!" cried the boy suddenly.

"What is the matter?"

"My ankle," said Nicholas, gingerly placing his weight on one leg. "Yes, it does hurt."

"Oh, Nicky, are you all right?" Pandora asked. "Can you walk?"

"I don't know," replied Nicholas, taking a few steps. He winced. "I think so, Pan. If we go slowly."

"Might I be of some assistance, Miss Marsh?"

Pandora swung around at the sound of a masculine voice behind her. She regarded the gentleman who stood before her with astonishment. It was Sarsbrook.

The viscount had been taking his usual morning walk when he noticed the kite. The sight of the high-flying object had filled his lordship with unexpected nostalgia. As a boy he had often flown kites. Having stopped to watch the kite's progress, Sarsbrook had noted the young lad and the lady beside him with the small terrier.

Never expecting to see Pandora Marsh, he had been stunned when the lady had turned around. Was it she? He had thought that he must be mistaken, but as he had come closer, he realized that it was indeed Pandora Marsh with the boy he had met at her home.

Seeing the object of so many of his recent thoughts had rather startled the viscount. He had not known whether to retreat or to boldly go up to the lady. Nicholas' fall had made him come forward immediately to offer assistance.

Pandora could only stare at him, dumbfounded. "Pan, it is Lord Sarsbrook!" said Nicholas. "Good morning, my lord."

Mr. Stubbs, delighted at the sight of another human, barked and tried to jump up on the viscount. Pandora pulled him back. "Bad Mr. Stubbs. I am sorry, Lord Sarsbrook. Mr. Stubbs is not the best-behaved of dogs."

The viscount looked down at Mr. Stubbs, but did not seem in the least disturbed by the terrier's bad manners. "Do you need help, Miss Marsh?"

Pandora looked rather embarrassed. "Nicky is having some difficulty walking. It is some distance home, but he does think he can manage."

"My home is very near here," said the viscount. "My groom can take a look at your brother's leg. He is very good with horses."

Pandora raised an eyebrow as her gray eyes met Sarsbrook's brown ones. "That would be very kind, but I do not like to trouble you."

"It is no trouble," said the viscount. "Come, lad. Can you walk? It is not far."

"Yes, my lord," replied Nicholas, walking slowly. It was clear by his expression that he was in pain.

"Wait. I'll carry you."

"Oh, no, Lord Sarsbrook, please do not . . . " Pandora protested, but the viscount had already lifted Nicholas up and had started across the park. "My lord, he is too heavy!"

The viscount continued on, oblivious to Pandora's words. "Get the kite, Pan!" called Nicholas.

Pandora picked up the kite and hurried after the viscount and her brother. Mr. Stubbs, thinking his master's plight most amusing, pulled on the leash and raced after them so that Pandora could barely keep up.

Upon arriving at Sarsbrook House, one of his lordship's footmen came out to take Nicholas from the viscount's arms. The brawny servant then carried Nicholas inside. "Take him to the drawing room," said Sarsbrook, "and fetch Willis."

The footman nodded. "Aye, m'lord."

Nicholas seemed very pleased to find himself in such a grand house and at the center of attention. When the footman deposited him on the sofa, he looked around the drawing room with keen interest. It was a magnificent room filled with splendid furniture, Italian and Venetian paintings, and Greek urns.

"You are very kind, Lord Sarsbrook," said Pandora.

He regarded her intently. "It is nothing," he said.

"It was a very great surprise to see you, my lord," said Pandora.

"I hope I did not alarm you, Miss Marsh."

"No, my lord."

The viscount thought it best to turn his attention to Nicholas. "And you, lad, how is that ankle?"

"Oh, I am sure it is not serious, Lord Sarsbrook. It does not hurt very much."

"Good," replied the viscount.

"Lord Sarsbrook," said Nicholas, "thank you for helping me with the Greek. For once Mr. Mawson thought I was not completely slow-witted. You must be very clever to know Greek, sir."

"I do not know about that," said Sarsbrook.

"Oh, indeed you must be," said Nicholas. "Even Pandora does not know Greek and she is certainly the cleverest person in our family."

"Really, Nicholas, do not bother his lordship with nonsense."

By this time Sarsbrook's groom had appeared, accompanied by the footman who had carried Nicholas. A small wiry man, the groom knelt down to examine the boy's ankle. "Does this hurt, lad?"

"No. Oh, now it does a little."

" 'Tis not broken, m'lord," said the groom, rising to his feet. "A sprain. 'Twill be right in a few days if the lad stays off it."

"Good. Thank you, Willis."

The servant bowed and left. "Your man certainly seemed to speak with authority," said Pandora.

"There is no better man with horses in all of London," said Sarsbrook.

"I should think he might wish to get a license from the Royal College of Physicians," said Pandora with an ironical look.

A trace of a smile appeared on the viscount's lean countenance. "There are many surgeons in London with a good deal less sense than Willis," he said. He turned to the footman. "Take the boy to the kitchen, Ned. Have Cook find him something to eat."

"Aye, m'lord."

The footman scooped up Nicholas and carried him off with Mr. Stubbs following behind, leaving Pandora alone in the drawing room with the viscount. He looked at her, noting the stylish pelisse and bonnet she was wearing. He did not pay much attention to ladies fashions, but it seemed that Miss Marsh's attire was very modish and attractive. She was a very good-looking woman, he found himself thinking once again.

Pandora was well aware that Sarsbrook was gazing at her with the same intense scrutiny that he had given her the first time they had met. She looked down, somewhat discomfitted.

"I am glad to have this opportunity to talk to you, Miss Marsh, and do not worry about your brother getting home. I shall take you in my carriage."

"That is too kind, my lord, but I could not think of imposing on you in such a way."

"It is a very small thing, Miss Marsh," replied Sarsbrook. "I assure you it is no inconvenience. Do sit down, madam. Seeing you in the park was most fortuitous. I do not think that our first meeting was entirely successful."

Pandora hesitated for a moment. She knew very well that it was not at all proper for her to be alone in a gentleman's drawing room, especially when that gentleman had taken her for the mistress of his uncle. She finally sat down on an elegant French chaise longue upholstered with peach-colored silk.

Sarsbrook remained standing. He continued. "As I am sure you are aware, your brother called upon me and explained everything."

"I am very glad, my lord," said Pandora. "I am assured he made your lordship understand the truth of the situation."

"Yes, your brother made things very clear," said the viscount, directing a somber look at Pandora. He hesitated, wondering whether to bring up the subject of a settlement.

Pandora expected Sarsbrook to apologize for his behavior in mistaking her for a fallen woman, but no apology was forthcoming. "I do think it best if the matter were forgotten," said Pandora.

"Yes," replied the viscount, deciding it best to say nothing further.

There was a rather awkward silence. Pandora felt decidedly uneasy in Sarsbrook's presence. There was something about him that caused a most unsettling feeling within her. Pandora looked about the splendid drawing room, gazing at the magnificent Renaissance paintings. She found herself wondering what it would be like to live in such a grand place. She turned her attention to one of the pictures. "Is that a Titian, Lord Sarsbrook?"

"Yes, indeed," returned the viscount, pleased that the lady seemed knowledgeable about art. "Do you like it, Miss Marsh?"

Pandora continued to gaze at the picture, which apparently portrayed a subject from Greek mythology. It was a rather turbulent scene featuring a good many horses and men with spears as well as centaurs. "It is magnificent, my lord." She glanced at the other paintings that adorned the walls. "You must be very devoted to art to have collected such works."

Sarsbrook shrugged. "It sometimes comforts me to know that a few members of the human race are capable of creating beauty. Art awakens in me that faint ember of hope that men are not entirely degenerate."

Pandora regarded the viscount curiously, thinking that it appeared his lordship did not have a high opinion of his fellow man. She was uncertain how to reply to such a remark. "I should be going home now, Lord Sarsbrook," she said. "If you would have someone fetch Nicholas, we shall take our leave."

"Very well," replied the viscount, not at all pleased with the shortness of Pandora's visit. Not knowing how to prolong it, however, he rang for a servant. "Fetch Master Nicholas," he told the footman who answered the bell. "And have my carriage brought round." Sarsbrook turned to Pandora. "I shall take you and your brother home in my carriage."

"I do thank you for offering your carriage. You need

not accompany us . . . " Pandora paused. "That is to say, if you are too busy, my lord."

"I am not too busy in the least," said the viscount eagerly.

"Thank you, my lord."

When Nicholas joined them, he was in very high spirits. The viscount's servants had made a great fuss about him, and he had charmed them with his manners and conversation. The footman who had carried Nicholas into the drawing room was only too happy to take him to his lordship's carriage.

The viscount handed Pandora into the vehicle, which was a splendid equipage pulled by four stately black horses. The viscount's coat of arms was emblazoned on the doors. Nicholas thought it very grand to find himself ensconced on the leather seat beside his sister. With Mr. Stubbs on his lap, he peered out the window as the driver directed his horses into the street.

"Those are very fine horses, my lord," said Nicholas, smiling at the viscount, who sat opposite him.

"I am told so," returned Sarsbrook, "although for my part I know nothing about horses."

"Indeed, sir?" said Nicholas, quite surprised. He had thought that lords would certainly know about horses. "Do you not like horses?"

"I do not like or dislike them," returned the viscount. "I give them little thought."

Pandora regarded the viscount with interest. He was an unusual man, she thought, very unlike other men of her acquaintance. Winfield and his friends were mad about horses.

"What about dogs, Lord Sarsbrook?" said Nicholas.

"What about dogs?" repeated the viscount.

"Do you like them?" said Nicholas, patting Mr. Stubbs.

A slight smile appeared on his lordship's face. "I do like dogs, young man," he said. This admission appeared to please Mr. Stubbs, who wagged his tail furiously and seemed ready to jump across to Sarsbrook.

Nicholas restrained him. "No, Mr. Stubbs, do mind your manners."

"Yes, Stubbs," said Pandora, "his lordship does not want you. You stay with Nicky." The dog cocked his head and regarded his mistress with a quizzical look.

The viscount smiled broadly at the terrier's expression. Surprised to see Sarsbrook look so amiable, Pandora found herself thinking that he was rather handsome when he smiled.

His lordship glanced from the dog to Pandora. Meeting his gaze, Pandora hoped she was not blushing, for again his scrutiny was making her feel most uncomfortable.

Unaware of the discomfort he was causing the young lady, Sarsbrook noted that she had particularly lovely eyes. The viscount could not help but wonder at how demure and refined Miss Marsh appeared sitting there across from him. How intriguing to think that she was the same Miss M. who had so delighted his uncle.

"Do you have a dog, Lord Sarsbrook?" said Nicholas.

The viscount reluctantly took his eyes from Pandora. "No, young man. I do not have a dog."

"Oh," said Nicholas. "That is too bad."

"Is it?" said Sarsbrook.

"Indeed so, my lord," said Nicholas. "They are very good companions. Perhaps your children have dogs."

"My children? Good God, I have no children. I am a bachelor, Master Nicholas."

"Oh," said the boy, pleased at this information. He had taken a liking to the viscount, despite that gentleman's somewhat formidable aspect. He was also very impressed that Sarsbrook was a lord who lived in an enormous house. It had occurred to Nicholas that the Viscount Sarsbrook would make a very good husband for his sister. "Do you not think it a good idea to marry, sir?" said Nicholas.

"Nicky!" exclaimed Pandora, very much embarrassed. "You forget yourself. You must not ask such questions. I pray you remain quiet."

"Oh, I do not mind answering," returned the viscount, eyeing Nicholas indulgently. "While some may think marriage a splendid institution, I believe it causes more misery than any other human folly. No, young man, any sensible person avoids marriage at all costs."

"Perhaps that is why Pandora does not wish to marry Mr. Underwood," said Nicholas.

"Nicky!" said Pandora in exasperation. "Lord Sarsbrook is not interested in discussing Mr. Underwood. I do not want to hear another word from you."

"Mr. Underwood?" said the viscount, directing a curious look at Pandora. "Indeed, Miss Marsh, I am quite interested in discussing him. Who is he? Has he asked for your hand?"

Pandora reddened. "Truly, Lord Sarsbrook, I do not think it is of any concern of yours."

"Oh, no, I suppose not. It is only idle curiosity." The viscount folded his arms across his chest. So Miss Marsh had a suitor. He frowned slightly. Perhaps she had dozens of them. Perhaps Uncle Humphrey had been a poor old fool in thinking his Miss M. was faithful to him. After all, she was a woman like any other and the female of the species was woefully unreliable.

Sarsbrook wondered why she didn't accept this fellow Underwood. He had assumed that a woman in her position would jump at a chance to marry. If she would take a husband, he would not have to be concerned about his uncle's wish that he take care of her. The viscount's frown grew deeper. He knew that he should be pleased with the thought of Pandora Marsh getting married, but the idea annoyed him.

Pandora watched Sarsbrook in silence, noting his unhappy expression. She wondered what he was thinking about. Turning to look out the window, Pandora reflected that it had been a most interesting morning.

11

Winfield Marsh had risen very late in the morning. Having been up most of the night carousing with his friends, he was suffering the effects of his improvident consumption of wine and spirits. What was even worse was the memory of having lost a woefully large sum of money at faro. Therefore, Winfield was not in the best of moods when he finally made his way downstairs to join his father and Lizzy in the drawing room.

"Ah, there you are, Winfield," said Mr. Marsh. "You are sleeping very late." There was a hint of disapproval in Mr. Marsh's voice, but he was not overly upset with his son. While Mr. Marsh thought Winfield's habits less than desirable, he was an indulgent father who knew that young men were apt to be rather wild. Although Mr. Marsh's own youth had been very tame by comparison, he did not begrudge his son enjoying himself.

"Good day, Father, Lizzy."

"Oh, Winnie," said his younger sister, "you are such a slugabed! I thought you would sleep the day away."

"Where is Pandora?" said Winfield, ignoring Lizzy's remark.

"She and Nicholas went to the park very early," replied Mr. Marsh. "That is what Martha tells us."

"And they are very late in coming back," said Lizzy.

"They went to the park?" said Winfield. He vaguely remembered Nicholas waking him up that morning, saying something about flying a kite.

"Yes," said Lizzy. "Martha said that Nicky took that silly kite of his. Poor Pan. How monstrous dull to stand

about watching a kite. Is that a carriage I hear?" Lizzy
hurried to the window. "Look! It is a carriage and it is
stopping here. And what a grand carriage it is. Oh, do
come look!"

Winfield and his father went to the window and
peered out at the splendid vehicle and its four magnificent black horses. "Good God!" said Winfield. "Whomever could it be?"

The mystery was quickly solved as one of the grooms
jumped down from the carriage to let down the steps and
open the carriage door. Out stepped Pandora.

"It is Pan!" cried Lizzy. "And look! Who is that gentleman?"

"Egad!" said Winfield. "That is Sarsbrook!" Winfield
had a sinking feeling. However did Pandora meet Sarsbrook? Did he say anything to her about having given
Winfield the necklace? If so, Winfield would be in considerable trouble.

"Sarsbrook?" said Mr. Marsh. "How is that possible?
And Nicholas! Is he injured?" Sarsbrook was helping the
youngest member of the Marsh family from the carriage.
"Oh, dear! Something is the matter! Let us go to them!"

"But wait!" cried Winfield. "I must say one thing. I
pray that neither of you mentions the emerald necklace
in Sarsbrook's presence."

"What?" said Mr. Marsh.

"I shall explain later, but suffice it to say that the matter was the cause of some embarrassment to Lord Sarsbrook and it would be better not to mention it."

"Yes, yes," said Mr. Marsh, rushing from the room
followed by Lizzy and Winfield. Reaching the front
door, Mr. Marsh flung it open. "Pandora! Nicholas!
What has happened?"

"Oh, it is nothing serious, Papa," said Pandora.
"Nicholas fell from a tree in the park, but there is no
need to worry."

Winfield hurried to Nicholas, who was leaning heavily against the viscount. "You are injured, Nicky."

"Oh, it is hardly worth mentioning," said Nicholas. "I

shall be fine. Lord Sarsbrook's man Willis said so. He knows all about bones and things."

"That is a relief," said Mr. Marsh. He looked at Sarsbrook. "I am very much indebted to you, sir."

"Papa," said Pandora. "I should like to present Lord Sarsbrook. My lord, this is my father, Mr. Marsh, and my sister, Lizzy. You have met my brother Winfield."

The viscount nodded to Pandora's kinsmen. Although Lizzy was nearly beside herself with excitement, she managed a very presentable curtsy.

"Let us go in," said Mr. Marsh. "I daresay we cannot stand about here. Do come in, my lord."

Sarsbrook seemed very willing to come in. He was very interested in the Marsh family. It struck him that they were all quite presentable, handsome, and respectable looking. Mr. Marsh seemed a pleasant, well-spoken gentleman, thought the viscount. He noted that the girl Lizzy was exceedingly pretty if one liked the willowy ethereal look, which his lordship did not.

Once everyone was seated in the drawing room, Pandora explained about her youngest brother's mishap and Sarsbrook's assistance. Mr. Marsh expressed the view that his lordship's appearance was wonderfully fortuitous.

Winfield smiled pleasantly, but he found himself feeling uneasy, wondering whether Sarsbrook had said anything to Pandora about the emeralds. Since his elder sister was not giving him any disapproving looks, he had reason to hope that the topic had not been discussed.

Sarsbrook sat among the Marsh family members, behaving with unusual civility. He directed most of his attention to Pandora, whom he found utterly charming, and very desirable. Indeed, he told himself, if he did not know himself better, he might have thought he was becoming enamoured of the lady.

After a short time, the viscount announced that he must depart. The Marsh family members again thanked him profusely for his kindness to Nicholas, and then Mr. Marsh escorted him to the door.

When he had left the drawing room, Winfield turned to his sister. "I cannot say how astonished I was to see Sarsbrook here."

"You must imagine how I felt when I turned around to see him standing there in the park," said Pandora.

"He seemed very civil," said Lizzy. "A pity that he is not very handsome."

"I would not call him unhandsome," said Pandora.

"Perhaps not, but he is not at all dashing," returned her sister. "Still he is a viscount and very rich."

"Indeed so," said Nicholas. "His house was very grand. It was just as Winfield described it. If only you could have seen it, Lizzy!"

"Yes, if only I could have been there," said Lizzy wistfully. "You are so lucky, both of you. But I cannot wait to tell Phoebe about this. Imagine! Meeting a viscount and having him in one's own drawing room. Phoebe will be green with envy. Nicky, do tell me eveything."

As Nicholas started to oblige his sister with a detailed account of his adventure, Winfield took Pandora aside. "Did he say anything? That is to say, did he mention the necklace?"

"Why, no, Winnie. I daresay he was probably embarrassed to have made such a mistake. He did say that you had explained everything. I told him that it was best to forget the matter."

"Yes, of course," said Winfield, very much relieved. At that moment Mr. Marsh came back into the drawing room to express his opinion that Lord Sarsbrook was an exceptionally fine fellow.

Nicholas, who had come to the same conclusion, looked from his father to Pandora. Would it not be wonderful if his sister could marry the viscount, he thought. Nicholas considered the matter, concluding that certainly there would be something he could do to promote such a match.

Leaving the Marsh family residence, Sarsbrook ordered his coachman to take him to the home of Mr.

Tucker. He arrived there shortly and was glad to find his friend at home. He was less happy to find that Mrs. Tucker was with her husband in the drawing room. Since Sarsbrook wanted very much to speak to Tucker alone, he regarded Mrs. Tucker's presence with disfavor.

Fanny Tucker could not fail to note that the viscount seemed less than pleased to see her. She had met her husband's friend on several occasions, and each time Sarsbrook had been cold and aloof. Fanny was a good-natured young woman who, like her husband, was popular with a wide circle of friends.

However, Fanny's attempts to be pleasant to the viscount had met with failure. She had the distinct impression that Sarsbrook disliked her, despite Tucker's assurance that this was not the case. It was a mystery to Fanny how her lovable and loving husband could have a friend like Sarsbrook.

As she greeted their visitor, Fanny tried to appear happy to see him. "How good of you to call, Lord Sarsbrook," she said.

The viscount nodded stiffly. "Good day, Mrs. Tucker. I fear, madam, that I have some private matters I wish to discuss with your husband. Do excuse us."

Rather startled by this abrupt dismissal in her own drawing room, Fanny managed to nod. "Yes, of course, my lord. Do excuse me." Casting a meaningful look at her husband, she left the room.

"Really, Robin," said Tucker, rather irritated with his friend. "I should think you might have been civil to Fanny. That was exceedingly rude."

"Was it?" said Sarsbrook. "Perhaps it was. I do apologize, Tuck."

"Oh, very well," said Tucker. "I shall forgive you, but I must insist that you make some effort to be polite to my wife, Robin."

Sarsbrook nodded solemnly. "Very well. I shall try to do better. I shall astonish Mrs. Tucker with my charm."

Tucker laughed, forgetting his vexation. "I shall be eager to see that. Now, do sit down, Robin."

The viscount nodded again and seated himself in a chair. Tucker took a place beside him. "I must talk to you about a certain matter," said Sarsbrook. "You will think me utterly ridiculous."

"I should not be surprised," said Tucker. He laughed at his friend's expression. "Oh, I am quizzing you, Robin. Do tell me. It appears to be serious."

"I should not call it serious," said Sarsbrook. "Dammit, I shall tell it straight out. It is that woman, Miss M."

"Miss M.?"

"I have just come from her."

"The devil you say!" exclaimed Tucker. "Good God, Robin, I have misjudged you. Tell me everything!"

"Your mind is in a lamentably debauched state, Tuck. What I did was spend a short time in the lady's drawing room with her father, two brothers, a sister, and a small terrier dog called Mr. Stubbs."

"Whatever were you doing there? You didn't call upon her?"

"I escorted her and her brother home. He had fallen from a tree in Hyde Park. I happened by."

"You happened by? By God, that sounds like fate to me, old lad. So what is it you wish to say? Have you fallen in love with this Miss M.?"

Sarsbrook looked thoughtful. "I don't know, Tuck. I scarcely know what love is. And I hardly know this woman. I have seen her but twice. But she disturbs me in a most profound way, Tuck. I have been thinking of her constantly since I met her. It is damnably irritating."

"Why, this is wonderful!" cried Tucker.

"I cannot see what is wonderful in the least," said Sarsbrook ill-temperedly. "I feel like a fool."

"Of course, every man in love feels a bit of a fool. Why, I am heartily glad for you, Robin. Now what will you do?"

The viscount shrugged. "I haven't any idea. I know nothing about such things. I fancy that my uncle was an exceedingly fortunate man."

"And now you want the lady for yourself."

Sarsbrook regarded his friend seriously. "I suppose I do."

"My dear Robin, I cannot see that this is such a great problem. I daresay the lady is in need of a protector. Having been one man's mistress, she is doubtless eager to find another man. I cannot imagine that she would not be pleased to have you, a rich, titled and handsome fellow."

Sarsbrook rose from his chair and paced across the floor. Turning, he frowned at Tucker. "It seems indecent."

"Well, it is rather a bit indecent," said Tucker with a smile.

"No, I mean, the fact that she was my uncle's mistress."

"My dear Robin, I should not worry about that in the least. Your uncle wished you to take care of her."

"I doubt this is what he had in mind," returned the viscount with a sardonic smile. "And even if I did not think it totally reprehensible to take this woman for myself, I do not know how to go about it. How does one take a mistress?"

Tucker grinned. "I am no expert, Robin, but I daresay taking a mistress is not unlike taking a wife. Perhaps it is a bit more difficult since one wishes to be discreet. You must woo the lady. Make your feelings known to her. Buy her things and promise her whatever she wants. From your uncle's diary, I would say this woman is quite a prize. Think of what delights await you, Robin."

Sarsbrook frowned. He had thought of little else since meeting Pandora. "You must swear you will tell no one, Tuck, not even your wife."

"Egad, do you think I would tell such a thing to Fanny? She would be quite shocked, I assure you. I shall keep your secret, Robin. You have my word."

"Then I shall go now, Tuck," said Sarsbrook, turning abruptly. "Thank you and good day." He stopped at the door of the drawing room. "Do tell Mrs. Tucker that I regret my hasty departure and that I shall look forward to seeing her another time. There, that was very civil of me, was it not?"

"Admirably civil," said Tucker with a smile. Sarsbrook smiled and hurried off, leaving his friend to shake his head in amusement at the surprising turn of events.

12

While Pandora Marsh tried very hard to appear as if Sarsbrook's visit was a matter of complete indifference to her, Lizzy did not disguise her excitement at the fact that a titled nobleman had called upon them for the second time. Lizzy seemed to think that Sarsbrook was so pleased with them all that he would call again, and that they would soon receive invitations to events frequented by the first circles of London society.

No matter how hard Pandora tried to restore her sister to reality, Lizzy refused to allow her enthusiasm to be dampened. The rest of the morning, Lizzy chattered endlessly about how they would soon be meeting the cream of the aristocracy. The younger Marsh sister was now quite resolved to marry a marquess or at the very least an earl, she told Pandora.

In the afternoon, Pandora accompanied Lizzy to call upon her friend Phoebe Reynolds. Pandora was never eager to visit the Reynolds household because she thought Phoebe a silly, bird-witted girl. To make matters worse, Pheobe's mother was an insufferable snob, who talked incessantly about her connections with the *haut ton*.

Lizzy, on the other hand, could not wait to see Phoebe and her mother to tell them about Sarsbrook's visit. They had no sooner positioned themselves on the Reynoldses' drawing room sofa before Lizzy began excitedly. "Oh, Phoebe and Mrs. Reynolds, you will never guess who came to our house this morning."

"I cannot imagine," said Phoebe.

"Why, it was Lord Sarsbrook. He is a viscount."

Mrs. Reynolds was a stout woman with graying hair and youthful countenance. "Lord Sarsbrook? Really?"

"Yes," said Lizzy. "When my brother fell from a tree in Hyde Park this morning, Lord Sarsbrook assisted him and Pandora. He brought them back home in his carriage. It was very grand."

"Good heavens," said Mrs. Reynolds. "That is quite remarkable. What is he like, Pandora?"

"I really don't know, ma'am," replied Pandora. "He was kind to help us."

"I have heard about this gentleman," said Mrs. Reynolds. "They say he is a cold fish. Yes, I have heard a number of things about him. His sister is Lady Verdon, one of the great ladies in society. I have met her and found her charming. I must say her ladyship showed the most admirable condescension in speaking with me at Almack's.

Pandora smiled. Mrs. Reynolds never passed up the opportunity to mention that she and her daughter had once received the treasured vouchers that allowed them to be admitted to the august assembly rooms frequented by London's elite society. Mrs. Reynolds continued, "They say that Sarsbrook is very rich, but one would not know it from how he lives. He avoids society, preferring to live like an old schoolmaster huddled away with his books.

"His uncle, Sir Humphrey Maitland, died recently. When the estate is settled, it is said Sarsbrook will receive another great fortune." Mrs. Reynolds sighed. "Can you imagine that a man of such rank and fortune is not married? I think that the height of selfishness, not to share such a fortune with a wife and children. How old is he, Pandora?"

Pandora shrugged. "He is not very old. Less than thirty, I should guess."

"Well, he may still redeem himself and marry. They say Sarsbrook claims to be a confirmed bachelor and that he detests females. I daresay that if he does marry, his wife will be a most unfortunate lady."

"But he is so rich," said Lizzy. "I cannot imagine how that would be so terrible."

"But Lizzy," said Phoebe, "what good does it do to marry a rich man if he is a frightful pinch-fist?"

"Yes, that is true," said Lizzy thoughtfully. "His carriage was all the crack, but he did not look very grand, did he, Pandora? I should think a viscount would look far more splendid."

"I think it presumptuous to fault a gentleman's tailor," said Pandora. "Indeed, I admire a man who is not a slave to fashion."

"Not a slave to fashion," repeated Mrs. Reynolds. "I do not like the sound of that. It conjures up a very slovenly appearance. A gentleman should pay attention to such things, Pandora."

"Yes, indeed," said Phoebe. "I could never look twice at a man who did not tie his cravat properly."

Pandora could only raise her eyebrows slightly and smile pleasantly at this remark. She was very glad when they returned home for tea. Lizzy and Pandora were joined by Mr. Marsh and Nicholas, who had just finished his Greek lesson. As they sipped their tea and ate slices of bread and butter, the conversation turned inevitably to Lord Sarsbrook.

"Mrs. Reynolds knew everything about Lord Sarsbrook, Papa," said Lizzy.

"That woman is a marvel," said Mr. Marsh. "She knows everything about everyone. What did she say about him?"

"That he is very rich and that he is a confirmed bachelor," said Lizzy.

"Confirmed bachelor?" said Nicholas.

"Yes, that means he does not wish to get married," explained Lizzy.

Nicholas looked over at Pandora. "But I thought he might marry Pan."

This comment caused the boy's father and Lizzy to

burst into laughter. "Oh, Nicky," cried Lizzy, "that is too funny."

"I do not see why it is so funny," said Nicholas, rather offended.

"Indeed, it is really not so funny," said Mr. Marsh. "What do you say, Pandora, do you think you'd wish to become a viscountess?"

Pandora hoped she was not blushing. She replied in a bantering tone. "I had hoped to become a duchess." Her father and sister laughed again.

"Would that not be wonderful?" cried Lizzy. "To be a duchess! That would be so very splendid. Of course, I would settle on being a marchioness or countess."

"You see, Nicholas?" said Mr. Marsh. "Your sisters think being a viscountess not grand enough. I fear they will disappoint Lord Sarsbrook."

"You are quizzing me," said Nicholas. "I daresay a viscountess is very grand."

"It is," said Pandora. "And that is why it is quite ridiculous. You see, Nicholas, gentlemen like Lord Sarsbrook do not think of marrying insignificant creatures like your sister Pan. Perhaps Lizzy is not out of the question, because she is beautiful."

"But you are beautiful, too, Pan," said Nicholas.

Pandora smiled fondly at her brother. "That is very sweet, Nicky, but I am certainly not beautiful. And I assure you that Lord Sarsbrook is not interested in marrying anyone, least of all me."

Nicholas frowned as he took another drink of tea. He did not see why it was so impossible for the viscount to marry Pandora. It seemed to him that Sarsbrook liked his sister very much.

While his sisters and father began talking about something else, Nicholas continued to think about the viscount. Surely there must be something one could do to encourage Lord Sarsbrook to become interested in Pandora.

Nicholas knitted his brow in concentration. Suddenly he had an idea. He would invite Sarsbrook to tea. Then the viscount could have another opportunity to see his sister and perhaps to decide to get married after all. Once having settled on this excellent plan, Nicholas smiled and took another piece of bread and butter.

After Sarsbrook left his friend Tucker, he returned home. After eating very little at luncheon, he paced about his residence, going from room to room as if looking for something. The servants noted their master's peculiar restlessness with great interest.

The viscount finally settled down at his desk in the library, where he tried to work on his Greek translation. After achieving little success on this project, he gave up, rising from his chair and wandering across the room to the window. There he stood looking out at the street, thinking about Pandora Marsh. Since leaving Tucker he had thought of little else but his conversation with his friend about her.

Tucker seemed to think it was all very easy, thought the viscount. According to Tucker, he would scarcely have to lift a finger and Pandora Marsh would fall into his arms and into his bed. Into his bed, he repeated to himself. Between the memory of his uncle's diary and his thoughts of Pandora's face and lovely body, the viscount began to conjure up the most pleasurable imaginings. "God," he muttered aloud. "I must have her."

Pacing restlessly, Sarsbrook turned his attention to the practical side of things. He would have to buy her a house, and he would give her family enough money to keep them happy.

The viscount wondered how much it would take for Mr. Marsh to accept the idea. Sarsbrook frowned at the thought. Of course, Marsh would hardly be the first father to look the other way at his daughter's dishonor, thought the viscount cynically. If the price were high enough, Marsh would doubtless come round. After all, it was the way of the world that those with money could have whatever they wanted. Sarsbrook frowned again. He did not like the world very much.

The viscount's reflections turned to Pandora herself. The key, of course, would be in getting her to accept him. His uncle had taken advantage of her innocence. Sarsbrook would be more forthright. But what if Pandora would not have him? After all, she had refused his offer of one thousand pounds and a yearly income. That in itself was remarkable.

Still, she appeared to be a sensible girl. Indeed, she seemed highly intelligent. Surely she would see the advantages of such an arrangement with him. He would be very generous. She would have clothes, servants, anything she wished.

As he pondered the situation, Sarsbrook remembered Tucker's words. His friend had said that the viscount should "woo her." How did one do that, he wondered. Doubtless it involved being very pleasant, writing letters and poetry pledging his undying affection. Sarsbrook frowned distastefully. He did not think he would be good at love letters. Of course, he had never tried writing any.

The viscount thought suddenly of his sister Isabelle. How surprised she would be to find that he had succumbed to a pretty face. Certainly Isabelle would not be at all pleased to know that he was directing his thoughts to a dishonorable relationship rather than doing his duty and finding a suitable wife.

It was a pity, considered the viscount, that Miss Marsh was such an unacceptable female. If he were to have to saddle himself with a wife, it would not seem so bad finding oneself attached to the lovely Pandora. But one could hardly consider marrying the mistress of one's late uncle, especially a mistress whose exploits had been so graphically chronicled in his uncle's diary.

Sarsbrook walked to the bellpull and rang for a servant. The butler answered his summons. "Yes, my lord?"

"Have my carriage brought round, Archer. I am going out."

"Very good, my lord," said the servant, bowing and then hurrying off to do the viscount's bidding.

A short time later Sarsbrook was in his carriage on his

way to the residence of his sister. He had seized upon the idea that Isabelle could assist him in providing opportunities to see Pandora. If she would invite the Marsh family to various society functions, he would have more opportunities to press his suit. Of course, he knew that Isabelle would be none too pleased if she knew of his goal of making Pandora his mistress. Yet, reasoned the viscount, there was no reason why Isabelle would have to know. After all, Sir Humphrey had been remarkably successful in keeping his private life secret.

Arriving at the Verdon home, the viscount strode purposefully to the door. He was admitted by the butler and led immediately to the drawing room.

Lady Isabelle Verdon was very surprised to hear that her brother had come to call. Since Sarsbrook was not in the habit of visiting, his arrival was most unusual. Intrigued at the servant's announcement that Lord Sarsbrook was waiting in the drawing room, Isabelle hurried to join him. "My dear Robert, how good it is to see you," she said, kissing him on the cheek. "My husband will be so disappointed to have missed you."

"It is you I have come to see," said the viscount. "I have a favor to ask of you."

"Indeed?" said Isabelle. She could not remember her brother ever asking her to do him a favor. It seemed very odd. "Ask away, Robert. I shall do my utmost to assist you."

Looking at his sister's eager face, he knew that he must tread carefully if he did not want her to jump to any wrong conclusions. "I believe I received an invitation to that annual ball of yours. When is it?"

"When is it?" echoed Isabelle. "Do not tell me you are going! Have you mislaid the invitation?"

"Indeed not. I tossed it into the fire."

"Robert!"

"But now I have decided to attend."

"That is very good of you," remarked her ladyship, eyeing her brother curiously. "It is in three weeks' time. I shall see you are sent another invitation."

"Thank you, Isabelle. And I should like you to invite someone else, that is, some people that I have recently met."

"Whomever can you mean, Robert? Do I know these people? I do hope they are none of your scholarly friends."

"No, not at all. I'm sure you do not know them. There is Mr. Marsh and his son Winfield Marsh."

"Marsh? I am not familiar with the family."

"There are also two daughters."

"Aha!" said Isabelle. "Two daughters! I do hope you are going to tell me that you have taken a fancy to one of these daughters."

"Don't be ridiculous," muttered the viscount.

Isabelle seemed pleased by this response. "Why, I believe you have. My dear Robert, I am very pleased. Of course, I do hope you have not taken a liking to some penniless, provincial nobody. Is she presentable?"

"I must disappoint you if you think I am contemplating marriage. I simply wish to assist this family in society. I should be grateful for your help. That is all. You are to take them up. Introduce them to all of your addle-pated friends."

"But who are they? And why would you wish to help them?"

Sarsbrook shrugged. "Perhaps it is simply a whim of mine."

"You are not a whimsical fellow, Robert. But I shall not argue. I shall take up these Marshes if that is your wish." She directed a shrewd look at him. "I shall be most eager to meet these daughters."

The viscount did not respond to this remark. "Will you call upon the Marsh family? This is the address." He took a paper from his pocket and handed it to her. "Do call upon them at once. I do hope you can persuade them to attend."

"Persuade them? My dear Robert, there are those who would sell their firstborn children to receive an invitation to one of my balls."

Sarsbrook smiled. "Then I shall be going, Isabelle."

"But you have just arrived."

"Yes, yes, but I know how busy you are. Good day, Isabelle." The viscount seemed eager to depart. When he was gone, Isabelle shook her head. Looking down at the slip of paper in her hand, she decided it would be very interesting to call upon the Marsh family.

Three days later, Miles Brackley arrived at Sarsbrook House. Brackley was dressed very carefully in a perfectly tailored coat of pea-green superfine, buff-colored pantaloons, and gleaming hessian boots.

A figure of sartorial splendor, Brackley was accustomed to impressing lesser personages. He was, therefore, rather affronted when Sarsbrook's butler opened the door and regarded him with obvious disfavor. Brackley directed an imperious look at the servant. "I am here to see my cousin, Lord Sarsbrook."

Having long been in the viscount's employ, Archer knew very well what his master thought of the gentleman who now stood before him. "I am sorry, Mr. Brackley," said the butler. "My master is not at home."

Brackley frowned. "That is of no matter," he said, boldly pushing past the startled servant and making his way into the house. "I shall wait for him."

"I do not think that wise, sir," said Archer. "His lordship may be gone a very long time."

"I do not mind waiting. Yes, I'll wait in the library. There is no need to show me the way."

Archer was horrified at Brackley's effrontery. Knowing that his employer would be furious if he returned to find Brackley there, Archer tried to stop him. "I am sorry, sir," he said firmly. "I must insist that you leave. I shall tell the master you called."

"And I said I shall wait," said Brackley in a loud voice, continuing toward the library. Archer hurried after him, unsure what to do. Entering the library, Brackley sat down on a chair. "I shall be fine here. Tell Sarsbrook I am here as soon as he arrives."

"Really, sir, I cannot allow you to stay here. You must leave, sir."

"Dammit, man, I will not leave!" said Brackley. "I've business with your master. If he will ignore my letter, I must come in person. I will not have a servant telling me what to do. Now get out!"

Archer hesitated. He was not a very big man and he did not think himself physically capable of tossing his master's obnoxious relative from the premises. And then, too, there was the matter of Brackley being a gentleman. It seemed, reflected Archer, there was nothing he could do but allow the young man to remain and suffer the consequences of the viscount's anger later.

The butler nodded stiffly to Brackley. He then retreated from the room, hurrying to the servant's hall to discuss the matter with his lordship's housekeeper.

Brackley was very pleased with Archer's distress. He did not doubt that Sarsbrook's servants had firm instructions not to admit him. Rising from his chair, Brackley strode about the room. He studied the bookshelves, thinking his cousin had wasted a good deal of money on books. Brackley had little use for books himself.

Walking over to Sarsbrook's desk, he picked up a volume from a stack of books sitting there. Opening the book and finding it to be in Greek, Brackley tossed it down disgustedly. His cousin was such a strange, bookish fellow, he told himself. How infamous that Sarsbrook had all the money.

Brackley sat down at his cousin's desk. Picking up some papers, he glanced through them. They appeared to be lines of poetry written in a neat, angular hand. He put the papers down disinterestedly.

There was a marble paperweight on the desk. Brackley picked it up and examined it absently. Finally replacing it, he examined the other objects on Sarsbrook's desk. There was a small wooden box, which he opened. It contained some papers. Brackley took them out and leafed through them. Finding them of little interest, Brackley put them back. As he did so, he noticed a key in the bottom of the box. Taking it out, he held it in the palm of his hand.

Noting a lock on one of the desk drawers, Brackley wondered if the key in his hand might open it. He placed it in the lock and turned it. It fit perfectly. Brackley smiled. What secrets might his cousin have hidden there? It would be amusing to see. Pausing briefly to glance at the door, he unlocked the drawer and pulled it open to find a book.

Taking it out, Brackley opened the volume. "A diary," he said, turning the pages. "I can think of nothing duller than my cousin's diary." He started to put the book back into the drawer, but opened it once again to take another look. "Why, this is not Sarsbrook's," he said as he read the first page. "It is my uncle's. Whyever would that old skinflint think anything he might write would be worth keeping for posterity?" Brackley thumbed through the diary. "What is this?" he said aloud, his eyes alighting on an interesting passage. "My God!"

Although Brackley normally detested reading, his eyes were now glued to the page. He could scarcely believe what he was seeing. Amazed and delighted, Brackley grinned. "The lascivious old goat," he said. After reading a few more pages, he paused to look toward the door. Fortunately, there was no sign of anyone. Brackley closed the diary. Tucking it inside his coat, he closed the drawer, locked it, and then replaced the key in the wooden box.

Rising from the desk, Brackley left the library and wordlessly exited the house. A few minutes later, Archer returned to the library accompanied by two footmen. Having consulted with his lordship's housekeeper, he had decided that Brackley must be routed from the house by whatever means necessary.

Archer was very much surprised to find the library empty. When one of the parlor maids reported seeing a gentleman leave the house and drive off in a curricle, the butler was perplexed. He was also relieved at finding a confrontation unnecessary.

When the viscount returned home, Archer told him about Brackley's visit. Sarsbrook scowled at hearing of his cousin's audacity but, much to the butler's relief, the viscount did not seem overly concerned.

Retreating to the library, Sarsbrook began to riffle through a stack of letters that had arrived in the afternoon post. As he went through them, he stopped at a letter addressed in a childish hand. Opening that curious missive, he read the following:

My Lord, I do hope you are well. I must thank you again for your kindness in helping me when I fell from the tree. My ankle is much better today. My sister Pandora thinks it was very good of you to assist us and to take us home.

I have been having a devilish lot of trouble with my Greek, my lord. Papa cannot help as he says his Greek is terribly rusty and Winfield says he never learned enough Greek to remember any. As you are so very expert on the subject, I was wondering if you might assist me. I know it is very forward of me and Pandora would be quite vexed with me if she knew I was asking you.

But could you come on Friday for tea? Four o'clock would be splendid. I should be most grateful to you.

Your Lordship's Most Obedient Servant,
Nicholas Marsh

The letter was marred by two large inkblots, but otherwise was a very serviceable effort for a ten-year-old. Sarsbrook smiled. He did not like children. He certainly didn't like his sister's offspring. Yet he thought Nicholas Marsh rather tolerable for a boy. It amused him to think of Nicholas inviting him to tea to ask his help with Greek.

The viscount was very pleased at the idea of seeing Pandora again. He took up a piece of paper and a pen and wrote a short note to Master Nicholas Marsh, accepting his invitation.

13

Nicholas Marsh had been very excited to receive the brief note from Sarsbrook saying that the viscount would have tea on Friday. He had been very fortunate that Martha had given him Sarsbrook's letter directly, so that other family members had not seen the viscount's crest in the sealing wax. Nicholas had asked Martha not to mention the letter to anyone else, explaining that it was something of a surprise. Since Martha was exceedingly fond of her young master, she was happy to comply.

Nicholas had then gone to the cook, informing her that he would have a very important guest on Friday for tea. Since the cook was a redoubtable woman who was not very fond of surprises, Nicholas had had to explain that the Viscount Sarsbrook would be the guest in question and that Pandora was not to be informed since it was a surprise for her. This information very much interested the cook, who was happy to think of her mistress being on such friendly terms with a viscount. It was also very gratifying to the cook to imagine such a high-born nobleman eating her tea cakes.

Thinking himself a veritable genius for arranging things with Sarsbrook and the cook, Nicholas then had to deal with the problem of how to get his other family members safely out of the way for the visit. Winfield was no problem, for he spent very few afternoons at home and Nicholas knew that there was to be a bout of fisticuffs taking place that Winfield would not want to miss. Mr. Marsh always spent Friday afternoons with an old school chum, a retired colonel who lived close by.

Lizzy, however, was another matter. Nicholas did not want the younger of his sisters there, since he thought it much better for Pandora to have the viscount's undivided attention. But how did one arrange for Lizzy to go somewhere? After all, when she went out of the house, she was almost always accompanied by Pandora or her father.

It was, therefore, most fortuitous when Lizzy received a note from her friend Phoebe asking her to accompany Phoebe and her mother to visit Phoebe's aunt. A carriage came for her shortly after noon and then Lizzy was safely out of the way.

Pandora found the rare quiet of the Friday afternoon very pleasant. Retiring to her bedchamber, she started work on a new gown. Pandora was finally making a dress for herself. Having found some wonderful peach-colored silk on her last visit to the linen drapers, Pandora had acquiesced to Lizzy's urging that she create her own gown.

There had been a design in one of the fashion magazines that Pandora thought would be perfect for her. It had been a long time since she had had anything new because she had been so busy with her sister's wardrobe.

Shortly before four o'clock Nicholas came to his sister's room. "Pan, it is time for tea."

Pandora looked up at her brother. The silk was laid out on her sewing table and she was carefully cutting the material. "I fear I am very busy at the moment, Nicky. When I am finished we will have tea. It will not take long."

"I just wanted to remind you."

"You must be hungry."

"I am, indeed."

"Oh, very well." Pandora put down her scissors. "I suppose it would be a good idea to stop for a time." She rose to her feet. "We could have tea now if you wish. Do tell Martha. Oh, there she is now." The maid had appeared in the doorway. "Martha, Master Nicky informs me he is hungry and wishes to have tea."

"Very good, miss," replied the servant. "Your visitor has arrived. He is in the drawing room."

"My visitor?"

Nicholas looked a trifle sheepish. "Actually, Pan, he is my visitor. I invited him to tea."

"You invited someone to tea without asking me?" said Pandora, very much surprised. "Whyever would you do such a thing? Who is it?"

"It is Lord Sarsbrook," said Nicholas.

"Sarsbrook!" cried Pandora, regarding her brother in bewilderment.

"Aye, miss, it is," said Martha.

"Nicholas!"

"I do hope you will not be angry, Pan, but I invited Lord Sarsbrook to tea. I sent him a letter. I asked if he could help me with my Greek. I thought it a good idea."

"Nicholas Marsh, I think it a very bad idea," said Pandora severely. "To have written to Lord Sarsbrook without my knowledge! And to have asked him to help you with your Greek! Oh, Nicholas, Lord Sarsbrook has much more important things to do than tutor a schoolboy."

"But he said he would be happy to have tea," said Nicholas.

Pandora directed a frustrated look at her youngest brother. Nicholas had invited Sarsbrook to tea and asked if the viscount would help him with his Greek? And the viscount had accepted? It was beyond belief.

Looking into the mirror on her dressing table, Pandora was appalled. Her hair was in disarray. She was wearing an old dress that had long since passed out of fashion. "You are in very serious trouble, young man," said Pandora.

"His lordship is waiting, Miss Pandora," said Martha.

"I am well aware of that, Martha," replied Pandora. "Nicky, you go down to entertain Lord Sarsbrook. I must change my dress and attempt to do something with my hair. Martha, you must help me."

Nicholas wisely suppressed a smile. He thought everything was going very well despite Pandora's vexation with him. Hurrying from the room, he went down to greet his guest, who was standing at the window looking out. "Lord Sarsbrook, thank you so much for coming," said Nicholas politely.

The viscount turned around. "Master Nicholas," he said, nodding at the boy.

"Do sit down, my lord," said Nicholas. "My sister Pandora will be here shortly."

"And where is your father?"

"Oh, he is visiting Colonel Herbert. They are very good friends. Colonel Herbert is a war hero, you know."

"Indeed, I did not know," returned the viscount.

"Well, Papa says that he is a hero. He was very brave in the Peninsula."

"He sounds admirable," said Sarsbrook, taking a seat on the sofa.

"Oh, he is," said Nicholas, coming to sit beside him.

"And your brother and other sister? Are they here?"

"No, my lord, Lizzy has gone out and Winfield has gone to see the bout."

"The bout?"

"Between Mad Jack Harper and George Jeffreys. Did you not know about it, my lord?"

"I fear I was not informed of this momentous event, young man."

"I only wish that I were old enough to go," said Nicholas wistfully. "I expect you wish you had known about it."

A slight smile appeared on the viscount's lips. "I may disappoint you, but I have no interest in pugilism. Seeing one overgrown ruffian pummel another has little appeal to me."

"Oh," said Nicholas, regarding his lordship curiously. "And you like Greek, my lord?"

Sarsbrook nearly burst into laughter at the boy's expression. It was obvious that Nicholas Marsh thought him an odd duck indeed. "I like Greek very much."

"I imagine one likes something if one is good at it," said Nicholas dubiously. It was hard for him to imagine anyone liking Greek at all.

"And you are having difficulty with the subject?"

"I am, sir. I can make neither head nor tail of it most of the time. Why, Mr. Mawson wants me to translate six entire pages. And I have only done one page. And I have made a muddle of that, I am sure."

"While we are waiting for your sister to appear, why don't you fetch your book? I'll have a look at what you've done."

"You are too good, my lord," said Nicholas, jumping up and dashing off to get his book.

When he was gone, Sarsbrook got up from the sofa and walked about the room. He paused in front of a seascape painting and stared at the waves caught on canvas. The viscount felt strangely agitated. He had not expected to find Pandora and Nicholas the only ones at home. He could scarcely believe his good fortune.

"Lord Sarsbrook."

The viscount turned from the painting. There stood Pandora. Sarsbrook thought she looked wonderful. She was attired in a dress of print muslin with long, tight-fitting sleeves. The bodice of the dress was cut very low, but in deference to modesty, there was a filmy piece of gauze from the edge of the bodice to the small ruffled collar. Pandora's red hair had been pulled neatly into a knot atop her head with a few strands of shorter hair curling about her face.

"Miss Marsh," said his lordship.

"But where is Nicholas?"

"He has gone to fetch his Greek text."

"Oh, dear, I am so sorry that he troubled you with such a thing. He is usually a very good boy. You must think him the worst-mannered child."

Sarsbrook shrugged. "I think nothing of the kind. He

is a pleasant-enough boy. I do not object in the least to assisting him with Greek."

"Do sit down, Lord Sarsbrook," said Pandora. "Tea will be ready soon."

The viscount took his place on the sofa once again. Pandora seated herself across from him. Sarsbrook fixed his gaze upon Pandora, noting how her splendid bosom was shown to such good advantage by the dress she was wearing.

Pandora tired hard to retain her composure, for being alone in the room with his lordship was once again making her feel decidedly uncomfortable. "You have certainly impressed my brother with your knowledge of Greek, my lord."

"I have confounded him to be sure," returned the viscount. "I daresay he thinks me eccentric."

"I am sure he does not."

"I daresay you think me eccentric."

"I? Indeed, I have not come to that conclusion." Pandora smiled. "Of course, perhaps I do not know you well enough. Upon further acquaintance I may decide that you are quite eccentric."

Sarsbrook smiled. "I am encouraged by the words 'further acquaintance,' Miss Marsh. I should like it very much if you would become better acquainted with me."

Pandora was rather flustered by the remark and the expression on the viscount's face. At that moment Nicholas reentered the room. "Here it is, my lord." He sat down on the sofa next to the viscount. "Pandora, his lordship is going to help me with this."

"Really, Nicky, I do not think it at all the thing for you to ask Lord Sarsbrook to tutor you."

"I assure you, Miss Marsh, I am happy to do it." Sarsbrook took the book from Nicholas, and the paper on which the boy had scrawled his translation.

"I do not think I have quite got it right, sir," said Nicholas. "The part about the Spartans and the battle. I know that is wrong."

The viscount scanned the page of text and then read

Nicholas' paper. "You have not done too badly. No, this is very good except for that line. That should be 'thrilled to the sound of battle.' "

Nicholas looked down at the book. "Oh, I see. Yes, now it makes sense. That was the one part I could not understand." He scribbled on his paper with a pencil.

"And you have the wrong declension there."

"Oh, I believe I know what it should be." Nicholas crossed out a word and wrote in another.

"Yes, exactly right."

Nicholas grinned. "I do thank you, sir."

"You have much work to do, Nicholas," said the viscount. "But I should think you may one day become an excellent scholar if you persevere."

"I should surprise everyone if I did, Lord Sarsbrook," said Nicholas. He paused and then added, "I did not know that lords could be scholars, sir."

"Oh, it is not very common, I admit." He glanced over at Pandora, who was regarding him with an appraising look. Martha entered the drawing room with the tea things.

Pandora poured the viscount a cup of tea. "You are very kind to help Nicholas."

"It is nothing," said Sarsbrook, taking his tea. His brown eyes met Pandora's striking gray ones. "I am enjoying myself."

Pandora looked down in some embarrassment. She busied herself with pouring tea for Nicholas and herself. "Do tell us how you have come to be so interested in the study of Greek, Lord Sarsbrook," she said, hoping her voice sounded calmly indifferent.

"I have always been interested in the ancients," said the viscount. "Their world always seemed infinitely preferable to our own."

"Do you truly think so, my lord?" said Pandora. "I have always thought that the ancient world, for all its artistic and literary glories, was plagued with slavery, war, and cruelty."

"Unlike our own time, Miss Marsh?" said the viscount with a sardonic smile.

"Oh, very well, I will admit our time is certainly not all that we might wish," replied Pandora.

"And think what wonders were to be found in ancient Greece. Think of Athens! The Parthenon, the Acropolis! Such perfection in art and architecture has never been equaled." Sarsbrook spoke with such enthusiasm that Pandora smiled. She had not thought noblemen were passionate about anything except hunting and hounds, horses, and gaming.

"I should have liked to have lived in ancient Greece," said Nicholas.

"And why is that, Nicky?" said Pandora. "I daresay I have not thought you so particularly fascinated with ancient history."

"If I lived there," said Nicholas, "I should not have to learn Greek, for I would know it already."

Pandora looked over at the viscount and they both laughed. "Admirable logic," said his lordship. Taking a drink of tea, the viscount realized that he was enjoying himself. He seldom really enjoyed himself except perhaps with his friend Tucker or when immersed in his books.

"I beg your pardon, Miss Pandora." Martha entered the room. She extended a silver salver toward her mistress upon which was a calling card. "There is a lady to see you, miss."

Pandora took the card. "Lady Verdon?"

"Blast," muttered the viscount. "She is here now?"

Pandora regarded him in surprise. "You know Lady Verdon, my lord?"

"She is my sister," returned the viscount.

"Do show her in, Martha." Pandora turned to Sarsbrook. "I shall be very glad to meet your sister."

Sarsbrook did not look altogether pleased. Although he had ordered his sister to call upon Pandora, he thought it ill luck that she happened to call the very afternoon that he was there. She would probably draw the

wrong conclusion, deciding that he was thinking of marriage. Sarsbrook realized that if his sister learned that
Pandora was Miss M., she would be very shocked.

As Isabelle walked into the drawing room, Pandora
eyed her visitor with surprise. Even though Phoebe's
mother had told her that Sarsbrook's sister was a reknowned lady of fashion, Pandora had not been prepared
to see such a grand-looking personage.

Isabelle wore a stunning pelisse that was fashioned
from lavender silk and decorated with satin rosettes.
Atop her head was a splendid bonnet trimmed with
lavender silk and festooned with a high plume of ostrich
feathers. Beneath the hat a profusion of fashionably dark
curls were visible.

"Robert!" cried Isabelle, recognizing her brother as he
rose from the sofa. "I did not expect to find you here."

"Nor I you, Isabelle," returned the viscount.

Rising to her feet, Pandora smiled at her new guest.

"I shall allow my brother to introduce us," said Isabelle, smiling in return at Pandora. Isabelle was regarding the young lady who stood before her with the same
keen interest with which Pandora was studying her.

The viscount's sister was pleased to find that the
young lady who had finally piqued her brother's interest
was a perfectly presentable female. While Isabelle's critical judgment pronounced Pandora no great beauty, she
concluded that she was pretty enough and suitably refined looking.

"Isabelle, may I present Miss Pandora Marsh and her
brother, Nicholas? Miss Marsh, my sister, Lady Verdon."

The ladies nodded politely to each other. Nicholas
made a very presentable bow. Isabelle, who was very
fond of children, smiled brightly at Nicholas. "How do
you do, young man?"

"Very well, thank you, my lady," said Nicholas, smiling at Isabelle in return. He was rather awestruck by Isabelle's magnificence. He thought she looked like a
queen.

"Do sit down, Lady Verdon," said Pandora. "How very kind of you to call. Will you have tea?"

"I should be delighted." Isabelle sat down on the sofa and Nicholas hurried to sit beside her. The viscount took a chair next to Pandora.

"I am so glad to find you home, Miss Marsh," said Lady Verdon as Pandora handed her a cup of tea. "My brother told me of meeting you. You sounded so perfectly charming that I was eager to make your acquaintance."

Pandora could not help but be surprised at this remark. She cast a sidelong glance at Sarsbrook, but his lordship's face was devoid of emotion. "It is a very great honor having you here, Lady Verdon," said Pandora.

Isabelle smiled graciously, pleased that the young lady seemed to recognize the distinction of such a visit. The great Lady Verdon did not often condescend to call upon lesser mortals. "I do hope I am not interrupting you," said Isabelle, looking at her brother.

"Indeed not," said Sarsbrook with a frown. "We were only discussing ancient Greece."

"Oh, dear. Miss Marsh, you will find that my brother's only topic of conversation. I find it so very tedious. I care very little for antiquities although they are quite the thing nowadays. But have you seen the Elgin Marbles, Miss Marsh?"

"No, I have not," said Pandora.

"The marbles?" said Sarsbrook. "You have seen them?"

"Why, yes, of course. I went to the British Museum only yesterday. It was a great crush of people to be sure. And I must say I cannot understand what the fuss is about. I am not so fond of old Greek statuary, Miss Marsh. Don't you agree that if a person pays such a great sum for statues, the heads and other appendages ought to be there?"

Pandora laughed. "I do suppose your ladyship has a point."

"My sister is a great philistine, Miss Marsh."

Isabelle directed a superior smile at her brother, but ignored his remark. "You must escort Miss Marsh and her brother to see the marbles, Robert," she said. "Although I should caution Miss Marsh that you would probably bore her to death with all your schoolmaster's knowledge of the subject."

"I should like to see the Elgin Marbles," said Nicholas eagerly.

"Then we will go and see them," said the viscount. "I shall be happy to take you. And your father and sister, of course."

"That would be very kind, my lord," said Pandora. She was eager to see the Elgin Marbles, which had just been put on display at the British Museum. The purchase of the ancient Greek statues from the Parthenon and the Acropolis had been much discussed in the newspapers. Many naysayers had been unhappy about the estimated hundred and sixty thousand pounds the British government had paid for the antique treasures.

"Remember I warned you, Miss Marsh, if you are bored to death," said Isabelle.

Pandora smiled. "Will you have a tea cake, Lady Verdon?"

"Oh, I fear I cannot stay, Miss Marsh," replied Isabelle, putting down her teacup. "I fear I have another engagement. I only stopped by to meet you and to bring you this invitation." Isabelle opened her reticule. Taking out an envelope, she handed it to Pandora. "It is an invitation to our ball. I would be so pleased if you and your family could come."

"That is very kind, Lady Verdon, but I am not sure—" began Pandora.

"Nonsense," said Isabelle with an imperious wave of her hand. "I shall not accept your regrets with good grace. You must come. I shall expect you."

"It is not unlike a royal command," said the viscount.

"And you did promise to come as well, Robert," said Isabelle. "My dear Miss Marsh, it is so difficult to get my brother to come to any function. He so disdains society."

"And with good reason," retorted the viscount.

"I'll listen to none of your nonsensical talk, Robert. Now, Miss Marsh, I must apologize for the shortness of my visit, but I fear I must go. Do forgive me."

Pandora hastened to assure her ladyship that she appreciated her visit, no matter how brief its duration. Isabelle smiled again, rose grandly from the sofa, and then took her leave.

"Your sister is very beautiful, Lord Sarsbrook," said Nicholas.

"Is she?" said his lordship. "Oh, I suppose some have said so."

"She is indeed," said Pandora. "And she was so very affable." She looked down at the invitation. "I cannot imagine why she would invite my family to such an occasion. My lord, I shall be a fish out of water."

"Nonsense," said Sarsbrook. "You will come?"

"Why, I shall try."

"Good," said the viscount. "And when shall we go to the British Museum?"

"Really, my lord, it is not necessary that you escort us there."

Sarsbrook's eyebrows raised slightly. "Miss Marsh, I assure you I never offer to do things that I do not wish to do. Why don't you consult with your father as to when you'd like to go and then write me? I shall be available any time."

"That is really too good of you."

The viscount smiled at her, and they returned to their tea. After another hour of conversation that ranged from Lord Elgin in Greece to the poet Byron and then back to Nicholas' Greek assignment, Sarsbrook took his leave.

Nicholas was beside himself with happiness at the great success of his lordship's visit. It was clear that Sarsbrook liked his sister very much. Nicholas was now even more enthusiastic about the viscount, thinking him the best of gentlemen save, of course, Nicholas's own father.

When Nicholas left to retrieve Mr. Stubbs, who had been banished to the kitchen, Pandora sat in the drawing room gazing down at the invitation Lady Verdon had given her. The afternoon had had an unreal quality about it. That one of the great ladies of society had favored her with a visit and then invited her family to a very elite ball seemed remarkable. What was even more remarkable was the fact that Sarsbrook had undoubtedly put his sister up to it.

Pandora knitted her brow in concentration. Could the viscount have serious intentions toward her? His sister seemed to be encouraging his attentions. Was it really possible that she could one day find herself Sarsbrook's wife? A few days ago the idea would have seemed utterly absurd, but now Pandora was not so sure. Sarsbrook was without a doubt the most intriguing man she had ever met. There was something about him she found very exciting. The thought of being his wife, of sharing his bed, did not displease her. Pandora studied the invitation again and smiled.

14

When Winfield Marsh returned home, he was in an exceptionally black mood. Having just lost fifty pounds betting on Mad Jack Harper, Winfield felt that things could not be worse. He had in only a few days lost most of the money he had obtained by pawning the emerald necklace. Rather than use it to pay his debts, Winfield had recklessly gambled the money away, thinking that his luck would change and he would make his fortune.

When Winfield entered the drawing room he found his father, sisters, and Nicholas all there. Nicholas hurried to him as he came through the doorway. "Winfield! You will never guess what happened! Lord Sarsbrook had tea with Pandora and me!"

"What? Here? Today?"

"Is it not horrible?" cried Lizzy. "I was off with Phoebe and her mother visiting her aunt. It was a dead bore, too, Winnie. And then I return to find that Lord Sarsbrook has been to tea. And can you imagine who called as well?"

"The prime minister?" said Winfield sarcastically.

Mr. Marsh and Pandora laughed at this response, but Lizzy was not amused. "Lady Verdon."

"Lady Verdon?" said Winfield. "Here? You must be mistaken." Winfield had heard of the lady, as had anyone with aspirations in society. She was one of the great hostesses who could make or break one's fortunes. To be accepted by Lady Verdon was a very great thing. "What would Lady Verdon be doing here?"

"She is Lord Sarsbrook's sister," said Pandora. "It seems his lordship asked her to call."

"This is dashed odd," said Winfield.

"And to think I was not here," cried Lizzy. "I shall die of disappointment!"

"I daresay you will live, Lizzy," said Mr. Marsh. "But it is a most interesting development. It appears that our Pandora has a highborn suitor. I had not thought about having a viscount for a son-in-law."

"Papa, you are very premature," said Pandora. "I think it a mistake to read too much into this."

Winfield folded his arms across his chest. It did not seem likely to him that Sarsbrook would consider his sister as a potential bride. Oh, he thought Pandora a remarkably fine girl and all that, but a man of the viscount's rank and wealth usually sought a bride among the pampered daughters of the nobility.

What was even more odd, considered Winfield, was that Sarsbrook was still under the impression that Pandora had been his uncle's mistress. A twinge of guilt came to Winfield at the idea of how unprincipled he had been in perpetuating the misunderstanding. It hardly seemed likely that Sarsbrook would consider Sir Humphrey's former mistress as a wife. Winfield frowned. Perhaps he might have other intentions, less-than-honorable ones at that.

"What is the matter, Winfield?" said Mr. Marsh. "Is something wrong?"

"Indeed not, Father," replied the young man. "I was but thinking."

"And you have not heard all of it, Winnie," continued Lizzy. "Lady Verdon has invited us to her ball!"

"The devil!" cried Winfield, quite astonished. "Lady Verdon's ball? Why, everyone from the first circles of society will be there."

"Indeed," said Mr. Marsh.

"I cannot wait to tell Phoebe," said Lizzy.

"Perhaps we have had a change of fortune," said Winfield.

"And if Pandora is to marry a viscount, I fancy I should like to marry an earl at the very least," said Lizzy.

"At the very least," repeated Winfield, his disposition suddenly improved. Everyone laughed, but, despite Winfield's jovial expression, he could not help but be a trifle uneasy about these most recent developments.

Sarsbrook had scarcely ever been in such a good mood. After leaving Pandora's residence, he had instructed his driver to take him to Hyde Park, where he got out and sent the carriage on home. He walked for a long time in the park, reflecting about his meeting with Pandora. As he walked, he seemed to be aware for the first time of the trees and flowers and the other people enjoying the excellent weather.

The viscount was undeniably infatuated. He found himself lingering on the memory of Pandora sitting in her drawing room regarding him with those fine gray eyes of hers.

It was a pity, thought his lordship, that Isabelle had arrived. He hoped that she would keep quiet, rather than shout it about that her wayward brother had finally found a female that suited him. Sarsbrook frowned, realizing that he had made a mistake in involving Isabelle. With his sister taking her up, all of society's attention would be focused on Pandora. That would hardly do if one wanted to be discreet. Why had he not thought of some other way to see more of Pandora, he asked himself. Well, Sarsbrook decided, Isabelle was involved and there was no turning back.

When the viscount arrived back at his house, his butler admitted him. "Fine day, is it not, Archer?" said Sarsbrook.

"Indeed it is, my lord," said the servant, rather surprised at the viscount's comment. His master was not accustomed to remarking on the weather or making small talk.

"I shall go to the library, Archer."

"And would your lordship wish to have dinner at the usual time?"

Sarsbrook nodded and then proceeded to the library. There he took up his neglected notes on his new translation and looked them over. After a time, the viscount's mind began to wander back to Pandora.

He thought suddenly of Sir Humphrey. It was very hard to imagine his uncle and Pandora; the very thought repulsed him. Yet there was the diary. Sarsbrook frowned. Perhaps he should destroy it. After all, it was so very compromising for Pandora, and indeed, he hated to look at it now that he had become so fond of her.

The viscount opened the wooden box on his desk and took out the key to the desk drawer. Unlocking it, he pulled it open. When he found the drawer empty, Sarsbrook could only stare in confusion. He pulled the drawer out as far as it would go. The book was gone!

"Good God," muttered his lordship. "This is monstrous!" Sarsbrook opened the other drawers, searching through them. Could he have put the diary somewhere else? he asked himself. No, he distinctly remembered placing it in the locked drawer some days ago. It was obvious that someone had taken it.

Sarsbrook rang impatiently for a servant. "My lord?" said Archer, entering the library.

"Archer," said the viscount, "there is something missing from my desk. It is very important. I suspect it has been stolen."

"Stolen, my lord? Are you sure?"

"It is not here," said Sarsbrook testily. "It was a book, a small book bound in blue vellum. It was locked in the drawer. I wish to know who has taken it."

"I cannot imagine that one of the servants has taken it, my lord," said Archer. "I believe every member of this household is trustworthy."

"Who then, Archer? We have few visitors here."

"There was Mr. Brackley," said Archer weakly. "He was in the library, my lord. I left him there for a short while. When I returned he was gone."

Sarsbrook slammed his fist down against the desk. "Dammit, Archer!" shouted the viscount. "If Brackley took this book, it is a very serious matter. How could you have allowed him in here? By God, had I not told you that he was not to be admitted?"

"I am so sorry, my lord," said Archer, eying his master with trepidation.

"Get out," said Sarsbrook. "Get out of my sight!" The butler scurried off. The viscount rested his head on his hands. Why had he not destroyed the diary? "Dammit," muttered the viscount again.

Dinner that evening was very strained for the servants at Sarsbrook House. One of the parlor maids had heard his lordship shout at Archer. It was a most unusual occurrence. Indeed, Sarsbrook did not normally have to resort to shouting to get a servant's attention. More often than not he found it sufficient to direct a look of displeasure at the offending employee.

After dining alone, the viscount sat sipping a glass of port in the drawing room. He stared glumly into the fire, thinking of the diary and its disappearance. "My lord?"

Sarsbrook looked up. Archer had entered the room. The viscount frowned at the servant, wishing he had not lost his temper. The man was an excellent butler who had been in his employ for a good many years.

"Yes, Archer." Sarsbrook hoped his tone would reassure the butler.

"A note has been delivered for your lordship." Archer extended a silver salver toward his master.

"Thank you, Archer," said Sarsbrook. Greatly encouraged to see that his employer's temper had subsided, the butler retreated from the drawing room. Opening the missive, Sarsbrook glanced at it. "Dash his impudence!" he said aloud. The letter was from Brackley.

The short communication read:

Cousin, I believe you may wish to speak with me about a matter of some interest to you. Meet me at

the Stag's Head on Russell Street at nine o'clock.
Miles Brackley.

While he was tempted to toss the note into the fire and
forget the idea of meeting his cousin, Sarsbrook soon
thought better of it. It would be best to see Brackley and
find out what he wanted.

Sarsbrook arrived at the tavern at precisely nine
o'clock. The Stag's Head was a lively establishment
jammed with noisy patrons who talked loudly as they
drank their fill of ale and gin. The viscount glanced
around the tavern, looking for his cousin. His eyes soon
alighted upon Brackley, seated at a table with a woman
on each arm. Catching sight of Sarsbrook, he waved.

The viscount made his way toward Brackley's table,
sidestepping around rowdy men in various states of inebriation. "Brackley," he said grimly.

"My lord cousin!" cried Brackley. "You are a prompt
one you are."

The women looked up curiously at the viscount, who
frowned at their painted faces and tawdry dresses. "Go
on then, my girls," Brackley continued. "I've business to
discuss with his lordship."

Rising reluctantly, the women left the table. Sarsbrook
sat down. "I suggest you state your 'business' as quickly
as possible, Brackley."

"Oh, I do intend to do that, Cousin," said Brackley.
He took up a flagon of ale that was sitting on the table
before him and took a long draught. "Would you like a
drink, then, my lord?"

"No," said Sarsbrook curtly.

"Very well, I shall get quickly to the point. I believe I
have something that you may wish to have returned to
you."

"Then you are a thief as well as a blackguard, Brackley."

"Come, come, Cousin, there is no point in your abus-
ing me in this manner. I believe I am the injured party
here. You led me to believe that you would settle some
money on my mother and me and I have not seen one

penny of it. You said I must write you, and I did, but you did not reply."

"Dammit, I have scarcely had the opportunity. You are dashed impatient."

"I need the money," said Brackley. "I do not have time to wait about forever. Now I will make a bargain with you. For ten thousand pounds, money that is owed me from my uncle, I shall return a certain book to you."

"Any why should I care about the book?"

"I don't know, but if a man locks something up in his desk, 'tis because he thinks it important."

Sarsbrook shrugged. "You may be disappointed, Brackley. What will you do if I do not give you the money?"

"Then I shall pass this book about to everyone in London. Perhaps I may have it published. Secretly, of course. There is a market for such things." An infuriatingly self-satisfied smile appeared on Brackley's face. "Our dear Uncle Humphrey will be notorious."

The viscount glowered at his cousin. The man's expression infuriated him. "You may go to hell, Brackley," he said. "I'll not give you anything. And your treachery has done you a disservice, for in truth I was going to settle money on you. Now you will get nothing and my conscience is perfectly clear."

Brackley looked startled. "You're lying," he said. "You never meant to give me anything."

The viscount's attempts to control his temper failed at that moment. Jumping up from the bench, he leaned across the table and grabbed his cousin roughly by the coat. "You damned villain! I should beat you within an inch of your life!"

Brackley was cowed by his cousin's unexpected fury. "Let me be!" he cried.

Sarsbrook released him. Without another word he left the tavern. Once inside his carriage, he cursed himself. He should not have lost his temper. He should have paid Brackley and retrieved the diary. His cousin would now make the diary public. It would be a great scandal, and

Sir Humphrey's name would be a laughingstock. The viscount frowned, but then shook his head stubbornly. How could he have faced himself in the mirror if he had allowed Brackley to get the best of him? Folding his arms across his chest, Sarsbrook wondered if perhaps his odious cousin had already done so.

15

There was a tiny walled garden behind the Marsh residence. Small as it was, the garden afforded Pandora a respite from the cares of life in town. She often retreated there to sit and enjoy the flowers.

The morning after Sarsbrook had come to tea Pandora rose early and made her way to the garden, where she sat on the cool stone bench amidst the primroses and columbines. Pandora had had a most disturbing dream just before she had awakened that morning, which had left her strangely restless.

In the dream Sarsbrook had appeared before her, opening his arms as if to embrace her. Pandora had been attired in her night dress, but that had not seemed odd to her. She had gone eagerly to his embrace, kissing him passionately on the lips. The viscount had smiled at her before wordlessly untying the ribbon at the throat of her gown, enabling the flimsy garment to slip to the floor. She had stood naked before him while his eyes roamed over her body. "You are very beautiful, Pandora," he had said, reaching out to her. She had then smiled, allowing his hands to caress her. And then she had awakened, confused and unsettled.

Pandora's cheeks reddened at the memory. How could she have had such unseemly thoughts, she asked herself. She looked down at the primroses at her feet, deeply embarrassed.

Surely it was wrong to imagine these things. A lady should not have such thoughts, she told herself. Yet when she had awakened from the dream, she had longed for Sarsbrook and had wished that he was there in the bed beside her.

After sitting for a time, Pandora left the garden to return to her room. Seeing the peach-colored silk lying on her sewing table, she told herself that she would have to work very hard if she were to finish the dress in time for Lady Verdon's ball. Pandora took up the pieces of the gown's bodice and began to pin them together.

She worked for an hour before Lizzy popped her head through the doorway. "Pandora—oh, you are hard at work." The younger of the Marsh daughters walked into the room. "That is a lovely color, Pan. I fancy you will look splendid."

"If I can finish it in time," said Pandora.

"Oh, of course you will, Pan. Is it not exciting? To think that we will be attending Lady Verdon's ball! It is too wonderful!"

"It is unexpected," replied Pandora, starting to sew tiny stitches into the material.

Lizzy smiled brightly. "I am so excited. I hope I do not make a cake of myself."

Pandora laughed. "You will be a very lovely cake in any case, Lizzy. I daresay the gentlemen will flock to you."

"I do hope so," said Lizzy. "I should not like to be a wallflower."

"I fear there is little chance of that."

"You are the best sister, Pan. I am so glad for you. That you have met Lord Sarsbrook, I mean to say. I cannot believe that I thought you should settle for Mr. Underwood. How ridiculous that seems now. Lord Sarsbrook suits you much better. And he is not so fat. Indeed, he is very thin. You do not think he is too thin?"

Pandora laughed again. "No, I do not."

"Good," said Lizzy. "And you do not think he is too ill-tempered?"

"I hardly know him, but I do not think him overly bad-tempered."

"Then you do like him?"

Pandora nodded. "I confess I do, Lizzy."

Lizzy smiled. "Good," she said. "Now, have you written to his lordship informing him when we will see the Elgin Marbles?"

"No, not yet, Lizzy."

"Pandora, you must do so at once. Papa said last night that Wednesday would be an excellent day. Do write him!"

"Oh, very well," said Pandora, putting down her sewing.

"It will be so thrilling," said Lizzy. "Now I will leave you, Pan, so that you may write to Lord Sarsbrook. Do not be long. It will soon be time for breakfast." Lizzy hurried away, leaving her sister to ponder what she would write to the viscount.

Tucker rapped smartly on the door of Sarsbrook House using the polished brass door knocker. When Archer opened the door, he smiled cheerfully. "Good afternoon, Archer. Is his lordship at home?"

"Do come in, sir," said the butler, pleased to see his master's friend. The viscount was in a bad mood, and the servant hoped that Mr. Tucker could bring him out of it.

Joining Sarsbrook in the library, Tucker grinned broadly at his friend, who was sitting as his desk. "Robin, old man, here you are again holed up in your library like a rabbit in a warren. 'Tis another beautiful day. Let us go to the park."

"I'm in no mood to go anywhere, Tuck."

"Indeed? Why, I did not expect to find you in high dudgeon. What is the matter?" Tucker sat down in front of the desk.

Sarsbrook shook his head. "You know my cousin Brackley?"

"I know who he is, but we have never been introduced."

"You are fortunate," replied Sarsbrook. "My cousin is a scoundrel." He paused. "And a thief."

"A thief? Good God, Robin, what do you mean?"

"He came here a few days ago, barged his way past my servant, and waited in the library. While here he evidently opened my locked drawer and stole Sir Humphrey's diary."

"The devil!" cried Tucker. "How did he know about it?"

"I daresay he did not know about it. He simply discovered it by chance. It seems he thought I would pay to get it back."

"Why, that is damnable!" said Tucker. "I can scarcely believe it! Your own cousin?"

"Would that he were not my cousin," said the viscount. "He sent word to me to meet him at a tavern last evening. There he demanded I pay him money or he would have the diary published."

"He would not dare. He could not publish something like that."

"He could have it printed secretly and distributed privately. I should say it would be very popular."

"I daresay you are right there," said Tucker with a smile. Seeing his friend's frown, he quickly adopted a more somber expression. "Why, I must say this is a devil of a fix, Robin. What did you do?"

"I told him to go to hell. But I wonder now whether I should have paid him. I meant to settle some money on him in any case. He so infuriated me that I could not bear to think of giving him anything."

"Do you think he will carry out his threat?"

"I am certain of it. He thinks there will be a great scandal."

"I daresay it will create a stir. But I do not know that it will reflect badly on you just because Sir Humphrey was your uncle."

"God in heaven, Tuck, that is not the point. It is that I cannot bear to think of others reading the diary. What it says about Miss . . . M. I dearly wish I had burned it."

"So it is Miss M. you are worried about?" said Tucker.

"My dear Robin, no one knows who she is. I would not concern yourself with that at all."

"I saw her again yesterday, Tuck. I had tea at her house. She is the most delightful lady."

"At her house? That sounds as though you are making progress on your campaign to win the fair Miss M. Do tell me what happened."

"Nothing happened," said Sarsbrook testily. "I had tea."

"Alone with her?" said Tucker eagerly.

"No. Her young brother was there."

"Her young brother? Why, young brothers are the best of chaperones. It is so easy to send them off with a shilling." Tucker was silenced by his friend's disapproving look.

"My sister arrived."

"Lady Verdon called upon Miss M.?"

"I had asked her to do so. At my request, she has invited the lady and her family to the Verdon Ball."

"Really, Robin, I daresay her ladyship would be sorely vexed to know who your lady really is."

"Then she had best not find out."

"Well, I shall be as silent as the Sphinx," replied Tucker, "but the Verdon Ball is such an important event. So many eyes will be upon your Miss M. Perhaps it might have been better if you had asked your sister to invite her to a less-public occasion."

"Perhaps so, but good God, Tuck, what is less public than my sister's ball? There are so many persons crammed into her ballroom, all of them fighting to be noticed, that one hardly sees anyone."

"You are doubtless right. But, my dear Robin, since you have brought up this matter of the Verdon Ball, do you not think you can convince your sister to invite Fanny and me as well? Fanny had been badgering me to ask you."

"Oh, very well, Tuck."

"And do you fancy she will do so?"

"I do not ask her to do me many favors," replied the viscount. "I daresay my sister will not refuse me."

"That is famous!" cried Tucker. "Fanny will be so thrilled."

"I cannot imagine why so many otherwise sensible persons are so eager to spend their time among such vapid and utterly silly individuals."

"Then you will not be attending the ball, Robin?" said Tucker, suppressing a smile.

"I assure you it is not my wish to do so."

"But then you would not have the opportunity to dance with a certain lady."

"I detest dancing," muttered Sarsbrook.

"That is only because you have not yet had the right partner," said Tucker with a knowing grin.

Sarsbrook smiled as he considered that his friend was probably right.

16

The British Museum was a venerable establishment that contained all manner of fascinating exhibits. Those with a scientific turn of mind as well as those with a liking for the curious and bizarre were apt to find it endlessly interesting.

The acquisition of the Elgin Marbles that year was a major coup for the museum. The display of ancient Greek sculptures from fabled Athens excited the imagination of the public, prompting a great craze for classical statuary.

Sarsbrook, despite his preoccupation with ancient Greece, had not yet had the opportunity to see the Elgin Marbles. He was, therefore, very eager to go to the British Museum. Of course, the viscount's love of ancient Attica was not the only reason he was so pleased to be traveling to the great museum in Bloomsbury. Indeed, Sarsbrook was actually much more interested in seeing Pandora Marsh than the ancient statues.

The viscount sat in his carriage, looking out the window as the vehicle approached the Marsh residence. He had taken particular care with his appearance, having admonished his valet that he had best make him look presentable. The valet, who had been long trying to get his master to have more interest in fashion, had been delighted.

The result of his lordship's unusual attention to his attire that day was decidedly positive. Sarsbrook looked very distinguished in his charcoal-gray coat and pale-buff pantaloons. His neckcloth was arranged, with his valet's assistance, in a suitably fashionable waterfall style. The viscount's hair, having been precisely trimmed by the barber that morning, was combed into the modish Corinthian style. Although no one would have taken his lordship for a member of the dandy set, Sarsbrook looked every inch the well-bred gentleman.

Arriving at the Marsh residence, the viscount jumped down from the carriage and made his way to the door. He was immediately admitted and led to the drawing room, where Mr. Marsh and Nicholas were waiting. They were joined shortly by the ladies. Lizzy, who could hardly contain her excitement at the venture, looked stunning in a peacock-blue dress and matching spencer. A fetching straw bonnet completed the ensemble.

While vaguely aware that Lizzy was a very pretty girl, Sarsbrook took little notice of the younger Marsh sister. His attention was fastened on Pandora. When she entered the drawing room, Pandora had smiled brightly at the viscount and he had been utterly entranced. He thought she looked splendid in a pale-green pelisse that was trimmed with ivory satin.

The outfit was several seasons old and it had been abandoned last year. Needing something to wear, Pandora had hastily resurrected it by redoing the sleeves and adding the ivory trim.

"We are all here, Lord Sarsbrook," said Mr. Marsh, eager to be off on the expedition.

"Then let us go," said the viscount, offering his arm to Pandora.

Lizzy and Mr. Marsh exchanged a meaningful glance as Pandora tucked her arm under his lordship's. They all then proceeded out to the carriage, where Sarsbrook solicitously assisted Pandora and then Lizzy into the vehicle. Nicholas climbed in after them, followed by his father. Sarsbrook was the last to enter. He sat down on the commodious leather seat where he gazed at Pandora, who was seated diagonally across from him.

Pandora noted that the viscount looked particularly handsome that afternoon. Smiling, she met his gaze.

Nicholas began to talk excitedly as the carriage started on its way. Lizzy and Mr. Marsh joined in, chatting happily. They were very much thrilled to be embarking on this outing, traveling in a fine carriage in the company of a viscount.

Sarsbrook answered any comments directed to him with brief answers, as he was not paying much attention to the conversation. Instead he watched Pandora. That young lady was well aware that his lordship's attention was focused on her. Indeed, she was aware of little else but his dark brown eyes upon her.

When they arrived at the British Museum, the viscount was first to alight from the carriage. He saw his guests safely down. Last to emerge was Pandora. The viscount extended his gloved hand to her, which she took as she walked down the carriage steps. Once safely on the ground, Sarsbrook did not seem inclined to release her hand. He held it for as long as he dared, finally freeing her with some reluctance.

"I expect you often visit the museum," said Pandora, thinking it best to make conversation.

"I do, Miss Marsh," said his lordship, extending his arm to her once again. "I most often visit the library."

Pandora took the offered arm. "It was so good of you to escort us," she said, looking up at him.

Fastening his dark eyes upon her gray ones, the viscount was filled with emotion. He wanted to take Pandora Marsh into his arms and cover her lips with his own. Instead he managed to smile. "I am only too happy to do so, Miss Marsh."

"It has been a very long time since I have been here," said Mr. Marsh, offering his arm to his younger daughter.

"I have never been here," said Nicholas eagerly. "I wish to see everything!"

"Nicky, I daresay there may not be time to see everything," said Lizzy. "We are here to see the Elgin Marbles."

"I know," said Nicholas, "but Winfield said there was a mummified cat."

Everyone laughed. "We will endeavor to see that as

well," said the viscount, and they made their way to the museum door.

The exhibit of the ancient Greek sculptures impressed the Marsh family very much. Even Lizzy, who had little interest in such things, was not unmoved at the sight of the stately friezes from the Parthenon. There was a great crowd of people in attendance, creating a festive mood.

Sarsbrook, who normally abhorred being among throngs of people, for once did not seem to mind. With Pandora on his arm, he was quite pleased when upon several occasions, the crush of onlookers forced her up against him.

Pandora felt contented and happy walking beside the viscount, discussing the famous sculptures. An expert on Greek history, Sarsbrook was a fountain of knowledge, but Pandora noted with approval that he was not in the least pedantic. For his part the viscount was happy to find that Pandora appeared to be quite well versed on Greek history.

There were many who noticed Pandora and the viscount as they walked together among the exhibits. Several romantically inclined ladies thought they were a very handsome couple who were obviously in love. A number of gentlemen viewed Sarsbrook with envy, seeing Pandora's radiant face.

One of the visitors to the museum was particularly interested in seeing Sarsbrook and Pandora. A pale young gentleman in dandified dress was surprised to find the viscount there in the company of two ladies, a middle-aged man, and a young boy. The gentleman, whose name was Wilcock, did not know Sarsbrook except by appearance.

Wilcock was a good friend of the viscount's cousin, Miles Brackley. Upon several occasions Brackley had pointed out the viscount to Wilcock, saying he was a monstrous, black-hearted creature. Viewing the sculptures with a bored look, Wilcock then directed his quizzing glass at Sarsbrook. "I say, Fielding," he said, addressing his companion, "I believe that is the viscount Sarsbrook. He is Brackley's cousin."

His friend, a tall, gangly young man in a claret-colored coat, stared at the viscount and Pandora. "I would not know, Wilcock. The man is almost a recluse. I have never met him."

"I know that is he," replied Wilcock. "I wonder who the lady is with him. Brackley always told me his cousin detests females and is a veritable monk."

Fielding eyed Sarsbrook with renewed interest. "I fancy Brackley is misinformed. See how he looks at her. Why, I think I know that lady."

"You do?"

"Yes, that is Winfield Marsh's sister. You know Marsh, of course. He always has such miserable luck at faro."

"Oh, yes, of course."

"Indeed," continued Fielding. "You see, there is Mr. Marsh, Winfield's father. He is a nice fellow. Yes, the lady is Pandora Marsh."

"That is very interesting," said Wilcock. "It seems the lady had made a very important conquest. The man is as rich as King Midas himself."

"If she snags him, I should say she will do well indeed," said Fielding. "Whatever Brackley might think of him, Sarsbrook is a great prize in the marriage mart."

Wilcock nodded. He would have to tell his friend Brackley about Sarsbrook and the lady. He was sure that Brackley would be very much interested.

Sarsbrook and Pandora continued on, completely unaware that they were generating so much interest. After seeing all of Lord Elgin's noted marbles as well as the mummified cat, it was finally time to leave the museum.

Once back inside the carriage everyone seemed filled with excitement and eager to discuss what they had seen. It was some time before a lull in the conversation allowed Nicholas to speak. "There is one thing that I do not understand, my lord, about the Greek statues."

"And what is that, Nicholas?" said the viscount.

"It is why the Greeks did not seem to like to put clothes on anyone."

"Nicholas!" cried Lizzy, horrified.

Pandora put her hand to her mouth to stifle her laugh.

"I think you would do better to keep your thoughts to yourself, Nicholas," said Mr. Marsh sternly.

"But the young man has asked a very good question," said the viscount, with an indulgent smile. "It was that the Greeks considered the human body the most perfect and wondrous creation. They saw no shame in viewing it." Sarsbrook looked at Pandora, thinking that the Greeks were right in their opinion.

"I think the Greeks were very interesting," said Nicholas.

Everyone laughed. Sarsbrook was enjoying himself immensely. He insisted that the Marsh family return with him to Sarsbrook House for tea.

Entering the viscount's home, Pandora's family was very much impressed by its grandeur. Mr. Marsh and Lizzy viewed the palatial residence with delight, noting its lavish furnishings and splendid paintings.

Seeing the house again had a sense of unreality for Pandora. Having allowed herself the fantasy of imagining herself as Lady Sarsbrook, being in Sarsbrook House now made that seem absurd. How could she, Pandora Marsh, think of becoming mistress of such a place?

"It is a magnificent house, my lord," said Mr. Marsh. "You must be very proud."

"It is a fine house," replied his lordship. In actuality he had never thought much about it. Having been raised there and in country houses even grander than Sarsbrook House, he had taken it for granted. "Would you like to see the rest of it?" Sarsbrook rather surprised himself, for he was not one to act as a tour guide to visitors to the stately mansion.

Offering Pandora his arm again, Sarsbrook led the Marsh family through the vast rooms and hallways of the home. He listened politely to Nicholas' questions and Lizzy's breathless exclamations at the wonders of the various rooms.

Walking along with the viscount, Pandora was

strangely silent. When the others were engrossed in studying the paintings in the portrait gallery, his lordship turned to Pandora. "Is something wrong, Miss Marsh? You seem so pensive."

"Oh, nothing, my lord," replied Pandora, looking up at him. "It is only that I am rather overcome by your house. It is very grand."

"I suppose it is," said the viscount. "When one is accustomed to it, it does not seem so."

"It is so very large, my lord," said Pandora. "One feels so insignificant."

Sarsbrook pressed her arm. "I do not think you should ever feel that, Miss Marsh." He paused. "Pandora."

This usage of her Christian name seemed to have an electrifying effect on Pandora. She looked up at him, her gray eyes searching his own. It took all of the viscount's considerable self-control to refrain from enfolding her in his arms.

"My lord, would you tell us about this gentleman here?" said Mr. Marsh, gesturing toward one of the pictures on the wall.

Sarsbrook looked away from Pandora. "Of course, sir," he said. "Come, madam. Your family wishes to know about my illustrious ancestors." Pandora leaned on Sarsbrook's arm as they walked over to join Mr. Marsh.

After concluding the tour of the house the viscount escorted his visitors to the drawing room, where a splendid tea was laid out for them. Having never before seen so many wonderful things to eat, Nicholas was glad that he was so hungry.

Pandora, on the other hand, was hardly able to eat anything, for she found her proximity to the viscount very unsettling. She tried to appear nonchalant as Lizzy chattered on about the wonders she was seeing at Sarsbrook House, but the visit was proving to be a trifle overwhelming. As she met Sarsbrook's gaze, Pandora could only smile and think that she had fallen in love.

17

Miles Brackley sat on a chaise longue in his bedchamber, idly sipping a glass of wine and thumbing through a sporting magazine. Although it was past noon, Brackley was still attired in his silk dressing gown. As usual he had been out very late the night before in the company of his convivial drinking companions.

Brackley and several other young gentlemen had spent a good part of the evening at what more moralistic persons might call a gambling den. There Brackley had had a rather profitable night winning at hazard and then enjoying the delights of a lady of the demimonde.

Now in the cold light of day, the memory of Sarsbrook came back to Brackley. He had thought of his cousin often since the unsuccessful meeting at the tavern nearly a week ago. Brackley frowned as he remembered. He'd been a bit surprised by Sarsbrook's behavior, for he had assumed that the viscount would be very willing to cooperate in order to get Sir Humphrey's diary back.

Getting up, Brackley went to the carved oak wardrobe that stood in his room. Opening the door, he took the diary from its hiding place. Reclining again on the chaise longue, Brackley began to read Sir Humphrey's words. His cousin forgotten, Brackley smiled as he read about Miss M.

A short time later, Brackley's butler appeared at the door, announcing that he had a visitor, Mr. Wilcock. Although he had not been eager to have company, Brackley was willing to see his very good friend. "I will see Mr. Wilcock. Show him in here."

The servant nodded, retreated, and returned shortly with the guest. "Brackley, I am so glad to find you in." Wilcock smiled blandly at his friend. He was attired in a tight-fitting plum-colored coat and ivory-colored pantaloons. His shirt points were outrageously high and his neckcloth puffed out at the base of his throat in snowy profusion. A jeweled quizzing glass hung from a satin ribbon about his neck, and his hessian boots were adorned with gold tassles. Wilcock was indeed a figure of sartorial magnificence.

"Where would I be at such an hour, Wilcock? What the devil are you doing about at this time?"

"My dear fellow, I rose with the sparrows this morning. And why not? I went to bed at such an ungodly hour. I daresay it was scarcely midnight. But I was doomed to spend last evening at home with my mother and sisters. You cannot imagine how I suffered. We were entertaining Sir Jeffrey Hawkins. He is such a dull fellow, but he is to marry Arabella. She thinks him a veritable paragon. He does have two thousand a year, but in my view it is his only virtue."

"Poor Wilcock," said Brackley with mock sympathy.

"And you do not know the half of it," said Wilcock, sitting down on a chair near his friend. "I spent yesterday at the British Museum, gaping at the Elgin Marbles. I daresay it was a frightful bore, but everyone is going to see then, so I felt as though I had to do so. There were so many people there. And I must tell you who I saw."

"I cannot imagine, Wilcock."

"Why, your cousin, Sarsbrook."

"Sarsbrook? Damn and blast the man."

"Yes, indeed," returned Wilcock with a smile. "He was with a young lady. And by my observation, he was absolutely fascinated by her."

"A lady? With my cousin? Did you know her?"

"I thought you would be interested. She was a good-looking wench. No, I did not know her, but Fielding recognized her. She was Miss Pandora Marsh, the sister of Winfield Marsh."

"Winfield Marsh?"

"You must remember him. He lost so badly at Mrs. Finch's a fortnight ago. He is a good-looking chap, dark hair. Very amiable fellow. He is a friend of Aldrich."

"Oh, yes, I do remember him," said Brackley. "We were never introduced."

"He has another sister. She was there, too. What a beauty! But I must say that your cousin seemed quite smitten with this Miss Marsh. I do not usually like redheads, but I thought her quite presentable."

"She had red hair?" said Brackley. He looked thoughtful. "Like Miss M."

"Miss M.?"

Brackley nodded. He closed the diary he was reading and handed it to his friend. "This is my uncle's diary."

Wilcock took the book. "Your uncle Sir Humphrey Maitland?"

"The very same. And you thought my uncle a colorless old recluse. Read a bit of that and you will change your mind."

"Must I?" said Wilcock. "I daresay I am in no mood to read an old man's memoirs."

"Read it," commanded Brackley.

Sighing, Wilcock opened the book. He read the first page and then went on to the second. By the time he got to the third page, he was very much interested. "Good heavens," he said, reading on.

Brackley grinned at his friend's expression. "Not in the least dull, is it?"

"Indeed not! How did you get this?"

"It was in the possession of Sarsbrook."

"He gave it to you?"

"No, let us say that, finding it at his residence, I borrowed it." Wilcock was barely attending. He continued reading, turning the pages of the book in rapid succession. "Come, come, Wilcock, you have seen enough. Give it back to me."

"You are a cruel fellow, Brackley. I am not done."

"Give it back to me." Wilcock reluctantly handed the

diary back to his friend. "Now tell me more about this lady that my cousin was with."

"I know very little about her. As I said she was a good-looking girl."

"But what of her family?"

"Provincial nobodies. Oh, they are respectable enough, but they have no money and no connections in society. I do wonder how Sarsbrook met her. If she marries him, she will have done very well."

"I can hardly think anyone marrying my cousin will have done very well," muttered Brackley.

"My dear fellow, I know how you detest the man, but he is so dreadfully rich. One cannot forget about that."

"Oh, I do not forget it for an instant," said Brackley. He looked down at the diary. "Do you not find it very curious that my cousin is suddenly squiring a lady about town?"

Wilcock shrugged. "I do not see anything odd about that, Brackley."

"And she has red hair?"

"Yes, but what of it?"

"Why, Miss M. has red hair."

"Miss M.?" Wilcock's eyes opened wide. "You cannot mean that you think Pandora Marsh is this Miss M.?"

"Is it a mere coincidence that she has red hair and that her name begins with the letter 'm'?"

"Still, I cannot see why you would jump to such a conclusion," said Wilcock dubiously.

"Any why not? My cousin had this diary locked in his desk."

"Locked in his desk? Then how did you get it?"

"That does not signify in the least, Wilcock. But it was locked away. Undoubtedly Sarsbrook obtained it from my uncle before he died. Perhaps his fortune was not all Sir Humphrey left to my cousin."

"Indeed?" said Wilcock. "It is an interesting theory. If so, your cousin has the most damnable good luck of anyone I have ever seen."

Brackley nodded thoughtfully and then offered his visitor some wine.

Winfield Marsh was most interested to hear about the excursion to the British Museum. Since he had not been home when his family members returned, he did not have the opportunity to learn about the trip until the following day.

Joining his father, sisters, and Nicholas for luncheon, Winfield did not have to wait long before Nicholas and Lizzy launched into a detailed description of the previous day's events. "And Lord Sarsbrook was most considerate," said Lizzy. "And he seems very fond of Pandora. I would not be surprised if he makes an offer very soon."

Pandora, although now hopeful of that very thing, thought it best to discourage this sort of speculation. "Now, Lizzy, I am not so sure of that."

"You would accept Lord Sarsbrook, would you not, Pan?" said Nicholas.

"Of course she would, Nicky," said Lizzy. "Why on earth would she refuse such an offer? She would be Lady Sarsbrook! And she would be very rich. Oh, that would be so wonderful! To think that my sister would be a grand lady."

"Then you would, Pan?" persisted, Nicholas, looking at Pandora.

She smiled. "I expect I would. Although I do find the prospect of being a grand lady rather daunting. To be mistress of Sarsbrook House! I am not sure that I could manage it."

"My dear," said Mr. Marsh, "you would do splendidly. There is no one with more intelligence and common sense than my Pandora."

Winfield was finding the discussion more and more disconcerting. His family had decided that Pandora was to be Sarsbrook's bride, and his usually sensible sister had evidently lost her heart to the fellow. He frowned. Having told the viscount that Pandora had indeed been

Sir Humphrey's mistress, Winfield could scarcely believe that his lordship would consider marriage to her.

Thinking as he did, Sarsbrook would consider Pandora a lady of easy virtue. It therefore seemed to Winfield much more likely that the viscount's intentions
were not in the least honorable. He did not know Sarsbrook, but Winfield was enough of a man of the world to
know that noblemen in Sarsbrook's position usually had
few scruples where women were concerned.

Winfield silently cursed himself for his behavior. He
was undoubtedly a vile knave, he decided. If Pandora
knew what he had told Sarsbrook, she would never
speak to him again. Frowning again, he thought of the
emerald necklace. The fact that he had taken it from
Sarsbrook bothered him constantly.

Pandora did not fail to note that her brother seemed
very unhappy and preoccupied during luncheon. When
they rose from the table, Pandora put her hand on Winfield's arm. "Is something wrong, Winnie?" she asked.

Winfield grimly watched the others leave the dining
room. "No, Pan, nothing is wrong."

"You seemed so perfectly glum. I would think you
would have been very happy to hear how amiable Lord
Sarsbrook has been."

"I don't think I should be so happy to think that he is
becoming so familiar with my sister."

Pandora regarded him in surprise. "Lord Sarsbrook
has been perfectly agreeable at all times."

"And I suppose you have lost your heart to him."

Pandora looked down. "I don't know. Perhaps I have."

"Damnation, Pan, you are no silly ninny like Lizzy,
thinking all sorts of romantic rubbish. Are you so sure
that Sarsbrook's intentions are honorable?"

"What do you mean?"

"A girl like you must take care, Pan. Do you truly believe Sarsbrook would marry someone with no money
and no position in society?"

Pandora's cheeks reddened angrily. "So you find the

idea so astonishing that Lord Sarsbrook could be fond of me?"

"No, of course not. I am sorry, Pan. Do forget what I said. I am a complete ass."

"I shall not disagree," said Pandora. She was rather hurt by Winfield's words, not that she found them unreasonable. In fact, what most upset her was the idea that he might be right. She knew very well that her position in life made it unlikely that she would make such a marriage. Perhaps she was being silly, thinking that Sarsbrook would care enough for her to make her his bride. She did not like to think she was acting like a naïve schoolgirl.

"Don't be angry," said Winfield. "I am only thinking of you. I don't want you to be hurt. Do take care, Pan."

Pandora made no reply. Winfield frowned and left her standing in the dining room, looking most unhappy. Winfield retreated hastily, thinking that he was a despicable bounder.

18

Mr. Marsh considered attending the Verdon Ball a very poor way to get one's feet wet in society. After all, to be among a great crush of people in an enormous ballroom was hardly conducive to making oneself known among London's elite.

Still, Mr. Marsh could not argue that the invitation to the ball had been very fortunate. One never knew who one might meet at such affairs. Certainly it would be a good opportunity for Lizzy and Winfield. Pandora, thought Mr. Marsh with a great deal of pride, seemed well on her way to becoming Lady Sarsbrook. Mr. Marsh could scarcely believe his good fortune.

Having spent his life on the fringes of high society, Mr. Marsh was cognizant of the importance of being invited to the Verdon Ball. It was well known that Lady Verdon, as one of the first ladies of the *haut ton*, invited only the cream of the aristocracy and gentry to her gatherings.

Mr. Marsh was therefore nearly as excited as his daughter Lizzy about attending the ball. The day of the great occasion seemed to come upon them very quickly. Pandora had suspected it would, since there had been so many preparations to make. She had worked so hard on her dress, sewing by candlelight until her eyes ached. Fortunately, she finished the gown with some time to spare.

Lizzy was so nervous at the prospect of going to the ball that she could eat nothing all day despite her father's pleas to take some refreshment. Pandora, although she did not like to admit it, was nearly as nervous as her younger sister.

Preparations for the ball started early with a good deal of attention devoted to the young ladies' coiffures. Since the occasion was so very special, Pandora had consented to obtaining the services of a hairdresser, Mr. Lewis.

Usually she and Lizzy worked on each other's hair assisted by the maid Martha. Mr. Lewis had been highly recommended by Lizzy's friend Phoebe and he proved to be an admirable and likeable man, who did an excellent job of arranging Lizzy's dark curls. He worked diligently on Pandora's red tresses, which he found to be more of a challenge. The result, however, was excellent. Looking into the mirror as Lewis affixed the final touch, a satin rose, Pandora could not help but be very pleased.

When both Lizzy and Pandora were ready for the ball, they stood in Pandora's bedchamber, critically surveying each other's appearance. "I must say, Lizzy, that you look positively stunning. I am a dashed fine seamstress, am I not?"

Lizzy laughed. "Oh, you are, Pan! But look at you! That gown is just perfect. You look so beautiful! Are you very nervous, Pan?"

Pandora nodded. "Oh, I admit I am a bit nervous, Lizzy, but I am sure that we will both enjoy ourselves very much."

"I do hope so. But even if we have a wretched time, it does not signify. After all, we will have attended the Verdon Ball! Poor Phoebe. She was quite shattered when I told her we were invited. But I promised I would tell her all about it."

Pandora glanced at the clock. "Come, Lizzy, Papa will be waiting for us."

The two sisters went down to the drawing room, where they found Mr. Marsh and Winfield dressed in their best evening attire. Pandora pronounced them both very handsome, while Mr. Marsh proclaimed that he had the two most beautiful daughters in all of England.

Nicholas told both his sisters that they looked wonderful, adding that he only wished he were old enough to go with them.

Since Mr. Marsh did not own a carriage, he had had to hire a vehicle to take them to the ball. Although Lizzy did not think the hired chaise quite up to snuff after riding in Sarsbrook's carriage, she prudently kept this opinion to herself. Once seated inside the conveyance, Lizzy chattered rather nervously while Pandora remained silent as they rode through the gaslit streets of town.

Lord Verdon, while not one of the wealthiest gentlemen in London, was reknowned for his fine hospitality. As eager as his wife to be a leader in society, Verdon did not begrudge the enormous expenditures that it took to maintain the Verdons' reputation as one of the foremost hosts and hostesses of London society.

The annual Verdon Ball was one of the season's most important events. It was known for the selectiveness of its company, fine music, and delicious refreshments. The spacious ballroom in the baron's residence was filled with light from brilliant crystal chandeliers.

By the time the Marsh family arrived, the ballroom was filled with people, all of them magnificently dressed and eager to be recognized. As they were announced, Pandora looked around the room. She did not expect to know anyone except, of course, Lord Sarsbrook and his sister. She did not spot Sarsbrook, although there was such a great crowd of people that it was difficult to see anyone.

Isabelle looked radiant as she greeted the guests entering the ballroom. She was attired in a pink satin gown trimmed with pearls. When she saw Pandora and her family, Isabelle made a special effort to welcome them. Lizzy was nearly overcome at meeting such a grand personage as Lady Verdon but she managed to retain her composure, smiling sweetly at her ladyship.

As the Marsh family members left Isabelle and made their way across the ballroom floor, Pandora had the distinct impression that they were being noticed. It seemed a good many heads were looking in their direction.

Smiling serenely, Pandora tried to appear cool and confident. She suspected that it was Lizzy who was generating the interest. Doubtless everyone was wondering who the beautiful young lady was.

It would have surprised Pandora very much to have known that she herself was the cause of so much interest among many of the guests at the ball. It would have surprised her even more to have known why so many thought her fascinating.

Over the past few days, Miles Brackley had done his best to spread the story throughout society about Sir Humphrey Maitland and his diary. Since no one loved anything more than fresh gossip, the story had spread quickly. Brackley had also circulated the rumor that Lord Sarsbrook had taken up his late uncle's mistress, who was suspected to be a young woman named Pandora Marsh.

More than a few fortunate gentlemen had been treated to excerpts from the now infamous diary. Those individuals were particularly interested to see what Miss M. looked like. When the Marsh family had been announced, word traveled quickly among the guests. There were many who could scarcely wait to have a look at the supposed Miss M. The fact that she was there seemed deliciously scandalous.

Viscount Sarsbrook stood at one side of the ballroom. Unaware of the gossip that had been circulating among a number of the guests regarding Pandora, he stood restlessly watching the company. He did not like balls. Indeed, it had been quite some time since he had attended one.

In other years when he had still felt some obligation to attend society functions, he had been rather put off by the efforts of the matchmaking mamas. These enterprising matrons had tried hard to get him interested in their daughters. It seemed that an endless number of ingénues had been paraded before him. That a man of his wealth and position did not wish to consider marriage seemed incomprehensible to those mothers seeking a good match for their daughters.

As he stood there, Sarsbrook appeared oblivious to the interest his presence generated at the ball. He remained an aloof personage, one that few dared approach.

When the viscount saw Pandora, a change came over his face. The expression of ennui was replaced with one of happy anticipation. More than one observer noted this fact and looked across the room to find what had altered his lordship's demeanor.

Sarsbrook thought that Pandora had never looked lovelier. She had outdone herself in creating a stunning peach-colored silk ball gown. Its simple classical lines flattered her excellent figure. The gown featured a very low-cut bodice, short full sleeves, and a high waist. Around Pandora's throat was a small cameo pendant and her red hair was styled in an elegant coiffure with short curls falling about her face in charming disarray.

The viscount hurried toward Pandora, who was standing with her father, brother, and Lizzy. "Miss Marsh."

Hearing her name, Pandora turned to see Sarsbrook approach. He was carefully attired in a black evening suit which made him look rather somber, but decidedly elegant. "Lord Sarsbrook." Pandora smiled at the viscount, and he could not fail to note that she looked genuinely glad to see him.

Coming along beside them, the viscount nodded to the others. "Miss Lizzy, Mr. Marsh, Winfield. I am so glad that you could come."

"We are happy to see you, my lord," said Pandora. "What a great crowd of people."

"Yes," said the viscount, wishing that the great crowd would vanish so that he could be alone with Pandora.

"I expect you know many people here, Lord Sarsbrook," said Mr. Marsh.

"Not very many," said the viscount. "I do not spend much time in society." The orchestra began to play and some of the guests moved toward the dancing area.

"Would you do me the honor, Miss Marsh, of allowing me this dance?"

"Yes, my lord. I should be very happy to."

Sarsbrook extended his arm to her, which she took readily. As she walked off, Mr. Marsh smiled broadly at his son. "You see, Winfield? There is no doubt that Sarsbrook is very interested in Pandora."

"Yes," said Winfield, watching Pandora and the viscount walk toward the dancers. Then, looking around the ballroom, Winfield espied an acquaintance of his. "There is Alec Thornton and his sister. Come, I shall introduce you." Mr. Marsh and Lizzy followed Winfield toward the others.

As they walked toward the dancers, Sarsbrook glanced over at Pandora. "You look so very beautiful, Miss Marsh. If Helen looked like you, I can well understand why the Trojan War was fought."

Pandora looked up at him and laughed. "I had not expected such outrageous flummery from you, my lord. My face is scarcely the sort to launch a thousand ships."

"If I were admiral of the fleet, it would indeed," said Sarsbrook.

"You are ridiculous," said Pandora, regarding him fondly.

He grinned. They arrived among the other couples and took their places. The music began. It was a lively round dance, one with steps the viscount had never mastered. He did his best to follow the other gentlemen but made a number of wrong turns, much to the amusement of the other dancers. His lordship thought the dance very trying. To make matters worse, with its fast pace and rapid switching of partners, the dance allowed Sarsbrook little contact with Pandora.

He was very glad when it was over. "I made a muddle of that," he said, leading Pandora away. "I daresay I provided much amusement to the company."

She smiled. "You did well enough."

"I was a laughingstock. I should be well advised to forget dancing."

"I hope not, my lord," said Pandora. "Your partner had no objections to your efforts."

"And you would be willing to venture another dance?"

"I should be very happy to do so," said Pandora.

Seeing Pandora smiling up at him, Sarsbrook did not seem to mind the idea of dancing. The orchestra began playing a mazurka. "I think I would be wise not to attempt that, Miss Marsh. Will you walk with me instead?"

"Of course, my lord." Accepting his arm, Pandora strolled with the viscount across the crowded room, taking no notice of the fact that a good many ladies and gentlemen in attendance watched them with interest. Indeed, Pandora was oblivious to the activity around her. She thought only of the viscount walking next to her. She felt supremely happy and contented beside him. "Lizzy was so excited about attending Lady Verdon's ball," said Pandora. "She could scarcely believe her good fortune in being invited."

"I always avoided my sister's balls and soirees," said Sarsbrook, smiling down at her. "But I am very glad to be here with you."

Pandora met his gaze. "I, too, am glad to be here, my lord."

"Excuse me." A masculine voice interrupted them. Winfield stood before them accompanied by a ruddy-faced, middle-aged gentleman whom Pandora had never seen before. Sarsbrook, unhappy at the intrusion, frowned at Pandora's brother, but Winfield only smiled. "Pandora, I have promised this gentleman that I would introduce you. May I present Sir Geoffrey Lytton? My sister, Miss Pandora Marsh. Have you met Lord Sarsbrook?"

"I have not had that pleasure."

"My lord, may I present Sir Geoffrey Lytton? Sir Geoffrey, the Viscount Sarsbrook."

Sarsbrook nodded stiffly to the other gentleman. He was decidedly irked at the interruption. Pandora smiled politely at Sir Geoffrey, but she thought her brother's appearance untimely.

"Sir Geoffrey was very eager to meet you, Pandora," said Winfield.

"Indeed so, ma'am," said Sir Geoffrey. "Would you do me the great honor of giving me the next dance?"

Pandora glanced over at the viscount. She did not want to dance with Sir Geoffrey, but it seemed rather impolite to refuse. "Yes, thank you, sir," she said. "If you would excuse me, Lord Sarsbrook?"

"I do so reluctantly, Miss Marsh," returned the viscount, unhappy at the idea of relinquishing Pandora to the broadly grinning gentleman. Pandora took Sir Geoffrey's proffered arm and left Sarsbrook with her brother.

"Are you enjoying the ball, my lord?" said Winfield.

"I was," said Sarsbrook, eyeing Winfield with displeasure.

"Pandora looks splendid, does she not?" said Winfield.

"She does indeed," returned the viscount, watching her cross the room with Sir Geoffrey.

"Sir Geoffrey is a widower," said Winfield. "I have it on good authority that he is in search of a wife."

The viscount regarded Pandora's brother curiously. It was obvious that he had made this comment for Sarsbrook's benefit. "And you are seeking a husband for your sister?"

"It would seem a brother's duty. Now do excuse me, my lord. I shall not monopolize your time any longer." Winfield bowed slightly and took his leave of the viscount, who frowned again. It appeared that Winfield Marsh did not approve of his attentions toward his sister. Apparently the young man did not believe Sarsbrook's intentions were honorable.

The viscount folded his arms across his chest. Of course, his intentions were not honorable, if by that one meant marriage. Not that he would not like to marry Pandora, but circumstances made that clearly impossible. If she would consent to become his mistress, he would take very good care of her. He would protect and cherish her like a wife.

Sarsbrook walked toward the dancers. He stood watching Pandora and Sir Geoffrey, a most unhappy expression on his face. The dance was a waltz, which allowed Sir Geoffrey to hold Pandora in his arms. The viscount eyed Sir Geoffrey resentfully as he and Pandora whirled about the dance floor.

While Pandora danced with her new partner, she could not help but wish he was Sarsbrook, though Sir Geoffrey was a good dancer. "You are a dashed pretty girl, Miss Marsh," he said, holding her a bit tighter than she would have liked.

"You are too kind, sir," Pandora murmured politely.

"I've not seen you before. 'Tis society's gain that you are among us, Miss Marsh."

Pandora acknowledged the compliment with a smile. "It is a lovely ball, is it not, sir?"

"It is splendid." He continued in a lower voice. "And you are the most desirable woman here, Miss Marsh."

This remark was accompanied by a wink and a tightening of his grip on her hand. Pandora was surprised and rather unnerved by her partner's familiarity. Making no reply, Pandora found herself hoping that the dance would end quickly and she could be rid of Sir Geoffrey Lytton.

Sarsbrook continued to watch Pandora, oblivious to the inquiring glances his behavior was generating. Unaware that a good many ladies and gentlemen were concluding that he was very much interested in Pandora, he kept his eyes fastened upon her.

"My lord, how good to see you."

The viscount turned around, vexed that anyone had deigned to speak to him. "Good God," he said, recognizing the young man who stood there. "Brackley! What are you doing here?"

"Oh, I was not invited, I assure you. But I am very good at finding my way into places where I am not invited."

"I suppose that is one of your few talents."

Brackley smiled unpleasantly. "I must say you are looking very well, Cousin. Black suits you."

Sarsbrook was outraged at his cousin's audacity. "I suggest you leave here at once, Brackley, before I have you tossed out."

"Oh, you would not wish to create a scene in your sister's house."

"I would not be so sure," muttered Sarsbrook.

Brackley smiled calmly at his cousin. He then directed his attention toward the dancers. "What a good-looking young lady. The red-haired girl with Sir Geoffrey Lytton. I saw you dancing with her before. I suspect you fancy her."

The viscount was quickly losing his temper. "I warn you, Brackley. If you do not leave here immediately, you will regret it."

Brackley seemed to take little notice of his cousin's words. "She is a pretty girl," he said, continuing to watch Pandora. "Her name is Pandora Marsh, is it not?" He turned to Sarsbrook and continued in a tone of studied indifference. "Or perhaps one should call her Miss M." Sarsbrook regarded Brackley in astonishment. He laughed. "Oh, I have amazed you. Yes, I have discovered the identity of your Miss M. And I must say, I envy you. Tell me, was she as good as Sir Humphrey's diary said she was?"

"You goddamned swine, Brackley," said the viscount in a low voice filled with rage. "I could kill you."

Brackley, well satisfied that he had infuriated his cousin, thought it best to retreat. "I am sorry to distress you, Cousin," he said sarcastically. "Oh, there is no need to do anything rash that you will regret. After all, thrashing me in your sister's ballroom would cause a very great scandal. I shall leave voluntarily, I assure you. Good evening, Cousin." Brackley executed a low, mocking bow and walked off.

Sarsbrook seethed with fury. That Brackley knew Pandora was Miss M. was intolerable! Knowing his cousin, the viscount did not doubt that Brackley had shared his discovery with anyone who would listen.

Pandora, meanwhile, was concluding her waltz with Sir Geoffrey Lytton. She was very happy when the dance was over. "Thank you very much, sir," she said.

"The pleasure is all mine, dear lady," said Sir Geoffrey, bowing over her hand. "Do say you will dance another with me."

"No, I fear I have promised Lord Sarsbrook the next dance," said Pandora, lying to be rid of him.

"The lucky fellow," said Sir Geoffrey. He leaned close and whispered in her ear. "If you tire of him, Sir Geoffrey Lytton is always here. I promise you a good ride, my dear. You'll not be sorry."

Pandora's eyes grew wide with shock. "How dare you, sir!" she said indignantly, turning to hurry away from him. What sort of man was he to speak so to her? she asked herself incredulously. She would have to talk to Winfield about the sort of acquaintances he wished to introduce to her.

The viscount, who had been occupied in watching his cousin's retreating form, had not witnessed Pandora's abrupt departure from Sir Geoffrey. When he turned his attention once more toward the dance area, he was pleased to see Pandora coming toward him.

"Did you enjoy the dance, Miss Marsh?" said Sarsbrook.

"No, my lord. I did not find Sir Geoffrey to my liking."

"Good," he said. Pandora noted that he seemed preoccupied. He hesitated for a moment, unsure what to say to her. "Pandora, I must talk with you. Come with me."

"Is something wrong, my lord?"

He frowned. "I have something I must tell you. Let us go to the garden."

Noting the seriousness of his expression, Pandora nodded. "Very well, my lord."

They made their way through the crowd. This time Pandora could not fail to note that a number of people were watching them. She did not seem to care, but allowed herself to be led from the ballroom.

Pandora felt the cool night air as she stepped outside. It was a welcome change after the closeness of the ballroom. The Verdons' garden was rather dark. Pandora noted that the moon was full and it cast a pale illumination into the garden, which was dominated by a fountain in the center.

Looking around the quiet garden, Pandora noted that they were alone. Although she knew that she should be alarmed at the idea of being there with a gentleman, she felt safe with Sarsbrook. She tightened her grip on his arm. "What is it that you must tell me, my lord?"

"Come, sit here beside me." Sarsbrook led her to a bench near the fountain, and they seated themselves there. She regarded him curiously, nothing that he seemed strangely agitated. Sarsbrook took Pandora's gloved hand in his own. He found himself thinking that it seemed so small and dainty. "Pandora, I believe you may already know that I have very strong feelings for you. Indeed, I did not think it possible that I would ever say this to any woman. I love you."

Pandora smiled. Her gray eyes met his. "And I love you."

"Oh, God," said Sarsbrook, taking her into his arms and crushing her to him. He was filled with such intense longing that he could hardly bear it. Pressing his lips against hers, he kissed her passionately.

Pandora returned Sarsbrook's kisses with an ardor that delighted and further inflamed him. "My dear sweet Pandora," he murmured, his lips moving to her neck and then to the roundness of her breasts, revealed in the daring décolletage of her gown.

"Oh, Sarsbrook," cried Pandora, entwining the fingers of one hand in his hair as he pressed his face against her bosom. She wanted to surrender completely to him, but at the same time a faint voice of reason was setting off an alarm within her. "My lord, you must stop," she said weakly.

Nearly overcome with desire, the viscount scarcely heard her. His kisses and caresses did not abate. "Sarsbrook!" cried Pandora in a stronger voice, pushing him away.

The viscount seemed to come to his senses. "Forgive me. I lost my head. Dearest Pandora, you cannot know how much I want you, how much I need you. Say you will be mine."

"Of course, I will be yours," said Pandora, smiling. "I love you with all my heart."

The viscount embraced her again. "I will take such good care of you, Pandora. You will have a house and a fine carriage and servants—everything you could possibly desire." Pandora pressed her face against his chest. At that moment she cared nothing for a fine carriage or servants. She wanted only Sarsbrook. He continued. "And I will look after your family. They will be well provided for."

Pandora snuggled happily in his arms. "You are very good, my lord."

He tightened his arms around her. "You will be the wife of my heart. I only wish it were possible that we might actually be wed."

These words shattered Pandora's bliss like a sledgehammer. She pulled away from him. "What do you mean?"

"Pandora," he said, fastening his brown eyes on hers. "You must know that what you have been to my uncle makes it impossible for you to be my wife."

"What . . . I have been—" said Pandora, so shocked that she could barely speak.

"It does not mean that I love you any less," continued the viscount. "Your brother Winfield told me how my uncle seduced you, taking advantage of your innocence. It was not your fault."

"Good heavens!" cried Pandora. "You still believe that I was your uncle's mistress!" She rose from the bench, horrified.

Sarsbrook jumped to his feet. He stood silhouetted

against the fountain. "You need not be ashamed that I know the truth. Your brother explained it all to me."

"My brother! You are telling me that my brother Winfield told you that I was Sir Humphrey's mistress?"

The viscount nodded. "When he came to me with the necklace. That is when he explained everything. You must wear the necklace sometime, my darling. I think emeralds would become you."

Pandora was so angry and confused that she could scarcely think straight. "I cannot believe that Winfield would lie to you. And why do you ask me to wear the necklace? I do not have it."

"I gave it to your brother," said Sarsbrook, rather alarmed at the expression in Pandora's gray eyes.

"You gave the necklace to Winfield? That is impossible!" She stared at him, trying valiantly to fight back tears. She did not know what to believe. "You think I was your uncle's mistress? You have never thought otherwise? And now you offer to make me *your* mistress?"

He stepped toward her, his arms outstretched. "My dear, Pandora, I love you."

"Keep away from me!" cried Pandora, pushing him away with such surprising force that Sarsbrook lost his balance. He fell backward, tripping on the wall of the fountain and falling into the water with a great splash.

"Pandora!" he shouted, rising from the water, soaking wet.

"I have never been anyone's mistress," cried Pandora. "And I have no intention of becoming yours, my lord!" She turned and rushed away. Entering the house, she hurried to the ballroom, where she scanned the crowd for Winfield and her father.

Spotting her brother dancing with a dark-haired young lady, Pandora moved toward him. When the music stopped, she pounced on him. "Winfield Marsh, I must talk to you!"

Winfield looked warily at his sister. "Pandora! I daresay you have not met Miss Cunningham. This is my sister, Pandora Marsh, Miss Cunningham."

"Do excuse us, Miss Cunningham," said Pandora. "There is a matter of some urgency which I must discuss with my brother." With these words she grasped Winfield's arm and pulled him away from a very disappointed Miss Cunningham.

"What is the meaning of this?" said Winfield as Pandora led him forcefully through the crowd. "Do you know who Miss Cunningham is? She is an heiress!"

"Winfield Marsh, I suggest you not say a word to me. We are going home."

"Home? We have just got here, Pan."

"We are going home! You shall tell Papa that I fell unwell and you will escort me home. You may then return as you wish, but I will not stay here another minute!"

"What on earth has happened?"

"I will not discuss it here. Tell Papa you are escorting me home!"

"Very well," said Winfield, alarmed at her expression. "I shall find Papa. I believe I saw him." Winfield went to find his father. He returned shortly. "Father is very worried."

Pandora said nothing, but walked quickly out of the ballroom. Winfield could only follow. When they were in the hired chaise going away from the Verdon residence, Winfield frowned. "Why don't you tell me what happened."

"Any why don't you tell me what you told Lord Sarsbrook?" demanded Pandora angrily.

"What do you mean?" Winfield shifted uncomfortably in his seat.

"The day you returned the necklace to him. Did you tell him that I had been his uncle's mistress?"

"Oh, Pan, I am sorry!"

"Winfield! How could you! Why would you do such a thing?"

Winfield hung his head. "Because I needed the money. I was desperate, Pan."

"So you kept the necklace?" He nodded reluctantly. "And what did you do with it?"

"I pawned it. Don't look at me so, Pan! I am sorry. I shall do anything to make this up to you." Pandora looked at her brother, and then out the carriage window. "What happened tonight? Did Sarsbrook take liberties with you? My God, he will rue the day he was born if he did!"

"I shall thank you to be quiet!" cried Pandora, tears welling up in her eyes. "You have caused enough misery, Winfield. I do not think I shall ever be able to forgive you." Hiding her face in her hands, Pandora burst into tears. Winfield could only stare at her dumbly, wondering what he could do to make things right.

19

Climbing out of the fountain dripping wet, Sarsbrook felt as if he were experiencing a particularly dreadful nightmare. Yet it struck him even then that the situation was decidedly ludicrous, and that anyone seeing him would have a great laugh at his expense.

The viscount walked from the fountain toward the house. How could she have done this to him? he asked himself. Frowning, Sarsbrook made his way toward the servants' entrance. Pandora had looked so shocked when he mentioned her having been Sir Humphrey's mistress. She had denied it so vehemently that he had been confused.

Sarsbrook frowned again, remembering his meeting with Winfield Marsh. Surely a brother would not say such a thing about his sister were it not true. Still, Winfield had struck his lordship as an unprincipled rogue when they had first met. What if he had lied, thinking to obtain money? What if Pandora was not Miss M.? Sarsbrook did not know what to believe.

When he arrived at the servants' entrance, he rapped on the door. It was opened by an astonished footman, who noted the newcomer's drenched evening clothes with undisguised horror. "What happened to you, sir?" he cried.

His outcry brought the Verdons' housekeeper, who recognized the viscount immediately. "Lord Sarsbrook! Do come in, my lord. Are you hurt?"

"No," muttered Sarsbrook.

"You must get out of those wet clothes before you

catch your death of cold," said the housekeeper. "Bob will take you to Lord Verdon's valet, who will find you some of my master's things."

"That is not necessary," said Sarsbrook. "If you would have someone find my carriage and have it brought round, I shall go home."

"Indeed not," said the housekeeper, a redoubtable lady with definite ideas. "I shall not wish to answer to her ladyship if I allowed you to leave here in such a state, my lord. Now do not argue, my lord, I pray you."

The viscount nodded. "Very well."

"Good. Then do go with Bob, my lord."

Sarsbrook followed one of the footmen up the back stairs from the servants' hall. Hearing music and voices from the ballroom, the viscount wondered if Pandora were still there. He resolved to find her and straighten out what seemed to be a very find mess.

Leading the viscount to Verdon's dressing room, the footman left Sarsbrook in the care of his brother-in-law's valet. This admirable fellow quickly fetched some towels and assisted Sarsbrook out of his wet garments. The valet then found some of his master's clothes and helped the viscount dress. Since his lordship was a good deal taller and thinner than the baron, Verdon's clothes did not fit him very well. Yet, thought Sarsbrook as he eyed his appearance in the mirror, it was hardly a time to worry about the length of one's sleeves.

"Robert! Whatever happened?"

Sarsbrook turned to see his sister standing in the doorway.

"Isabelle."

The viscount's sister regarded his lordship with disfavor as she entered the room. "I was told you came to the servants' hall soaked to the skin. I wish to know what happened." Noticing her husband's valet standing beside the viscount, she dismissed him. "That will be all, Hill."

"Very good, my lady," said the servant, bowing and leaving them.

"Now what did happen, Robert?"

"I fell into your fountain."

"Fell into the fountain? Good God, Robert, are you drunk?"

"I am decidedly sober. Perhaps it is more accurate to say that I was pushed into the fountain."

"Pushed!" cried Isabelle. "By whom?"

"Miss Pandora Marsh."

"Good heavens," said Isabelle, frowning at her brother as if he were a wayward schoolboy. "She pushed you into the fountain? I should not doubt that you quite deserved it. I must say this entire business about you and Miss Marsh is quite shocking. And to think that you would have me invite that young woman to my ball as if she were a respectable person. You have made a fool of me and I am furious with you."

"What are you talking about, Isabelle?" said Sarsbrook impatiently.

"There is no need to act as if you don't know what I mean."

"I assure you I have no idea what you are talking about."

"Very well, then I shall tell you. I was informed tonight about Miss Marsh. Can you imagine how I felt when I was told that she was our uncle's mistress? And then to hear that she is now your mistress! How could you, Robert! Everyone was talking about it. If you have to take a mistress, why could you not be more discreet!"

"She is not my mistress," said Sarsbrook, appalled at his sister's words. "Who told you this?"

"The news was all over the ballroom. I was informed of it by Georgina Cathcart, who heard it from Lord Thomas Atherton. Can you imagine my humiliation at being told such a thing by that detestable woman?"

"It is a lie," said Sarsbrook, who was growing increasingly irritated by his sister. "Why do you listen to such ridiculous gossip?"

"Is it ridiculous?"

"I have told you so. Miss Marsh is not my mistress."

Isabelle eyed him skeptically. "Perhaps you would

like to explain what you were doing with her alone in the garden and why she pushed you into the fountain?"

Sarsbrook frowned. "I should prefer to drop the subject. Do tell your husband I am indebted to him for the loan of his clothes. Do excuse me, Isabelle."

"I shall not excuse you," said Isabelle. "I feel I deserve a better explanation than this and I must tell you I am quite angry with you, Robert. I find your behavior utterly astonishing.

"To urge me to bring this Marsh family into society! I thought that this Miss Marsh was some respectable girl for whom you had developed a *tendre*. I was very pleased at the idea. Yes, I was willing to accept the fact that she was beneath you, a penniless nobody from a family I had never heard of. Indeed, I could overlook that to see you wed. And now to find that she is a strumpet, whom everyone believes to be your bit of muslin! This is truly monstrous, Robert! Do you not care what people are saying?"

"I do not care one damn what anyone says," replied the viscount angrily. "And I caution you to say nothing further about Miss Marsh. Indeed, I caution you to say nothing further about anything!" Sarsbrook did not allow his sister the opportunity to reply, but strode from the room.

As he walked down the corridor, Isabelle called to him. "Robert! Come back here at once!"

Ignoring her, Sarsbrook continued to walk quickly away.

By the time Winfield and Pandora arrived at their home, Winfield was nearly distraught. His sister was sobbing, refusing to speak to him. There was nothing he could say to her to make things right. Indeed, in all of Winfield's young life, he had never been so completely at a loss.

Pandora refused to allow him to assist her down from the carriage, angrily pushing his proffered hand aside and then hurrying into the house. Once inside, she went to her bedchamber, slamming the door behind her.

Winfield stood outside Pandora's room. "Pandora," he said.

"Go away!"

Winfield stood for a time, knowing it was futile to attempt to say anything more. "Very well, Pan," he said, turning from the door and then going out of the house and into the rented vehicle to return to the ball.

Once inside her room, Pandora regained her composure enough to change into her nightgown. She sat at her dressing table, glumly brushing her hair, while tears continued to trickle down her cheeks.

Pandora found herself reliving the scene with Sarsbrook by the fountain and felt a sense of bitter betrayal as she remembered his kisses and the touch of his hands. What a fool she had been to think he was asking her to marry him, she told herself. And all this time he thought she was a light-skirt, unfit to marry.

And Winfield! Pandora frowned at the thought of her brother. That he could have told Sarsbrook that she had been his uncle's mistress! It was incredible! Putting down her hairbrush, Pandora stared miserably at her reflection in the mirror.

There was a knock at the door, and the maid Martha entered. Having not expected anyone to return so early, she wondered what was amiss. "Do you need anything, miss?"

"No, Martha. Do go to bed. I do not need you." Pandora managed to speak in a calm voice although she felt very much like bursting into sobs once again.

"Very well, miss. You are not ill, are you?"

"No, no, Martha."

"But where is the master and Miss Lizzy? Did they not come home with you?"

"No, they did not, Martha. Now I assure you, there is nothing to worry about. Do leave. I wish to go to bed. Close the door behind you, Martha."

The servant hesitated, but then nodded. "Good night then, miss."

Martha left the room, closing the door behind her. It was obvious her mistress was in distress. Whatever could have happened at the ball, she wondered. Going downstairs, Martha heard a knock at the door. Assuming it would be Mr. Marsh and Lizzy, she hurried to answer it and was very much surprised to find a tall gentleman she recognized as Lord Sarsbrook standing there. He looked very much agitated.

"I must see Miss Marsh."

"Indeed, my lord, it is very late. Miss Marsh has gone to bed."

"It is very important that I see her," said Sarsbrook insistently.

"No, my lord, that is quite impossible," said Martha firmly. "I shall tell her you called."

"No, you do not understand," said the viscount, entering the house. "I must see her. Where is she?"

Martha was somewhat taken aback by Sarsbrook's behavior. He had a wild look and she suspected that he had been drinking. "You must leave, my lord," said Martha.

Sarsbrook looked toward the stairway that led upstairs. "Her room. Is it upstairs?"

"Really, my lord, you must go."

"Stand aside." The viscount walked past the startled maid and hurried up the stairs.

Martha ran after him. "My lord! This will not do!"

Sarsbrook took no note of the servant. Spotting the closed door, he seemed to know instinctively that Pandora was inside. He knocked sharply on the door. "Pandora! It is I, Sarsbrook."

Pandora rose from her dressing table in horror. "Sarsbrook!"

The viscount flung open the door. "Pandora, I must talk with you."

She stared at him in stunned silence for a moment. "How dare you come here!"

"I am sorry, miss," cried Martha, quite dismayed.

Sarsbrook looked at Pandora. Standing there in her nightgown in the soft light of an oil lamp, she looked startlingly beautiful. Her red hair fell about her shoulders and the nightgown revealed the voluptuous curves of her body. "Pandora, you must listen to me."

"I will not!" said Pandora.

"By God, you will!" cried Sarsbrook, advancing into the room.

Pandora regarded him angrily. At that moment she felt she hated him. "Martha," she said with admirable calm. "Fetch Andrew."

Martha hesitated. Andrew was the only male in service at the Marsh household. Nearly seventy years old, he was hardly a match for Lord Sarsbrook. "Very well, miss," she said finally. Martha turned and rushed away.

"Pandora," said Sarsbrook. "I think you might listen to me. You nearly drowned me in that accursed fountain."

"I wish that I had," said Pandora. "Now get out! I never want to see you again. Have you not done enough?"

"Pandora, I love you. You said you loved me."

"I do not love you, my lord," cried Pandora, trying very hard to keep from bursting into tears. "Indeed, I despise you! Get out, I pray you!"

"No," shouted the viscount. Springing forward, he caught her roughly by the arms. "You will listen to me."

Looking into his brown eyes, Pandora felt a momentary weakness. "No," she said, attempting to pull away from him.

He held her tight. "I love you," he repeated.

She glared up at him. "And is this how you show your love? Barging into my bedchamber in such an infamous manner? Oh, I know you are under the impression that I am accustomed to entertaining men in my bedchamber."

"Pandora." Sarsbrook released his grip on her arms. "You know I think no such thing."

"But you believe I was your uncle's mistress."

"What am I to think when your own brother tells me

that you were? Is it my fault? By all the gods, Pandora, be reasonable."

Pandora's gray eyes flashed angrily. "Reasonable? I suppose you think the reasonable thing for me to do is to become your mistress. I fear I shall remain unreasonable, Lord Sarsbrook. Now I must insist that you go!"

"Pandora—" The viscount's reply was cut off by a male voice.

"You best be going, m'lord."

Sarsbrook turned to see an elderly servant standing beside the maid who had admitted him. White-haired and stooped with age, the servant did not appear very menacing although he carried a blunt stick which he brandished in one hand. The viscount looked from the servant to Pandora. "I shall not dare defy your formidable man, Miss Marsh. I shall go." He started to turn to leave, but stopped. "Pandora, I am sorry."

"Please go."

Sarsbrook nodded and then walked out of the room. When he was gone, Pandora collapsed onto her bed and once again burst into sobs.

Mr. Marsh, Lizzy, and Winfield returned home less than an hour after Sarsbrook had left. Mr. Marsh had been quite mystified by his elder daughter's hasty departure from the ball. When he had not received a satisfactory explanation from Winfield, he had insisted that they go home as well.

Lizzy had been crushed at having to leave the ball. She had been having a marvelous time. Her beauty had attracted a horde of interested gentlemen who were eager to make her acquaintance. She had danced with a number of male admirers, several of whom were sufficiently handsome and dashing to excite her interest. It had seemed dreadful to Lizzy to have had to disappoint so many promising young men to whom she had promised dances. Still, there had been no alternative but to make her farewells and go home to see what was the matter with her sister.

Entering the house, Mr. Marsh was greeted by Martha, who informed him that Pandora was in her bedchamber. "Is she ill?" he asked, a worried look on his face.

"No, sir," replied the maid. She hesitated, unsure whether to say anything about Sarsbrook. Deciding her master should be informed, Martha continued. "I fear Miss Pandora was very upset about Lord Sarsbrook coming to the house."

"Coming to the house?" cried Winfield.

"He was here?" asked Mr. Marsh.

"Aye, sir. Not an hour ago. Miss was in her room. I told him she was abed, sir, but it did not matter. He went up to her bedchamber."

"Good God!" cried Winfield. "I shall murder him!"

"But there was no harm done, sir," said Martha. "Andrew and I sent him on his way. But Miss Pandora was very much distressed."

"I don't understand," said Lizzy. "Why would Lord Sarsbrook come here and behave in such a shocking manner? I thought he was fond of Pandora. This is very odd. I must go to her." Lizzy started to go toward the stairs. As she reached them, she was startled to see her sister coming down attired in her dressing gown. "Pan! Are you all right?"

"Yes, Lizzy," replied Pandora, continuing down the stairs.

"What is this business with Sarsbrook?" said Mr. Marsh. "Martha said he was here. What is the meaning of this, Pandora?"

"I shall tell you all what happened," said Pandora with a trace of weariness in her voice. "Come, let us go and sit down."

After seating themselves in the drawing room, Mr. Marsh and Pandora's brother and sister waited expectantly. "Do tell us what this is about, Pan," said Lizzy. "I did not know what to think when Papa said you had gone home. And Winnie would scarcely say anything at all."

Pandora nodded. "I have been a very great ninnyhammer. You see, I thought Lord Sarsbrook was very fond of me. I had even thought he might wish to marry me. At the ball I learned the truth. His lordship did not want to marry me. Instead, he asked me to become his mistress."

"What the deuce!" cried Mr. Marsh, horrified.

Lizzy's eyes opened wide with astonishment. "Oh, Pan!"

"There is something that I never told you, Papa. I did not wish to upset you, but when Lord Sarsbrook first appeared here about the emerald necklace, he had made a frightful mistake. You see, the necklace was for his late uncle's mistress, whom he knew only by the name of Miss M. He assumed I was that lady."

"He thought you were his uncle's mistress?" cried Mr. Marsh, aghast at this revelation.

"Oh, I very vehemently denied it." She frowned over at Winfield. "And I thought that he had come to believe that it was all some dreadful mistake, Yet, tonight I found that Sarsbrook continued to think I was this Miss M. person. He professed affection for me, but since he assumed I had lost my virtue, he could not consider me to be his wife. Instead, he proposed to make me his mistress."

"Oh, Pan!" cried Lizzy. "What did you do?"

"I pushed him into Lady Verdon's fountain," replied Pandora.

"Good girl!" cried Mr. Marsh. "That is my Pandora! My poor dear, I am so sorry that you had to endure such a grievous insult. The man is a villain, to be sure. And he had the audacity to come to our home!"

Pandora frowned. "He was very upset as well."

"I cannot imagine how he had the unmitigated gall to show his face to you. I took him for a gentleman. I thought him a decent fellow."

"I am sorry I ruined your ball, Lizzy," said Pandora. "You would have danced every dance, I am sure."

"Oh, Pan," replied Lizzy, "I do not care in the least for the ball. Oh, it was great fun, I do admit that, but I should have been so miserable had I stayed longer and then found out about what had happened."

"I do not fancy that Lady Verdon will be sending us any more invitations," said Pandora.

"Hang the woman," muttered Mr. Marsh, "and her brother."

"Yes," said Lizzy stoutly, although in truth she was not too happy to think that her sojourn into high society was coming to such an abrupt end.

Winfield remained stonily silent. He felt tremendously guilty and it was even worse that his sister was so nobly shielding him from his father's wrath. He vowed to do anything he could to make amends, but he realized it would be difficult at best. After all, he had behaved despicably.

"Enough of my gloomy tale," said Pandora, attempting to make light of the evening's disastrous events. "Lizzy, tell me about the ball."

Lizzy was only too happy to oblige. She began to talk excitedly about her adventures at the Verdon ball.

20

When the viscount returned to Sarsbrook House after his ill-fated meeting with Pandora, his servants noted that their master was in an exceptionally foul temper. Although the viscount's valet thought it exceedingly odd that his lordship had come home from the ball in a different suit of clothes, he made no comment on his master's attire. The worthy servant prudently attended to his duties as if there was nothing in the least unusual.

Once divested of the ill-fitting garments, the viscount ordered his valet to return them to Lord Verdon. The servant asked no questions. Instead, he bowed and left the viscount.

Restless, Sarsbrook prowled about his bedchamber before retiring to bed where he lay awake, thinking about Pandora. As he remembered the events of the evening, his face took on a grim expression. Things had not worked out at all as he had anticipated. Indeed, his lordship had a vivid imagination and he had given a good deal of thought to the blissful nights he would have when Pandora agreed to become his mistress.

This made it particularly wretched to have to lie there alone, thinking of Pandora and how she had rejected him. Sleep eluded him for most of the night and he was glad when the light of dawn finally peered through the narrow opening between the draperies in his room.

Rising from his bed, Sarsbrook soon found himself walking restlessly through the streets of London. He walked for hours, pondering his lamentable situation and wondering how he could make things right with Pandora.

The viscount mused that he could very well understand that she would be upset. He supposed a woman did not much appreciate being asked to be a man's mistress. After all, respectability, or at least the veneer of respectability, was vital to the female of the species.

As he strode briskly along the street, he considered what he might do. He would marry Pandora, he resolved firmly. Surely she would agree to marriage. After all, she did say she loved him. And he was a good catch as far as his wealth and title were concerned. Sarsbrook was aware that he did have failings in his personality, but he thought he would be a good husband to Pandora. He did love her very much. And he liked her as well. Yes, that was an excellent feature for he disliked so many people. Indeed, the viscount reflected, Pandora Marsh was perhaps the only woman in the kingdom with whom he could be happy.

The idea of marriage to Pandora cheered him considerably. Of course, he knew that his sister, Isabelle, would be very unhappy, but he did not much care what Isabelle thought. After all, she was obliged to be civil to him no matter what since he held the family's purse strings.

Brackley came suddenly to mind, clouding his lordship's improved mood. That Brackley had stolen the diary was bad enough, but the fact that he had spread the rumor that Pandora was Miss M. was quite appalling. Isabelle had said that everyone at the ball was discussing the story that Pandora had been Sir Humphrey's mistress and was now his.

Sarsbrook frowned. This was rather serious even for one who did not care a fig for society's opinion. He did not like the idea of all the chowderheads in town spreading scandal about Pandora. And if Brackley passed the diary around to his friends and they thought Pandora was Miss M., that would be utterly disastrous.

Brackley must be dealt with severely, Sarsbrook decided. Surely with all his wealth and power, he could make his obnoxious cousin come to heel. Ways of controlling Brackley preoccupied his lordship for the rest of his walk and it was some time before he arrived back at Sarsbrook House.

Although he had been gone for hours, it was still very early when the viscount returned. He went to his beloved library, where he tried to read the morning newspapers.

Some time later, the butler entered the library. "Yes, Archer?"

"A young gentleman is here to see your lordship," he said.

"Dammit, Archer, I wish to see no one. It is too damned early to have visitors."

"It is Mr. Winfield Marsh, my lord."

"Oh?" Sarsbrook frowned. "I shall see him. Have him come in."

The butler bowed and retreated, returning shortly with Winfield, who looked well dressed and dapper. Winfield regarded the viscount warily. "Good morning, Lord Sarsbrook."

"You are an early riser, Marsh," commented his lordship.

"I do not normally rise before eleven, my lord," said Winfield. "However, I could not sleep. I needed to speak with you."

"Sit down," said Sarsbrook, motioning toward a chair across from his desk.

Winfield nodded. "Thank you," he said as he took a seat. "I shall first say that my sister has told me what happened last night, of how you came to our house and forced your way into her bedchamber. And I know that you asked Pandora to become your mistress." He frowned at the viscount. "I find your behavior totally reprehensible, my lord."

"You find my behavior totally reprehensible?" repeated the viscount, surprised at Winfield's impertinence. "You are an audacious fellow, Marsh. I must ask you a question. Did you or did you not tell me that your sister was the mistress of my uncle?"

Winfield looked down. "I did."

"And was she?"

"No," said Winfield shamefacedly. "My sister is a lady of unsullied virtue. That is what I came here to tell you."

"Damn and blast, sir," said the viscount. "Then you confess that you lied to me about your own sister's honor? And you have the effrontery to call my behavior reprehensible?"

"I cannot excuse what I did, but I was desperate. You see, I was in a dashed bad situation. You cannot know how much I needed money."

"And knowing that I felt obligated to provide for my late uncle's mistress, you decided that you would slander your own sister?"

"I did not think anyone would know about it. And I didn't think Pandora would have to find out. You must believe that my sister never knew anything about what I did until last night when she discovered it from you."

"And what of the emerald necklace? You never gave it to your sister?"

Winfield shook his head. "I pawned it, my lord. I needed the money. Pandora knew nothing about it."

"Dammit, that was a very valuable necklace. Where is it now?"

"I took it to a man named Jenkins on Rosemary Lane."

Sarsbrook regarded Winfield disgustedly. He found himself thinking that his first impression of Winfield Marsh as an unscrupulous young man was an accurate one. "Did you think you could keep this matter secret from your sister, Marsh?"

Winfield shrugged. "I did, my lord."

"Well, you have made a mess of things," muttered the viscount disgustedly. "Are you aware that the whole of London society believes that Pandora was my uncle's mistress?"

"What?" cried Winfield. "You spread such a tale?"

"Dammit," said Sarsbrook, "Do you take me for some

tattlemonger? The rumor was passed about by my cousin, who obtained my uncle's diary. In the diary, he spoke of his mistress, a certain Miss M., a red-haired lady like your sister. Observing my interest in Pandora, my cousin assumed that she is Miss M. He lost no time in telling everyone in town."

"Good God!"

"And that is not all," continued Sarsbrook. "My cousin is also spreading the rumor that Pandora is now my mistress."

"And it appears you were eager to make that rumor true, my lord," said Winfield.

Sarsbrook ignored this remark. "There is one more thing. My uncle's diary was most indiscreet and I fear my cousin intends to pass it about. My uncle described his . . . shall we say, amatory adventures in vivid detail."

Winfield looked pale. "And you thought this Miss M. was Pandora?"

Sarsbrook shifted uncomfortably in his chair. "Blast your eyes, Marsh, you told me so yourself! I rest the blame for this calamitous state of affairs squarely on your shoulders."

Very much upset, Winfield rose from the chair. "Then my sister is ruined! Our family is ruined!"

"Stop your blathering," muttered the viscount irritably.

"And you feel I am to blame?" Knowing that he was guilty made Winfield defensive. "Well, perhaps it is my fault, I admit that, but I do not hold you guiltless, my lord," said Winfield.

"Me?"

"It was you who allowed my sister to think you cared for her, that you had honorable intentions toward her. And from the first, you schemed to make her your bit of muslin!"

"You go too far, sir," said Sarsbrook angrily. "If there was any scheming done, it was by you! By God, it seems incomprehensible that Pandora could have such a brother. Now get out of my sight."

Winfield glared at the viscount. "I will obey your command with pleasure, my lord," he said. Making an ironical bow, he left the room, leaving Sarsbrook sitting there with a very disgusted look on his lean face.

As Winfield walked back to the Marsh residence, he cursed himself. He had not improved matters at all. Why had he lost his temper and angered Sarsbrook? He had not meant to do so. In fact, he had planned to confess that he had lied and then beg the viscount's forgiveness. Indeed, he had hoped that if Sarsbrook was truly fond of Pandora, he might be able to convince him to do the honorable thing and marry her.

Winfield frowned. He did not think Sarsbrook at all likeable. He appeared to be a cold fish and it confounded Winfield that his sister seemed to have lost her heart to him. Winfield consoled himself with the thought that Sarsbrook would never have considered marriage to Pandora in any case.

When Winfield returned home, it was nearly eleven. Martha informed him that neither Mr. Marsh nor Lizzy had yet risen. Pandora, however, had been up for some time and might be found in the garden.

Winfield went immediately there to find her. Pandora was seated on the stone bench, silently contemplating the flowers. She was neatly attired in a dress of striped muslin, but she looked very forlorn.

"Pandora."

She looked over at her brother. "Winfield? I was quite astonished to hear that you had gone out so early. It is unlike you."

Winfield smiled, happy to see that she was speaking to him. He sat down beside her on the bench. "I did not sleep very well last night. I daresay you did not either.'

"No, I slept quite well. It was surprising."

"Poor Pan, how dreadful this is for you, and it is all my fault. I am so sorry, Pan. Will you forgive me?"

Pandora looked over at her brother. "I don't know, Winfield. I'm not sure. I am still trying to understand how you could have behaved in such an infamous manner."

"I know, Pan." Neither of them spoke for a time. Finally Winfield broke the silence. "I have something I must tell you. I went to see Sarsbrook this morning."

"Winfield! How could you!"

"I wanted to explain things to him, to say that I had lied. He was very angry. But, Pan, he told me something that I feel you must know. I pray you will not be too upset."

"What is it?" said Pandora impatiently. "Winfield Marsh, I warn you that I cannot bear much more wretched news."

Winfield frowned, wondering if he should have kept silent. "It seems that Sarsbrook's uncle had a diary in which he wrote about his mistress, Miss M. It was most indiscreet. In it he described his . . . well, I expect it was rather shocking.

"Sarsbrook's cousin stole the diary and is passing it about. When he discovered Sarsbrook appeared to be interested in you, he surmised that you are Miss M. and the subject of the diary. He has told everyone in town that you are this scandalous lady."

Pandora's eyes widened with dismay. Suddenly it became clear why Sir Geoffrey Lytton, the man who had danced with her at the ball, acted as he had. He had thought she was Miss M. "And Lord Sarsbrook read this diary?"

"I don't know, Pan. I suppose that he did."

Pandora looked stricken as an unsettling realization came to her. Sarsbrook's interest stemmed from thinking she was the licentious female described in his uncle's diary. He did not care for her at all, but thought she was someone else, a woman of ill fame. What a goosecap she had been to think he loved her! What a silly, romantic idiot she had been.

Pandora rose from the bench. "What else did he say to you?"

Winfield got to his feet as well. "What do you mean?"

"Did he say anything about me? Did he give you any message for me?"

"No, Pan, he did not. But there is one more thing. I don't know if I should tell you."

"Winfield Marsh, what is it?" demanded Pandora.

"There is also a rumor about, spread by Sarsbrook's cousin, that you are the viscount's mistress."

"That I am Sarsbrook's mistress? So that is what everyone thinks! This is monstrous! How can I face anyone?"

"Come now, Pan, we will set things right."

"How?" cried Pandora. "There is nothing that can be done that will not make things worse. I don't want to talk about this anymore, Winnie. Now go away! I pray you leave me!"

Winfield stood awkwardly for a moment. "I am sorry, Pan," he said, leaving his sister in the garden. As he returned inside the house, Winfield felt worse than he ever had before. The viscount was right, and everything was his own fault. Not wanting to see his father or Lizzy, Winfield left the house, deciding to find one of his friends and get blissfully drunk.

After Winfield Marsh's visit, Sarsbrook sat in the library for a time, reflecting about what to do next. He felt that he had mishandled the visit with Winfield. Why had he not told the fellow that he intended to marry Pandora? Why had he not told Winfield to return to his sister saying that Sarsbrook loved her very much and was sorry for the distress he had caused her?

The viscount frowned. Pandora's brother had made him angry. In fact, he had never wanted so badly to throttle anyone as when Winfield stood before him. How would he endure having such a scoundrel for a brother-in-law? Well, he would somehow, for Pandora's sake.

The butler arrived to interrupt his musings. "My lord. There is another caller. It is Mr. Tucker."

"Mr. Tucker? Send him in at once," said Sarsbrook,

glad to see his friend. There was no one, save Pandora of course, that he wanted to see more.

"Robin, I know it is an odd time to call," said Tucker as he strode into the library.

"My dear Tuck," said the viscount, greeting his friend with a handshake. "The gods must have sent you. I need to talk to you."

Tucker raised an eyebrow and smiled. "Then it is very fortunate I have come."

"Sit down over here, Tuck," said the viscount, leading his friend to a comfortable armchair, then sitting down beside him. "I have so much to tell you."

"But what happened at the ball? Did you leave early? I arrived very late and did not have an opportunity to talk to you. I did catch a glimpse of you crossing the room with a lovely red-haired lady. Miss M., I presume? What a lucky man you are, Robin. But I fear it was all over the ballroom about you and the lady. I daresay she will not be admitted to any drawing rooms."

"You can be sure Lady Sarsbrook will be admitted to any drawing room in town."

"Lady Sarsbrook? What can you mean, Robin?"

"I mean that I intend to marry Miss Marsh. And she is not Miss M."

Tucker regarded his friend in wonderment. "You intend to marry her?"

"Yes, if she will accept me."

"But she is not Miss M.?"

"Indeed not."

"Then she was not your uncle's—"

"No, she was not," said Sarsbrook emphatically. "It is a damnably long story, Tuck."

"I cannot wait to hear it," said the amiable Tucker, settling back in his chair. Sarsbrook launched into the tale, explaining everything. When he told of his plunge into Isabelle's fountain, Tucker laughed heartily despite the viscount's warning look.

"And that is what happened," said Sarsbrook at the conclusion of his tale.

"I must say that this Winfield Marsh is a knave. Your poor Miss Marsh. But, Robin, this business with your cousin. It will not do having him pass that diary about. You know how people talk. If they have it in their heads that Miss M. is your Miss Marsh, I daresay it will be hard to get them to change their opinion. I recommend you try to stop Brackley. Get the diary back."

"I have already considered that," said his lordship. "I shall deal with my cousin. Do not fear."

Noting the resolute look on his friend's face, Tucker was glad that he was not Brackley. He had known Sarsbrook long enough to know that the viscount could be a powerful adversary.

"Well, I am convinced all will work out well in the end, Robin," said Tucker. "And I am very pleased to hear you will join the ranks of married men."

Sarsbrook smiled. "So am I," he said.

21

Eager to hear all about the ball, Nicholas Marsh was sorely disappointed to discover that Pandora had not had a wonderful time. At luncheon Lizzy cheerfully related her experiences at Lady Verdon's, while Pandora remained silent.

Since Nicholas was a very perceptive young man, he knew enough not to persist in questioning his elder sister about Lord Sarsbrook. For Nicholas' benefit, Mr. Marsh tried to act as if the ball had been a great success. However, the youngest of the Marsh family sensed that, at least where Pandora was concerned, the ball had not gone well.

After luncheon, Nicholas went to meet his tutor while Mr. Marsh retired to his library to write letters. Pandora and Lizzy retired to the drawing room, where Lizzy took up her embroidery and sat regarding her sister with a sympathetic look.

"Do not worry about me," said Pandora. "I am only sorry that things did not work out for your sake, Lizzy. I daresay we will receive no invitations from the *haut ton*."

"Oh, that does not signify in the least," said Lizzy bravely. "I much preferred our old company."

"That is pure fustian, Lizzy," said her sister.

"No, it is the truth. I shall be glad that Phoebe will be my friend again. She was so dreadfully jealous that I was going to Lady Verdon's ball. Oh, Pan, you did remember that I promised we would call on Phoebe this afternoon?

She made me swear that I would do so to tell her all about the ball."

"Oh, yes," said Pandora, who had actually forgotten all about it. Although she did not feel at all like seeing anyone, she managed to smile. "I shall be happy to see Phoebe and Mrs. Reynolds. And perhaps we might stop by some of the shops on the way."

Since Lizzy loved nothing better than to meander through the shops, she nodded eagerly. "Then perhaps we should go very soon."

"Of course," said Pandora. "Let us make ready. Indeed, I am in need of an outing. And I must return my book to the library."

The two young ladies were soon attired in their best walking dresses and pelisses. It was not very far to walk to the shops. Pandora and Lizzy went first to the circulating library, where Pandora returned her book, but declined to take another. They then stopped at the linen drapers, the milliner's, and finally at the confectioners, where Lizzy bought some of her favorite sweetmeats.

Pandora was glad for the distraction, although she was not really able to keep from thinking about Sarsbrook. She could not help but wonder where he was and what he was thinking. She did not know if she could bear to see him again after what Winfield had told her that morning.

After lingering for a time at the confectioner's, the sisters proceeded on to the residence of Lizzy's friend Phoebe. Considerably more well-to-do than the Marshes, Phoebe's family lived in a large, comfortable townhouse. Arriving at the house, Lizzy lifted the brass door knocker and rapped upon the door.

When it opened, the Reynolds' butler greeted them. "Good afternoon, Miss Marsh and Miss Lizzy."

"Good afternoon, Wood. I believe we are expected."

"I am sorry, miss, but Mrs. Reynolds and Miss are not at home."

"Not at home? But I told Phoebe that I would call."

"Miss left a letter for you," said the butler. "I shall

fetch it." The servant closed the door, leaving the Marsh sisters standing on the doorstep. He returned a few moments later to hand Lizzy a neatly folded piece of paper. "Good day, ladies," he said, closing the door.

"That was very peculiar, Pan," said Lizzy, unfolding the missive. "I know Phoebe told me that she would be at home this afternoon."

"What does the letter say?"

Lizzy scanned the short note. "Oh, dear! Pan, Phoebe does not want to see me again."

"What?" said Pandora.

"You read it, Pan," said Lizzy, tears beginning to fall from her eyes.

Taking the letter, Pandora began reading. "My dear Lizzy," it said. "Mama did not want me to write, but Wood said that he would give you this note. I fear that Mama has said that we may not receive you or any of the Marsh family. She has heard of a very great scandal about your sister, Pandora. Oh, I cannot believe it of dear Pandora, but Mama says that everyone is talking about it so it must be so. I am so sorry, Lizzy. I shall miss you. Phoebe." After she had finished reading, Pandora looked at her sister. "I cannot believe that this rumor has already reached Mrs. Reynolds. It must be all over town."

"But if we tell them it is not true, Pan, will they not believe it?"

"I daresay we will not have that opportunity. And when society has judged one to be unacceptable, it is very difficult to reverse that judgment."

"Then we will not be welcomed anywhere!" cried Lizzy. "Oh, Pan, what will we do?"

Pandora folded the paper and deposited it in her reticle. "Let us go home and tell Papa."

The two young ladies hurried away, returning to their home as quickly as possible. They found their father in the drawing room going through the afternoon post. "Papa," cried Lizzy. "Something terrible had happened! Phoebe and her mother have snubbed us! They refused

to see us. It is because Pandora is too scandalous!" With
that remark, Lizzy burst into tears and fell into the com-
forting embrace of her father.

"What is the meaning of this, Pandora?" said Mr.
Marsh as his younger daughter sobbed into his waistcoat.

Pandora took the letter from her reticule and handed it
to her father. "You may read it for yourself, Papa," she
said. "It seems the Reynoldses have heard that I am a
fallen woman. They will not receive us."

Mr. Marsh scanned the letter. "Do sit down, Lizzy.
That's a good girl."

"Oh, Papa," Lizzy managed to say between sobs,
"what will I do now? No one will invite me anywhere!"

"Dear Lizzy, don't worry," said her father, "we will
think of something."

Pandora sat down wearily upon the sofa. "This is very
serious, Papa."

Just as Mr. Marsh was going to reply, Martha entered
the drawing room. "Mr. Marsh, there is a man to see Mr.
Winfield."

"You know very well that he is not at home, Martha."

"Aye, sir, but the man will not believe me. I did not
want to admit him, but he came into the entry hall."

"Did he give his name?"

"No, sir, and he is no gentleman to be sure," said
Martha.

"Doubtless he is dunning Winfield for money," said
Mr. Marsh disgustedly. "He is not the first. The situation
is becoming dashed intolerable."

"I shall see to him, Papa," said Pandora, rising from
the sofa. "Do stay with Lizzy. Oh, do not worry, I can
deal with such a person very well." For all her apparent
confidence, Pandora had a sinking feeling as she followed Martha from the room. In recent weeks Winfield's
creditors had been showing up at the house. They were
becoming increasingly bold and obnoxious in their de-
mands for payment.

Pandora tired to adopt a regal posture as she approached the visitor. He was a short, middle-aged man in a tight-fitting brown coat and beige pantaloons. "May I help you, sir?" she said. "I am Miss Marsh, Winfield Marsh's sister."

"Oh, so you are Miss Marsh?" said the man, eyeing her with interest. He smiled unpleasantly, revealing a set of bad teeth. "I wish to see your brother, Miss Marsh."

"He is not here, sir."

"Then I should appreciate it if you might give him a message, ma'am."

"I should be happy to do so, Mr. . . . ?"

"Oh, my name is not important, ma'am. Mr. Winfield Marsh owes my employer Jonas Graves fifty pounds. He'll know that name. You tell him I can take no more excuses. Now that your circumstances have changed, Mr. Graves expects to be paid."

"Circumstances changed? I do not know what you mean."

"I believe you do, ma'am. I know that you have a very wealthy protector now, Miss Marsh. Fifty pounds is nothing to a man like that."

Pandora regarded the man first in surprise and then with indignation. "Get out of here!" she demanded. "I say get out!"

"Very well, Miss Marsh, but I will be back." Smiling again, he turned and left.

Pandora closed the door firmly behind him and returned to the drawing room. "Papa, that was an odious man who said that Winfield owed fifty pounds to a Mr. Jonas Graves."

"Winfield," said Mr. Marsh. "I must talk to him. He is acting so irresponsibly."

"Yes, he is," murmured Pandora, frowning at the thought of her brother's deviousness.

"I think I shall go to my room," said Lizzy. "I have a headache."

"Yes, go on, my dear," said Mr. Marsh. "Perhaps you need some rest. This is very difficult for you."

"Oh, I shall be fine, Papa," said Lizzy, kissing her father on the cheek and leaving the drawing room.

Pandora sat down on the sofa once again. When her sister had gone, she frowned. "I fear we are going to have to leave London, Papa."

"Leave London?"

"That man, the one who was just here, knew about the rumor. I daresay there is not a man or woman in all of London who has not heard it."

"Heard that ridiculous nonsense about you and Sarsbrook's uncle? That is so preposterous, no one will believe it."

"I fear people are willing to believe the worst of anyone, Papa. But that is not the only rumor. You see, Winfield visited Lord Sarsbrook this morning."

"This morning? What on earth for?"

Pandora hesitated. "I'm not sure, Papa. But Sarsbrook told him that another rumor was being circulated, that I am now his lordship's mistress."

"That damnable villain!" cried Mr. Marsh in a rare display of passion. "How could he spread such villainous calumny?"

"It was Sarsbrook's cousin who spread the rumors," said Pandora.

Her father shook his head. "And I had thought Sarsbrook such a decent man."

Pandora looked down. "I, too, Papa."

"I shall go to him and demand an explanation!"

"No, Papa, that would serve no purpose. I do not want to hear anything more of Lord Sarsbrook as long as I live."

"My poor Pandora, I know how distraught you must be. But, my dear, in time things will sort themselves out."

"I cannot imagine how, Papa. We must face certain realities. We are totally ruined in society. How will Lizzy find a husband? Surely no one in all of London will wish to have anything to do with the Marsh family. And then there is Winfield."

"Winfield," said Mr. Marsh, frowning darkly.

"We will be constantly hounded by his creditors. We must leave here, Papa. And we must go at once."

"Do not be hasty, Pandora. Where would we go?"

"We could return to Suffolk."

"But the house is sold."

"We could stay with Aunt Agnes for a time. We will find another house."

Mr. Marsh looked thoughtful. He missed the country, and the idea of leaving London did not displease him. "It would take some time to sell the lease on this house," said Mr. Marsh.

"But I should like to leave here at once," said Pandora. "Please, Papa, I do not wish to stay even one day more where everyone will be whispering about me. Lizzy and I could leave on the coach in the morning."

"In the morning?"

"Yes, it will not take long to pack what we will need. When things are settled here, you and Nicholas and Winfield could join us."

Although he thought his daughter was acting in an unduly hasty manner, Mr. Marsh did not wish to argue. Knowing how upset Pandora must be at the disastrous turn of events, he could understand why she would wish to leave London. "Very well," he said.

Pandora rose from the sofa. "Then I must go, Papa. There is much to do. I do hope Lizzy will agree it is the best thing." With these words, Pandora hurried from the drawing room to find her sister.

22

Later that afternoon Sarsbrook debated calling at the Marsh household. He very much wanted to see Pandora, but he suspected that he would not be admitted. After much reflection and pacing about the room, the viscount decided it would be best to wait before calling. After all, his impulsive visit the night before had been disastrous.

Sarsbrook's thoughts turned to Brackley. Perhaps, he considered, it was time to pay a call on his cousin. The viscount rang for a servant. "Have Reeves bring my carriage, Archer," he ordered his butler. "I am going out."

"Very good, my lord."

In a short time Sarsbrook was riding in his fine equipage, staring intently out the window. Brackley lived in a stylish townhouse in a neighborhood not too far distant.

When he arrived at his cousin's home, he knocked at the door and was admitted by Brackley's butler.

"I am Lord Sarsbrook," he said. "Tell your master I am here."

"Yes, my lord."

The butler hastened off. Like all the servants in the Brackley household, he had heard of his master's cousin. Brackley and his mother were sitting in the drawing room when the servant entered. "What is it?" said Brackley.

"Lord Sarsbrook is here, sir."

"Sarsbrook?" cried Mrs. Brackley, quite astonished. "What is he doing here?"

"I daresay we will only find out by admitting him," returned her son. "Show him in, Martin."

Although Brackley exhibited admirable aplomb, he was actually rather disturbed at the idea of his cousin showing up at his door. Remembering Sarsbrook's fury at the ball, he knew that the viscount's visit would hardly be a pleasant family occasion. And while he very much enjoyed causing trouble for his hated cousin, Brackley did have some qualms about angering a man of such enormous wealth.

As the viscount strode into the room, Brackley rose to his feet. As always, Sarsbrook's cousin was dressed with meticulous care. His lordship was indifferent to Brackley's well-cut coat and gleaming hessian boots. He did, however, direct a curious look at the lady sitting on the fine Italian sofa. He had never actually met his aunt, although she had been present at the reading of his uncle's will. She was a very attractive woman who bore her fifty years of age exceedingly well. The viscount thought he detected a faint resemblance to his late mother.

"Sarsbrook," said Brackley. "This is, indeed, an unexpected honor." His cousin's words were tinged with sarcasm, but the viscount seemed indifferent to it. "May I present my mother?" continued Brackley. "Mother, this is your nephew Sarsbrook."

"I am very pleased to meet you," said Mrs. Brackley, extending her hand.

Sarsbrook bowed politely over his aunt's hand. He was somewhat surprised at her civility. "Madam," he said.

"I had hoped that we would meet one day, Sarsbrook," said Mrs. Brackley. "Do sit down. I hope that you will stay for tea."

"I fear I cannot do so," returned the viscount, remaining standing. "Perhaps another time. I have some business to discuss with my cousin, madam. I should like to discuss it privately."

"I do not know what you could say to me that you

could not say to my mother, cousin," said Brackley, who thought his mother's presence a good idea.

"Very well," said the viscount, "if you wish your mother to hear what I am going to say, I shall not object." He looked at his aunt. "Your son, madam, is the worst sort of villain. He is a man without a shred of honor or decency, who has most unwisely set himself against me."

"How dare you say such things about my son?" sputtered Mrs. Brackley.

"Because they are true, madam." He looked at his cousin. "Brackley, you have something that you have stolen from my house. I want it back."

"What does he mean, Miles?" Mrs. Brackley asked.

"He is spouting fustian, Mother," returned Brackley. "I think it best if you left now, Sarsbrook. Have you no regard for my mother?"

"If you have any regard for her, you will listen to me. It appears you are in a position of some difficulty, Brackley." Sarsbrook smiled at his cousin. "You see, I have ordered my agents to buy up all of your debts, which apparently are considerable."

"What?"

"My dear cousin, I have set my mind on ruining you and I assure you I will have no trouble doing so. When I have your debts, I shall have you."

"You damned blackguard, Sarsbrook," said Brackley, growing rather pale.

"Sarsbrook," cried Mrs. Brackley, very much distressed. "Why do you seek to destroy us?"

"Because your son has sought to destroy my happiness, madam. I do not know what you take me for, Brackley. Did you think I would not seek to have my revenge on you?"

"Do your worst then!" cried Brackley, a scornful look on his handsome face. "I do not care."

"Miles!" said Mrs. Brackley, alarmed that her son was further angering their wealthy relative. "Sarsbrook, I entreat you to reconsider. I am your own mother's sister.

And we have been very much wronged by my family. My son is a rash young man. Perhaps he acted unwisely. There must be something that can be done to persuade you to desist from this course of action."

"I shall be happy to do so, madam. Your son has but to meet two conditions and I shall be satisfied. He must return what he has taken from me and he must swear that he will never again attempt to contact me in any way. I shall settle the sum of two thousand pounds per year upon you, but I never want to see or hear of you again."

"Two thousand pounds?" said Mrs. Brackley, brightening. "Miles, Sarsbrook is being quite generous. I do not know what you think my son has taken from you, Sarsbrook, but I am certain it is some misunderstanding. Miles, if you have something that your cousin wishes returned, do so at once."

Brackley scowled at Sarsbrook, who was regarding him with a self-satisfied look. "Two thousand pounds," he muttered. "What a clutch-fist you are, cousin. Do you think we can live on such a sum?"

Sarsbrook raised his eyebrows. "You are the most brazen fellow, Brackley. Perhaps I should withdraw the offer."

"My son is not thinking clearly," said Mrs. Brackley. "Do not listen to him. Go get whatever your cousin is talking about, Miles."

Brackley frowned, but did as his mother instructed. He left the room and returned quickly with Sir Humphrey's diary. Wordlessly, he handed it back to his cousin.,

"Then I shall assume we are in agreement?" said Sarsbrook, taking the book.

"Yes," said Brackley.

"Then I shall take my leave of you. Good day, madam. We will not meet again." He turned abruptly and left them.

Once inside his carriage, Sarsbrook appeared thoughtful. He did not like giving Brackley any money. It seemed that the fellow was being rewarded for his infa-

mous conduct. Still, he did get the diary back and he
would be rid of Brackley for good. Making his cousin
and aunt dependent upon him was undoubtedly a clever
move, for one could always threaten to withhold the
money. Indeed, mused his lordship, he should have done
something like this some time ago. It might have saved a
good deal of trouble.

The viscount looked down at the diary, which he had
placed on the seat next to him. He thought of Miss M.
His uncle had instructed him to provide for her and he
had never fulfilled this obligation. He would have to find
the real Miss M. and see to her welfare.

Sarsbrook pondered the matter. He thought suddenly
of the emerald necklace intended for that lady. He remembered that Winfield had said he had pawned it at a
shop on Rosemary Lane. It would be only right if the
necklace could be given to the lady for whom it was intended.

The viscount instructed his driver to change course.
Some time later he arrived at a narrow street lined with
shops and crowded with people. It did not take long to
discover the whereabouts of the man Winfield had mentioned. After some negotiations, Sarsbrook emerged
from the shop with the emerald necklace.

He was very pleased to have retrieved the necklace.
By rights, he told himself, the emeralds belonged to the
mysterious Miss M. Yet since he had no idea who she
actually was, Sarsbrook was not sure how he could get
the necklace to its rightful owner.

As he started to enter the carriage, an idea struck his
lordship. "Go to my late uncle's house, Reeves," Sarsbrook directed his driver.

Seated inside, the viscount stared at the necklace
again. How well it would look on Pandora, he thought.
Sarsbrook was soon lost in reverie, envisioning Pandora
and how she had looked the night before, clad in her
nightgown, her beautiful hair loose and in charming disarray.

When the carriage pulled to a stop in front of the

home of the late Sir Humphrey Maitland, the viscount was roused from his daydreams. Climbing out of the carriage, he made his way to the door.

Although most of Sir Humphrey's servants had long since gone, a few remained to take care of the house while arrangements were made for its sale. When he opened the door, Sir Humphrey's butler was surprised to see the viscount.

Sarsbrook came quickly to the point, asking the servant bluntly if he had known about his late master's mistress. At first the butler seemed reluctant to answer, but finally he admitted that he did know of the lady.

"I must have her name," said the viscount. "Come, come, man, I have no time to waste. Her name and address."

"Her name is Miss Monferdini, my lord," returned the butler, deciding that he could not withhold information from anyone as formidable as his lordship. "She lives at Sixteen Gloucester Place, my lord."

"Sixteen Gloucester Place," repeated Sarsbrook. Knowing that Pandora's address was 16 Clarence Place, it suddenly became clear to him how the mistake might have been made. Clarence and Gloucester were both the names of royal dukes, brothers of the Prince Regent. It would have been easy for his elderly uncle to mix them up. "Miss Monferdini?"

"Yes," replied the servant.

Sarsbrook handed him a coin, which the servant accepted with profuse thanks. Then the viscount returned to his carriage, ordering his driver to go immediately to 16 Gloucester Place.

When he arrived there, the viscount noted that the residence was not unlike that of the Marsh family. It was a respectable townhouse on a nice, but unfashionable street.

Sarsbrook took up the jewelry case and got out of the carriage. The butler answered the door. "Yes, sir?"

"I wish to see Miss Monferdini. I am Lord Sarsbrook. You may tell her I am Sir Humphrey's nephew."

"Of course, milord," said the servant, ushering the viscount inside. He was an older man and he spoke with an Italian accent. He led his noble visitor to the drawing room. "If milord will wait here, I shall inform Miss Monferdini."

Left alone in the room, should looked around curiously. Miss Monferdini's drawing room was decorated in a vivid oriental style. The ceiling, which was elaborately painted in a geometric pattern of gold, azure and sea green, resembled something that one might expect to find in a Turkish palace. Sofas and chairs of deep crimson lined the blue walls, which were adorned with several paintings of the baroque style. On the floor were splendid Persian carpets.

Sarsbrook found himself wondering if his uncle had paid for the room's costly decorations. It seemed so out of character for the miserly Sir Humphrey to have spent money in such a fashion. Of course, reflected the viscount as he studied one of the paintings, he would not have thought his uncle would have been one to keep a mistress, and buy her an expensive emerald necklace.

"Lord Sarsbrook!" A powerful feminine voice made the viscount turn from the painting to face the lady he had come to visit. "How good to meet you, milord. Your uncle spoke of you so many times to me."

Sarsbrook smiled politely and bowed slightly. "Miss Monferdini." The viscount hoped his face was not showing the surprise he felt at finally seeing Miss M. The woman who now stood before him was not, by a very long shot, the woman of his fantasies.

Very short and exceedingly plump, Miss Monferdini had dark eyes and curly, henna-dyed hair that was piled atop her head in a style reminiscent of coiffures worn by Parisian ladies of the last century. The viscount found himself wondering how old she was, for her face was so heavily powdered, painted, and rouged that it was hard to determine her age. Sarsbrook studied Miss Monferdini's face with interest, noting her prominent nose, square chin, and wide, painted mouth.

She was dressed in a tight-fitting gown of purple satin whose low-cut bodice revealed a good portion of the lady's ponderous bosom. At her feet were two pug dogs who displayed a good deal of interest in his lordship's boots.

Thinking of his uncle's diary, Sarsbrook found himself having an impulse to burst into laughter. In reading Sir Humphrey's graphic memoir, he had never envisioned someone like Miss Monferdini. No, he had instead imagined Pandora Marsh.

"Will you sit down, milord?" said the lady, gesturing toward one of the crimson sofas. Sarsbrook nodded, taking a seat. Miss Monferdini sat down next to him and the pug dogs hopped up beside her. "I must say I am very surprised to see you."

"I am sorry for not calling sooner, Miss Monferdini. You see, I didn't know who you were until today." He handed her the jewelry case. "Before he died, my uncle bought you this."

"For me?" said the lady, eagerly taking the case from his lordship. Opening it up, she cried delightedly. "Oh, that dearest man! Emeralds! Oh, how lovely they are." She reached out and grasped the viscount's hand. "Thank you so, Milord Sarsbrook!"

"It was nothing, I assure you," said Sarsbrook, pulling his hand away from her impassioned grip.

"You are a kind man, milord," said Miss Monferdini. "I think you are very like your uncle. I do hope you will visit me often. I have many interesting guests. Perhaps you will come for dinner one evening soon."

"That is very kind, Miss Monferdini," said the viscount, somewhat unnerved by the flirtatious way in which the lady was looking up at him. "Perhaps one day. But I fear I must be going. I have other engagements this afternoon."

"Oh, do stay a little longer, milord," said Miss Monferdini imploringly.

"I am sorry, but I cannot, madam," he said firmly.

"But I must also say that my uncle wished some financial provision to be made for you."

"That dear gentleman!"

"Yes," returned Sarsbrook. "I shall arrange for you to receive one thousand pounds immediately and then five hundred per year from my uncle's estate."

"Oh, Milord Sarsbrook!" cried Miss Monferdini, grasping his hand once again and pressing it to her bosom. "You are an angel!"

Hastening to retrieve his hand, Sarsbrook rose from the sofa. "I must take my leave, madam."

"Oh, do not go. You have only just arrived!"

"Truly, madam, I must. Good day. And you may expect to receive your money very soon."

Miss Monferdini made more protests at Sarsbrook's hasty departure, but he managed to take his leave, eagerly leaving Miss M. and returning to his carriage. As the vehicle drove off, the viscount felt relieved. Glancing down at the carriage seat, he saw his uncle's diary. So that was the sensuous Miss M., he said to himself. He burst into laughter.

When he arrived back at Sarsbrook House, the viscount's first act was to toss Sir Humphrey's memoir into the fire. Smiling, he watched it burn.

23

The White Horse Inn was one of the busiest establishments in all of London. Coaches bound for all parts of England departed from its courtyard and throngs of travelers could be found there at all times, waiting to begin their journeys.

It was early morning when Pandora and Lizzy arrived at the White Horse, accompanied by Mr. Marsh, Winfield, and Nicholas. Relations were so strained between Pandora and her brother Winfield that they said nothing to each other. Winfield, who had received an unusually spirited dressing-down from his father the night before, appeared very solemn.

It was altogether a very somber affair with everyone in the family gloomy and unhappy. Lizzy did not wish to leave London, but she had accepted the idea of returning to Suffolk with surprising equanimity. She had made little protest when Pandora had said they must go to the country, agreeing that, under the circumstances, it was the best course of action.

Now, however, in the cold light of morning, Pandora was not so sure they were doing the right thing. To run off seemed an admission of guilt and they were guilty of nothing. Still, the idea of seeing Sarsbrook again so distressed her that fleeing London seemed the only thing to do.

Nicholas Marsh stood beside Pandora, watching the hostlers harnessing the horses to a coach. "I do wish I was going with you, Pan," he said.

"You will come very soon, Nicky," said Pandora. "Once Papa arranges things."

"I do hope it will be soon. Mr. Stubbs is eager to go to the country. He does not like town overmuch."

"At least Mr. Stubbs does not find the country dull," said Lizzy.

"Now, now, Lizzy," said Mr. Marsh, "I am certain it will not be in the least dull."

Lizzy looked unconvinced but said nothing. When it was time to board the eastbound coach, Lizzy embraced Mr. Marsh, Winfield, and Nicholas. Pandora hugged her father and Nicholas, but turned to frown at Winfield. "Pan," he said, "I am sorry."

She hesitated, noting the look of contrition on his handsome face. Sighing, she embraced him as well. "Good-bye, Winnie."

There were tears in Winfield's eyes. "I *am* sorry, Pan. I shall change. I swear it."

Fearing she would burst into tears, Pandora only nodded and allowed her brother to escort her to the coach and assist her up the steps. As the lumbering vehicle started off, Pandora watched her father and brothers standing there. Nicholas waved and Pandora realized how much she would miss him.

Once the coach was on its way, Pandora sat back on the worn leather seat and appeared thoughtful. One of the other passengers, a slender middle-aged woman in a Leghorn hat, introduced herself as Mrs. Baxter. She was traveling with her husband, a portly, taciturn man who promptly fell asleep despite the way the coach jostled its passengers as it maneuvered through the busy streets of town.

The lady in the Leghorn hat was a talkative woman, who was overjoyed to find two young ladies with whom to converse. She was soon chattering merrily to Lizzy and Pandora. Lizzy, who was happy for the diversion, was cheered by the loquacious lady. Pandora, however, while civilly answering a few questions, found her mind wandering.

She thought of Suffolk with its bucolic landscape and rural inhabitants. Pandora loved the country. She told herself that it was a very good thing that she and Lizzy would soon be away from the dirt and noise of the city.

Thinking about the quiet village where they had lived, Pandora tried to convince herself that everything was for the best. They would find another house and live simply within their means. She would work as a dressmaker to make extra money and they would do very well. Lizzy would meet a nice young man and get married and they would be very close to Cambridge and her brother Augustus.

Pandora stared out the carriage window. She knew that she was deceiving herself. It would be a very long time before she would be happy in Suffolk. Her thoughts of Sarsbrook would prevent that. Pandora frowned as the viscount came clearly to mind. "And do you agree with your sister, Miss Marsh?"

Pandora was brought out of her reverie by the question. She looked at Mrs. Baxter. "I am sorry, ma'am. I was not attending."

Mrs. Baxter appeared to take no offense, but happily repeated the question under consideration. Pandora entered the conversation as the coach continued on its way.

When Sarsbrook had risen early in the morning, he had been able to think of nothing but seeing Pandora. Knowing very well that one did not pay calls at seven in the morning, he had occupied himself with some trivial business matters until ten o'clock.

Deciding that he could not wait any longer, the viscount called for his carriage and set out for the Marsh residence. A short time later Sarsbrook arrived at the door, which was opened by Martha. The servant regarded his lordship with undisguised disapproval.

"I wish to see Miss Marsh," he said abruptly.

"She is not at home, my lord," replied Martha.

"I will wait," said Sarsbrook, boldly stepping into the entry hall.

Martha, who had not formed a very favorable opinion of his lordship from their previous encounter decided it was best not to deal with him herself. She hurried off to fetch Mr. Marsh.

Nicholas, who had been gazing out the window of his room, had seen Sarsbrook's carriage pull up. He hurried down to see the viscount. At his heels was his faithful companion, the terrier Mr. Stubbs. "Lord Sarsbrook!" said Nicholas.

"Master Nicholas," returned the viscount, smiling at Pandora's brother. "I have come to see your sister, Pandora." He stooped down to scratch Mr. Stubbs behind the ears. "I daresay your maid disapproves of me. Will you tell Pandora I must see her?"

"But she is not here, my lord," said Nicholas.

"Not here?"

Before Nicholas could reply, his father appeared in the entry hall. "Lord Sarsbrook," he said, frowning at his unwelcome visitor. "My daughter is not at home. And I will tell you, my lord, that were she at home, I should not allow you to see her. You are not welcome here, sir. I must ask you to leave. You have caused enough harm to my daughter."

"Mr. Marsh," said his lordship, "I well understand that you are angry with me. But I must see Pandora."

"That is impossible. Now I must ask you once again to leave, my lord."

"I will not leave until I see Pandora. I shall wait all day if need be."

"You will not!" cried Mr. Marsh, growing red in the face. Usually a mild-mannered gentleman, Pandora's father was furious. Standing before him was the nobleman who had ruined his beloved daughter's reputation. Mr. Marsh's indignation made him uncharacteristically hot-tempered. "If you don't go, I shall fetch a riding crop and drive you out."

"Mr. Marsh," said the viscount, "do listen to what I have to say."

"By God!" shouted Mr. Marsh. "I will not! I warn you I shall fetch my riding crop!"

"Very well, I shall go," said Sarsbrook, not at all happy at the thought of goading his future father-in-law to violence. "But I shall return."

The viscount turned and left the house. Mr. Stubbs raced after him as he made his way to the carriage. "Mr. Stubbs!" shouted Nicholas, racing after the dog. "Come back, sir!" Ignoring his young master, Mr. Stubbs hurried to Sarsbrook and barked. Arriving beside the viscount, Nicholas scooped up his wayward terrier.

"Come back to the house, Nicholas," commanded Mr. Marsh from the doorway.

Nicholas looked at the viscount. "You are fond of Pandora, are you not, my lord?"

"I love your sister, young man," replied Sarsbrook. "I wish to marry her."

"Indeed?" said Nicholas, smiling brightly at the idea. "I had hoped she might marry you."

"Nicholas!" Mr. Marsh called again.

"I must go," said Nicholas, hesitating for a moment. Then he whispered. "Pandora and Lizzy left for Suffolk on the coach from the White Horse Inn this morning." Turning, he dashed off back to the house.

The viscount watched Nicholas vanish inside. He then turned to his driver. "Reeves, a coach left the White Horse Inn this morning for Suffolk. I wish to catch up with it."

"Aye, m'lord," replied the driver. " 'Twill not be too difficult, not with these beauties." He gestured toward the viscount's magnificent horses.

The groom, who had hopped down from his position beside the driver, opened the door for the viscount.

"Then make haste, Reeves," said Sarsbrook, climbing up into the vehicle. When his master was safely inside and the groom once again in his place, the coachman started the horses off at a smart pace. The viscount folded his arms across his chest and hoped that he would see Pandora.

After more than four hours, the coach that had left the White Horse Inn with Pandora and Lizzy aboard had traveled nearly thirty miles. Pandora was growing exceedingly weary of the bumpy ride and Mrs. Baxter's incessant prattle. She was very glad when the equipage came to a stop at a village inn. There the passengers would have a brief rest while the horses were changed.

Pandora and Lizzy were able to disengage themselves from Mrs. Baxter, who had to wake her sleeping husband and see to his comfort. "I daresay, Lizzy," said Pandora as the two sisters stretched their legs, walking about on the grounds around the inn, "it is good to escape from Mrs. Baxter for a time."

"Indeed," said Lizzy with a smile.

"She means well," said Pandora, "but I do wish she would occasionally allow one to complete a sentence."

Lizzy laughed. She was glad to see that her sister appeared to be in a better humor. The weather was very fine, sunny and pleasantly warm, and the scenery was picturesque. Lizzy's spirits improved quite a bit as the two young ladies continued walking. "It is lovely here," she said, looking out into the countryside.

"Yes," said Pandora, stopping to survey the area. The inn was located near the edge of the village, which was a prosperous-looking place with tidy homes and well-kept shops. It was not unlike their own village in Suffolk. Pandora looked out at the road. She saw a carriage approaching, but took little notice of it. "Shall we have something to eat, Lizzy? We do have a little time."

"I should like that," said her sister.

Pandora and Lizzy entered the inn. Mrs. Baxter waved to them. "Do join us, my dear girls," she called. After exchanging a glance the sisters went to the table where Mr. and Mrs. Baxter were sitting. "Sit down," insisted Mrs. Baxter. "You must share our food. The cold mutton is quite delicious. And do have some gingerbread."

Pandora and her sister had scarcely sat down when the door to the inn opened and a tall gentleman walked in. Lizzy, who was facing the door, was the first to see him. Her mouth dropped open in surprise as she recognized the newcomer as Sarsbrook.

"What is it?" said Pandora, noting her sister's expression.

"Lord Sarsbrook!" cried Lizzy.

Pandora whirled around. It was indeed Sarsbrook. Pandora was utterly astonished. He saw her instantly. "Pandora!" he said, hurrying to the table.

Mrs. Baxter viewed the viscount with considerable interest, having heard Lizzy say *Lord* Sarsbrook. She was very eager to make the acquaintance of a titled gentleman.

"Pandora, I must talk with you."

"No, my lord, that is impossible," replied Pandora, looking down in some confusion.

"I beg of you!" said Sarsbrook.

"And I beg of you, my lord," cried Pandora, "go away! I do not wish to talk to you."

Mrs. Baxter felt obliged to step in at this point. "Is something wrong, Miss Marsh?" She turned to her husband. "Richard, the gentleman is upsetting Miss Marsh."

Mr. Baxter looked up from his glass of beer, but appeared disinclined to involve himself in the affairs of strangers. He only regarded the viscount with a questioning look.

"Pandora, please listen to me. I have been a fool."

"I shall not listen to you, my lord," said Pandora firmly.

The viscount, who was growing very frustrated, suddenly reached out and grabbed Pandora by the elbow. "Pandora, come with me," he said, pulling her to her feet.

She was so amazed at this treatment that, for a moment, she could only look at him in horror. "Let go of me!"

His lordship only tightened his grip. "You are coming outside, Pandora Marsh. I must speak with you in private. I want no argument!"

Pandora became angry. "No!"

The viscount responded by encircling Pandora's waist

with his arm. "If you do not come with me, Pandora, I shall pick you up and carry you out of here!"

"Oh, dear!" cried Mrs. Baxter. Her husband raised his eyebrows.

Pandora looked into Sarsbrook's face. "If I listen to you, do you promise that you will go?"

The viscount nodded. "Yes, of course."

"Very well," she said finally. "I shall go outside."

"Pan," said Lizzy, rather worried.

"Stay here, Lizzy," said Pandora. "I will be but a moment."

Sarsbrook brought her out of the inn and into the sunlight. Leading her to the side of the inn, out of sight of the grooms and coachmen, he stopped. "Pandora, I pray you give me a hearing."

"Very well, my lord. I shall do so, but do not think you will change my mind about you." She paused. "How did you find me?"

"Your brother Nicholas told me that you had taken the coach to Suffolk."

"Nicholas?" said Pandora in surprise.

"I went to your house this morning, where your father threatened to take his whip to me."

Pandora smiled. "Good," she said.

"Dammit, Pandora," said Sarsbrook. "You are too hard on me. Am I a monster for wanting you? My dearest Pandora, I love you more than I thought it possible to love anyone."

She turned away. "You don't even know me, my lord. And you thought I was someone else. It was Miss M. you wanted, not Pandora Marsh. I should only disappoint you."

"You are speaking nonsense," said Sarsbrook, taking her by the arms. "Don't you know how much I love you, Pandora? I want you to marry me. Say you will be my wife."

"That is impossible!" cried Pandora.

"Why?" demanded his lordship, taking her into his arms.

"I don't know," said Pandora weakly. The closeness of his body was awakening strong sensations within her and she felt suddenly powerless.

The viscount pulled her to him. His desire for her was nearly overwhelming. "Pandora," he murmured.

"No, please—"

Sarsbrook stopped her protest by covering her mouth with his own. He kissed her hungrily, with a consuming passion that left her breathless. "My dear Pandora," he whispered.

"Oh, Sarsbrook, I do love you," said Pandora, her misgivings melting away. She kissed him with a fervor that matched his own, inciting him to even greater ardor.

"Pandora! Pandora!" It took some time for Lizzy's voice to divert Pandora from the viscount's lips and hands. "Pandora!" Lizzy shouted at the top of her lungs.

Pandora pushed Sarsbrook away. "Lizzy!" She turned to find her sister regarding her in alarm. Beside her were Mr. and Mrs. Baxter.

"Are you all right, Miss Marsh?" said Mrs. Baxter, staring wide-eyed at the viscount. She had heard that lords had deplorable morals, but she had never before seen such vivid evidence of it.

"Oh, yes," said Pandora. She looked at Sarsbrook who, although not at all happy at being interrupted, appeared to be in a decidedly good humor. "My lord, may I present Mr. and Mrs. Baxter? Mr. and Mrs. Baxter, this is Lord Sarsbrook." Noting that the Baxters were regarding his lordship with disfavor, she continued. "I am engaged to marry Lord Sarsbrook."

Lizzy's eyes grew wide. She smiled delightedly. "You are to marry Lord Sarsbrook, Pan?"

Pandora nodded.

"You have said so in front of witnesses, Miss Marsh," said the viscount, taking her hand. "You cannot escape me now."

Pandora looked up at him, and her expression told Sarsbrook that she had no intention of trying to escape. He grinned, and despite the shocked look of Mrs. Baxter, he took Pandora into his arms and kissed her once again.

Epilogue

Nicholas Marsh looked up at the mantel clock in the drawing room. "Papa," he said, turning to his father who was seated upon the sofa, reading the newspaper, "It is nearly three o'clock. Pandora's letter said they would arrive today. I thought they would have called on us."

Mr. Marsh looked up from his newspaper. "Do not be so impatient, Nicholas. If they do not come today, most certainly they will call tomorrow."

Nicholas frowned. He was so looking forward to seeing Pandora and Sarsbrook, who had been gone for more than three months on a wedding trip to Greece. Nicholas walked across the room to stare dolefully out the window. The terrier, Mr. Stubbs, followed him, his tale wagging. "I so wished to see them today, Mr. Stubbs," he said. The little dog looked up at his master and cocked his head.

Lizzy was seated beside her father, studying a drawing of a stylish morning dress in a fashion magazine. She smiled over at her brother. "There is no need to be blue-deviled, Nicky. You will see Pan soon enough."

Nicky turned away from the window. "Do you think she will be changed, Lizzy? I mean, now that she is a viscountess."

"Don't be silly," said Lizzy, looking down at her magazine once again.

Mr. Marsh glanced over at his youngest son. "Your sister is a great lady now with many responsibilities, but she is still your sister. I fancy you will find her little changed." Returning to his newspaper, Mr. Marsh smiled to himself. He shared his son's eagerness to see Pandora again, for he had missed her very much. Indeed, he had not been pleased with his new son-in-law for taking his beloved daughter out of the country to strange foreign lands. He knew that he would rest far more easily when Pandora was once again safely returned to England.

Pandora's father grew thoughtful as he remembered the shock he had felt when Sarsbrook, Pandora, and Lizzy had returned home. When Sarsbrook had announced his intentions to marry Pandora, Mr. Marsh had not been at all happy. Yet Pandora's pleas had made him relent and he had accepted the idea of the wealthy nobleman joining the family.

It had not taken long before Mr. Marsh had come to see Pandora's marriage in a favorable light. After all, Sarsbrook was a man of such enormous wealth and noble rank that a father could scarcely wish a better match. The fact that Pandora and the viscount were so obviously in love made it all the better.

Sarsbrook had quickly provided the family with financial assistance, settling all of Winfield's debts. Deciding idleness was part of the problem, the viscount had also arranged for Pandora's wayward brother to obtain a post in the foreign office. It had been a great surprise to Mr. Marsh to find that Winfield had taken so well to his new post, diligently working at his duties and favorably impressing his superiors.

Nicholas looked out the window again, hoping to see Sarsbrook's carriage approaching. After watching the activity on the street for a long time, he turned away. There was no point in standing about all day waiting, he told himself. Taking one last look out at the street, Nicholas' eyes opened wide. There was a carriage coming! "I see them!" cried the boy. "I do see them! They are here!" Nicholas' excited shouts caused Mr. Stubbs to erupt into frenzied barking.

Rising eagerly from the sofa, Lizzy and Mr. Marsh

rushed to the window. "It is Pandora and Sarsbrook!" cried Lizzy.

"Indeed it is!" said Mr. Marsh, who was just as excited as his son and daughter to see Pandora.

Unable to wait until the visitors came inside, Nicholas raced from the room with Mr. Stubbs close behind him. Meeting Pandora on the walk beyond the front door, he gleefully flung himself into her arms. "Oh, Pan! I am so glad you are home!"

"And so am I," said Pandora, hugging her brother tightly. Mr. Stubbs ran around them in circles, barking merrily and showing his great joy by leaping into the air. "My, you have grown, Nicky," said Pandora after finally releasing her brother from her embrace.

"I am taller," said Nicholas proudly. Turning to Sarsbrook, he grinned up at the viscount. "Welcome home, sir."

Smiling, Sarsbrook opened his arms. Nicholas quickly hurried to embrace his brother-in-law. Mr. Marsh and Lizzy had followed quickly after Nicholas. Lizzy burst into tears as she fell into Pandora's arms. Mr. Marsh shook the viscount's hand warmly and then ushered the travelers back into the house.

Once everyone was seated in the drawing room, Mr. Marsh smiled fondly at Pandora and her new husband. He found himself thinking that they made an exceptionally handsome couple. Pandora looked splendid dressed in a cerulean blue satin spencer over a pale gray cambric muslin round dress. Atop her head was a bonnet trimmed with blue silk and tied with satin ribbons.

Sarsbrook was dressed simply, but with scrupulous care. Mr. Marsh noted that he seemed relaxed and happy. The viscount was the picture of civility, smiling at everyone and appearing very pleased to be among them.

"Do tell us about Greece, Pan," said Lizzy.

"Oh, Lizzy," returned her sister, "I scarcely know where to begin." Tucking her arm under Sarsbrook's, she looked up at the viscount. "It was so wonderful."

Sarsbrook smiled down at her. "It was indeed." The

two of them exchanged a meaningful glance. Their time in Greece had been glorious. They had been favored with smooth seas and fine weather on the voyage. In Greece they had spent most of their time in a magnificent villa overlooking the Aegean Sea.

Pandora and Sarsbrook had traveled to Athens and had visited the Parthenon and other fabled sites, but for the viscount, what he would remember most about the time in Greece was being with Pandora. He would not soon forget the nights that he and Pandora had spent in the villa, making love as the cool breezes from the sea rustled the gauze draperies.

"We will tell you all about Greece," said Pandora, "but, Lizzy, you must first tell us the news from here. We did get some of your letters, but I fear not all of them."

"Your sister is the belle of London," said Mr. Marsh. "Her beaux are too numerous to mention."

"Oh, Papa," said Lizzy, blushing.

"Have you met anyone you like, Lizzy?" said Pandora.

"But that is the problem, Pan," said Lizzy, "I have met so many charming gentlemen. It is so vexatious having to choose among them." She smiled at the viscount. "Lady Verdon has been so gracious, my lord."

"Do call me Sarsbrook, Lizzy," said the viscount amiably. "You must all do so."

"I, too?" said Nicholas.

"Especially you, Nicholas. After all, if you hadn't invited me to tea that day, I might never have become your brother-in-law."

Nicholas grinned. "It was a good idea, was it not, my writing and saying I needed help with my Greek?"

Everyone laughed. Sarsbrook smiled at Pandora. "I shall never forget that day. And it was a great surprise that Isabelle chose that same afternoon to call."

The viscount had made amends with Isabelle shortly after his proposal to Pandora. While her ladyship had been very upset with her brother, she had soon come

around. Once she had been convinced of the truth about
Pandora, she had not opposed the match. She had taken
it upon herself to restore Pandora's good name in society, a formidable task considering the damage Miles
Brackley had done. Yet Lady Verdon's influence in society was so great that she had been able to straighten
things out. Within a short time Lizzy and the other members of the Marsh family were once again welcome in
London's finest drawing rooms.

"And how is Winfield? And Henry and Augustus?"
said Pandora.

"Oh, they are all exceedingly well," said Mr. Marsh.
"Henry and Augustus will be coming to town in a few
days. They are so eager to see you both. But Winfield! I
know that you will be quite pleased to see how well he is
doing."

"Yes," said Nicholas. "He is very important. He
spends his time preventing wars and doing other useful
things."

Pandora laughed. "I am so glad, but I daresay that I
hope there are others in Whitehall responsible for preventing wars."

"I am very glad to hear he is doing well," said Sarsbrook. The viscount had been a bit reluctant to obtain a
post for Winfield, considering that young man's apparent
failings of character. Still, one had to give him a chance.

Conversation turned back to Greece with Nicholas
asking a host of questions about what was to him a very
exotic location. Tea was served as Lizzy, Nicholas and
Mr. Marsh listened intently to Pandora and Sarsbrook
tell of their travels.

When it grew late, the viscount and his lady reluctantly took their leave. Pandora embraced everyone in-
cluding Mr. Stubbs and commanded her father, Lizzy,
and Nicholas to call upon them the next day at Sarsbrook House.

When Pandora and Sarsbrook were seated inside the
carriage returning to their London residence, Pandora
pressed the viscount's arm. "It appears all is well here,

thanks to you, my dear Robert. You have done so much for my family."

Sarsbrook took her hand and pressed it to his lips. "I am happy to do what I can, my darling, when I think what you have done for me in making me the happiest man in the world."

"Oh, Robert," said Pandora, "how I love you!"

The viscount put his arm around her shoulders, pulling her close and kissing her ardently. "You must be exhausted, Pandora," he said softly.

"No, I am feeling quite well."

"That is unfortunate," said his lordship.

Pandora looked into his dark eyes questioningly. "Unfortunate?"

"I had thought that when we returned, I would tell the servants that her ladyship was so exhausted that she must retire at once"—he grinned at her—"to bed."

"You are incorrigible," said Pandora, laughing and placing a kiss on his cheek. She smiled mischievously. "In truth, I am very tired."

"Good," said the viscount, smiling again and kissing his lady tenderly on the lips.